ALSO BY CHRISTOPH HEIN

The Tango Player

The Distant Lover

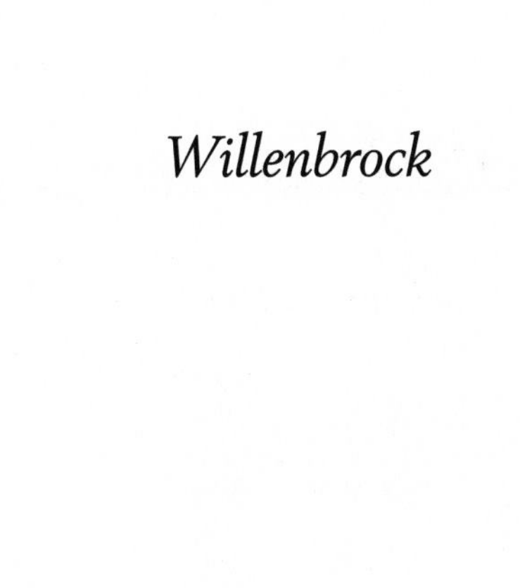

Willenbrock

Christoph Hein

Translated by Philip Boehm

METROPOLITAN BOOKS

HENRY HOLT AND COMPANY

NEW YORK

willenbrock

a novel

Metropolitan Books
Henry Holt and Company, LLC
Publishers since 1866
115 West 18th Street
New York, New York 10011

Published in Canada by Fitzhenry & Whiteside Ltd.,
195 Allstate Parkway, Markham, Ontario L3R 4T8.

Originally published in Germany in 2000 under the title *Willenbrock*
by Suhrkamp Verlag, Frankfurt.

The translator is grateful to the Ledig House International
Writers' Residency for support of this project.

Library of Congress Cataloging-in-Publication Data
Hein, Christoph, 1944–
[Willenbrock. English]
Willenbrock : a novel / Christoph Hein ; translated by Philip Boehm.
p. cm.
ISBN 0-8050-6731-0
I. Boehm, Philip. II. Title.
PT2668.E3747W5513 2003
833'.914—dc21 2003048814

Henry Holt books are available for special promotions and
premiums. For details contact: Director, Special Markets.

First American Edition 2003
Designed by Fritz Metsch

Printed in the United States of America
1 3 5 7 9 10 8 6 4 2

Willenbrock

1

He crouched in front of the small cast-iron stove and held a match to the paper wadded beneath the stack of kindling. Then he closed the door and waited. When he heard the flames crackle he opened the lid and tossed in a few pieces of wood. He wiped his fingers on a rag lying next to his desk and sat down, then took a magazine from one of the drawers and leafed through the pages while he fished a cigarette out of his jacket pocket and lit it. In the night he had dreamed he was running along an endless iron footbridge that spanned some railroad tracks. Now, as he studied the naked girls in the magazine, he wondered where he might have seen the bridge before. In the dream he'd been chasing a man running ahead of him. He couldn't catch up with the man; he just kept running after him, always the same distance behind. He didn't know why he was chasing the man or if they knew each other. He had no idea who the man might be or what, if anything, bound them together. All he could remember was the endlessly long bridge and the diagonal trusses he passed as he ran, the metallic clang of his steps and those of the man he was pursuing. The bridge seemed familiar. He sensed he had crossed it before, but the vague, blurry pictures in his head refused to sharpen into focus, no matter how hard he tried.

It's just a stupid dream, he told himself, and went on leafing through the magazine, jaded and halfheartedly, looking at the girls who smiled invitingly as they thrust their breasts at him. He closed the magazine and stashed it back inside a drawer packed with similar publications.

There was a noise outside the trailer. He glanced up and saw the door handle move. He rose from his seat, unlocked the door, and pulled it open. Standing by the steps were six men who eyed him expectantly but said nothing.

"Nine o'clock," he said, tapping his wristwatch. "We open at nine."

He realized that he had forgotten to close the gate after driving into the yard that morning. The men smiled up at him blankly, so he repeated: "Nine o'clock." When they did not react, he translated into Russian: "*Devyat' chasov,*" then nodded his head several times, looked out over the fenced-in lot, and stepped back inside the trailer. He locked the door, went over to the stove, and, using a pair of coal tongs, added a few briquettes to the burning wood before returning to the desk. One by one he opened the drawers, checked the papers inside, then shoved each drawer back so that it closed with a bang. In the bottom drawer he found a clamped sheaf of contracts; he took them out and flipped through them until he found the one he was looking for. Next he took out his cell phone, dialed the number, and spent several minutes arranging the delivery of an air-conditioning system. After that he again searched through the papers, dialed another number, and spoke to the manager of a body shop.

He heard a rap on the window, stood up, and opened the door, without interrupting his phone conversation. Nodding to the man he had let in, he sat back down and propped his legs on the desk. Once he finished talking, he put the small phone in his jacket pocket and turned to the man now seated on the threadbare couch.

"What are we doing wrong, Jurek?"

"Wrong? What do you mean?"

"They've been lined up out there for an hour waiting to take these old rustbuckets off my hands. I've got half of Warsaw at my doorstep. Are my prices too low? Am I asking too little? Should I tack on another thousand for each car?"

"We have a good name, boss. People know we've got top-quality goods. All the Poles who come to Berlin know that whatever Jurek is selling is guaranteed first-class. Better you should give the thousand marks to me."

"I'll think about it, Jurek. After all, what difference does it make whether the taxman ruins me or you do? Want some coffee?"

The Pole declined. "Time to open up, boss."

Willenbrock grabbed a stack of papers and the two men stood and went outside. From the top of the trailer's small wooden staircase, the car dealer silently surveyed the men below and the spacious lot packed with cars. Jurek went down and spoke with the men, one at a time, asking questions and taking notes. Then he gestured to one of them and led him across the yard. The others—mostly young men dressed in cheap dark suits—trailed behind, keeping a respectful distance while making sure nothing escaped their attention as they sized up the rows of cars, determined to buy.

One man remained by the trailer. He pointed to a sign

bearing the name of the business and its hours of operation. "Are you the boss?"

The man on the staircase nodded. Then he came down the last two steps and introduced himself: "Bernd Willenbrock. What can I do for you?"

The other man pointed to a car parked in the driveway and asked whether Willenbrock would be interested.

"How old is it?"

"Eight years," said the man, taking some papers out of his coat pocket and handing them to Willenbrock. They went to the car. The dealer walked around the vehicle, ran his hand over the paint, opened the driver's door, and sat behind the wheel for a moment. Then he climbed out, again walked around the car, and gave each tire several kicks.

"How much are you asking?"

"I don't know. You're the expert. How much would you pay me?"

"You really want me to name the price? In that case, one hundred marks."

The man forced a smile. "I was thinking more like five thousand. That's what they said at my repair shop."

"Then sell it to your shop."

"They don't buy used cars."

"Then their figure doesn't really mean much, does it? I can give you two thousand marks."

"It's only had one owner. And I haven't driven it much—you can check the odometer."

"You haven't driven it *enough*. Numbers like that look suspicious. Another few thousand kilometers would be easier to believe."

"The tires are brand new."

"I saw. That's why I'm offering as much as I am. They're the best thing about it. I'd take the tires without the car."

Willenbrock asked the man to open the hood and start the engine, then looked across at the group of men huddled around a small van parked by the barbed wire and called for Jurek. When the Pole turned around, Willenbrock held up his right arm and summoned his worker with a brief, bossy wave.

"Take a look, Jurek. Think it's worth two thousand?"

Jurek stuck his head under the hood, listened to the motor, checked the cables and hoses and ran a finger over the vibrating engine block. Then he stood up, carefully wiped his hand on a rag, and looked at his employer.

"It's losing oil. Probably the head gasket. But otherwise no problem. We've got worse machines on the lot."

He cast a passing glance at the owner, then went back to the men at the fence.

"So, two thousand," Willenbrock said. "Is it a deal?"

"I was counting on more."

"Of course you were—I'd say the same thing in your shoes. But that's the best I can do. After all, I've got to resell the car."

Willenbrock waited for a reaction from the man, who was examining the vehicle intently, as if for the first time.

"All right. But you're getting a real deal—I don't have time to shop it around."

"Of course I'm getting a deal. That's why I'm in this business. What did you think? Come on in."

He stepped inside the trailer; the man followed. Willenbrock asked him to take a seat on the couch and began filling out some forms, constantly glancing at the documents the man had provided.

"Who buys all these cars?" the man asked.

"Practically everything goes to Eastern Europe. Poland, Russia, Romania—it's a bottomless pit."

"So business is good?"

"Business is excellent." If I weren't getting fleeced on my taxes I'd be so rich I couldn't bear it."

"So then why don't you pay me what my car's really worth?"

Willenbrock stopped writing and looked up. Then he laughed.

"You need a receipt? If not, I could throw in another three hundred marks."

"I don't need a receipt. What for?"

Willenbrock pulled a wad of bills from his pocket and counted out the agreed-upon amount plus the bonus.

"Look at it this way. You're getting rid of your old car, and I'm taking a problem off your hands."

He slid over two forms for the man to sign, then stamped the documents, slipped one inside an envelope together with the keys and placed it in a drawer. Then he stood up and handed the counted bills and the second form to the man on the couch. The seller gave a look of disapproval and stuck everything inside his pocket without saying a word.

"What used to be here? I know it was something different, but I can't remember exactly what."

"A garden shop," said Willenbrock. He sat back down and looked out over the lot. "The owner couldn't afford the rent anymore so he moved to the outskirts of town. Makes more sense, somehow. How are cabbages and flowers supposed to grow in the middle of the city? It's healthier for the plants out there."

"Looks like cars are better business than flowers."

"You got that right. Best idea I've had these past ten years. Though my wife isn't crazy about it. She thinks all car dealers are crooks and refuses to set foot on the lot. I wanted to hire her to keep the books and do the taxes—you need family for that, if you know what I mean. But she wouldn't hear of it. No interest whatsoever. Fine, so I set her up with a little boutique. Classy rags for ladies who like pearl necklaces and matching outfits—that should keep her happy. Thank God we don't have to rely on the little she brings in."

Willenbrock took a metal box out of the desk and unlocked it. He pulled the remaining cash from his pocket, ran his thumb across the edge of the wad, and added it to the rest in the box.

"Do you mind if I ask what you used to do, before you started this business?"

"I'm an engineer. I spent twenty years working at the Triumphator Calculator Company. After the reunification, we tried to keep things going, but we didn't have a chance. None of us had any connections. Didn't know the right people. And of course the company didn't have enough capital resources to keep things afloat. The place ran on empty for three months and finally went broke. To this day, somebody owes me three months' pay, but there's nobody to hold responsible. Then I was out of work for nine months, looking for something in my field. No luck there—you can't imagine how many engineers the East churned out. Back then there were never enough, then all of a sudden there were loads too many. I'd go to the unemployment office and run into half my class from the engineering school. Not what you'd call a pleasant reunion, either."

He fanned the bills and put them back in the box, letting his fingers rummage among the other papers inside. Then he snapped the lid shut, locked the box, and stowed it back inside the drawer.

"No, it definitely wasn't pleasant, but it was eye-opening, all right. One day I finally figured out how the world really works, and then I went into action. My brother-in-law pointed me in the right direction. He's the one who suggested the used-car business. He runs a well-construction company outside Bremen—started with two people, now he has fifteen. The guy's a genius, he's got a sixth sense, a real nose for it, if you know what I mean. He's always landed on his feet, no matter what. Always will, too. When the government collapsed, he saw his chance. He left one of his drillers in charge of his well business and opened four or five used-car lots. For three years he made a killing, then gave it up and expanded his old company. He pushed me to go into business for myself, left me some cars he couldn't sell—that's how I got started. Today he acts like he *gave* them to me, but he made something on that deal, too, I assure you. He always does. Needless to say, my wife doesn't think much of her brother. She's into higher things, you know, like art, but the man does have a perfect nose. He got me set up and wangled me a loan. You can imagine how the banks were tripping over each other to extend credit to an unemployed engineer. But with his backing, the heavens just opened, and money started raining down on this wretched sinner's head."

His hands, which had been illustrating the money raining from heaven, stopped in midair. Suddenly he leaned over, grinned at the man, and said: "But enough about me. What do you do, if I may ask?"

"I'm a painter."

"Houses or oils?"

"If that's how it breaks down, I'm on the oils side."

"Aha, an artist. A ray of light in my dreary hovel! Are you famous?"

"No."

"But you make enough to live on?"

"I manage."

"Hard times, huh? Who buys paintings these days?"

He took the contract back out of the drawer and studied it. "Your name does seem familiar. You've had exhibitions?"

"Sure. Quite a few, in fact," said the man.

"In Berlin?"

"Yes."

"I knew it! I thought I recognized your name. Personally, I'm not much for art, but my wife's wild about it. She sees all the shows, goes to the theater, everything. I bet my wife knows you. I'm sure she does, in fact."

"I'm sure you're right, Herr Willenbrock. Well . . . you have my car, and I've got my money, so I should be on my way. Tell your wife I said hello."

"My God, when I tell her who was in my office today, she won't believe it. Do me a favor, Herr Berger, just one tiny favor. Could I get a picture of the two of us? Would that be too much to ask?"

"It's a lot to ask, but I don't seem to have much choice, do I?"

The two men stood up. Willenbrock took a camera from a cupboard and asked the painter to join him on the steps. He went out first and held the door open.

"Jurek," he called across the lot.

"Just a minute, boss."

"No, right now. Come here."

The Pole came running to the trailer.

"Do you know who this is, Jurek? This is Johannes Berger, the famous painter."

"I see. Can I go now? We have customers."

"No, I need you to take our picture. Here's the camera. Make sure you get the two of us together."

"But boss, my hands are greasy."

"Don't worry, it doesn't matter, the picture's more important."

Willenbrock turned to the painter. "Just one second, my friend, it'll only take a second. It's an instant camera. We'll see right away if it came out. What's the matter, Jurek?"

"I don't know, boss. Something isn't working right."

"Here, let me see it."

He climbed down the two steps to where Jurek was standing, took the camera, and turned it over.

"It's empty. There's no film, Jurek. Didn't you get a new cartridge?"

"You never said to, boss."

"This is crazy," he said to Jurek, then turned to Berger. "I'm sorry. This is really annoying. What am I going to tell my wife? Johannes Berger shows up and we're out of film. It's a disaster."

"Can I go now, boss? The customers are waiting."

"Go on, go on. If you're in the neighborhood again, Herr Berger, please stop by. It'll just take a second. I'll make sure to keep a fresh cartridge on hand, just for you."

"Well, goodbye, then," the painter said and laughed.

"Wait! You know, you're right about the car. It really is in good shape. Maybe I should throw in another two hundred marks. I don't want to gyp you or anything. Although I do have to sell the car. And you can see for yourself my customers aren't exactly rolling in money. They're always scouting around for the lowest price they can find. They buy from me, then probably turn right around and resell the cars back home."

"Forget it. We made a deal, and I agreed. Let's leave it at that. Goodbye."

"Don't forget to stop back. Promise. Otherwise my wife's going to be heartbroken."

The painter laughed again and nodded significantly at Willenbrock, then crossed the yard and left. For a moment Willenbrock watched him go, then turned his gaze on Jurek, who was showing a car to a small, elderly man with protruding ears, while the rest of the group waited at a discreet distance, intent on not missing a word of Jurek's explanations. Willenbrock went back in the trailer, where he sorted through the papers on his desk. Then he reached for a large album—an illustrated history of World War I aircraft—leaned back in his chair, and buried himself in the pictures and descriptions of biplanes and monoplanes.

An hour later Jurek knocked on the window and signaled

that he'd sold three cars. Right away he brought the elderly man into the trailer. Willenbrock offered the man a seat on the couch and listened while Jurek relayed the details of the sale and the negotiated price. He took one of the girlie magazines and handed it to the customer.

"On the house," he said and signaled to Jurek to translate into Polish, then started filling out the papers as Jurek explained. Embarrassed, the customer leafed uneasily through the magazine. When Jurek asked for the agreed sum of money, the man took a bundle of bills from a small leather pouch concealed beneath his shirt, and counted them carefully before laying them on Willenbrock's desk.

"Did you give him the keys?" asked Willenbrock.

The Pole nodded.

"Then hand him the papers and say something nice." He beamed at the man with the protruding ears and locked up the box.

"I also sold your friend's car—the famous painter," Jurek said after the man had left the office.

"For how much?"

"Four. That's good, isn't it, boss? Very good."

"I don't know, Jurek. The car's worth more. Another thousand would be better."

"You don't want to sell? Should I say it's no deal?"

"No, Jurek, let's go ahead. It's good business to keep the inventory moving."

That afternoon Willenbrock said he had to go out for a couple of hours. He drove to the bank to make a deposit and transfer some funds, then sat in his car, swiveled the rearview mirror, and examined his face. He took a small portable shaver from the glove compartment and shaved, checking in the mirror and feeling his face with his fingers. Then he put the razor back, fished out a bottle of aftershave, and dabbed some on. Twenty minutes later he parked outside a hairdresser's near the Lehrter Freight Station. He went inside. It was a ladies' hair salon, and the hairdressers and clients stared at him in surprise. A heavyset woman with dyed blond hair combed into a high pile was sitting by the cash register. She asked Willenbrock how she might be of assistance. He said he was looking for Frau Lohr.

"The pedicurist is in the next room, behind the door," said the woman. "But if you're here to schedule an appointment, you can do that with me."

"I need to speak to her myself," said Willenbrock.

He gave a short rap on the door and stepped into the next room, which was partitioned into a small reception area and three tiny cubicles by a series of white curtains hanging from the ceiling. It was quiet; although he couldn't see anyone, he sensed he was not alone. A woman's voice asked who was there. Willenbrock answered by clearing his throat.

"Who is it?" the voice asked again, adding, "Just a moment, please. I'm almost finished."

Willenbrock sat on one of the plastic chairs. He heard women's soft voices and a rhythmic metallic clinking of instruments that reminded him of a leaky water faucet. He felt uncomfortable. It bothered him to be sitting in a ladies' salon, and he was overcome by the urge to whistle loudly. A curtain was pushed aside; an elderly woman dressed in black came out and looked at him in silence. She was followed by a young woman wearing a white smock. When she saw Willenbrock her face turned a bright red.

"Oh, it's *you*," she said. "I'll be done in a second."

She stood next to the desk, filled out a receipt, and handed it to the lady.

"So we'll see each other four weeks from now," said the young woman.

"Four weeks," the lady repeated and nodded, then went out.

The young woman stopped in front of Willenbrock, who was watching her from the chair. He looked her in the eye, then let his gaze glide down her short smock to her legs.

"I don't have the faintest idea what you want from me," said the girl coquettishly. She planted her hands on her hips and tapped her right foot, as if she could barely contain her energy. Willenbrock smiled.

"You call up, out of the blue, and come waltzing over. Honestly, I don't know what to make of you."

"I sold you a car and I want to make sure you're happy with it. All part of our customer satisfaction program. So, how about joining me for a coffee?"

The girl burst out laughing and shook her head. Then she slid open a different curtain and went into another cubicle, where she unbuttoned her smock and reached for a dress that was draped on a clothes hanger. Before changing she discreetly drew the white curtain. When she came out she stopped at the little mirror, put on some lipstick, and combed her hair. Her eyes met Willenbrock's in the mirror.

"Go wait for me in front of the jewelry store," she said, and went on leisurely combing her hair. At her words, Willenbrock felt himself relax. He took a deep breath and left the salon.

When the girl came out, Willenbrock was leaning against his car. He jumped up and opened the door for her. She wanted to take her own car, but he promised to bring her back after coffee. They drove to a hotel at the Gendarmenmarkt. He pulled up to the entrance, handed the porter his keys and some money, and asked him to park the car. The porter was taken aback. He asked whether Willenbrock was a guest of the hotel. In a bored voice Willenbrock said he was. He led the young woman into the lounge and ordered coffee and two glasses of champagne. Once they were comfortably seated, the girl said she knew he would call, and Willenbrock replied that he knew that she knew.

After paying for the drinks he went to the reception desk and asked for the keys to the room he had reserved. As they stepped out of the elevator on the third floor, the girl said she had to be home by seven or else she'd be in trouble. Willenbrock said he had no intention of causing her trouble, quite the opposite.

She looked the room over and called to show him the bath. Willenbrock produced a bottle of wine, uncorked it, and poured two glasses. The young woman sat on a chair across from him and looked at him pertly.

"So," she said, "what happens now?"

"Let's have a glass of wine, Rita. To your health, and to our having met."

"I'm not drinking another drop. I can't go home reeking of alcohol."

Willenbrock took a sip of wine, stood behind her, and rested his hands on her shoulders. Slowly he let them drop to her breasts.

"Wait a second," she said, "this dress shows every little stain."

She got up and with one quick movement was out of her dress and standing before him in her slip.

"What's the matter with you? Do you need a special invitation?"

He wanted to pull her over and kiss her, but she fended him off.

"First get undressed," she said, then stripped off her slip and climbed into bed. Pulling the covers up to her neck, she watched him as he took off his clothes.

"I knew it," she said. "As soon as I saw you I knew you had the hots for me."

"And you?"

"I'll tell you later. I never know until after."

Two hours later he drove her to her car, which was parked outside the hair salon. As they were saying goodbye, the girl asked whether they'd see each other again.

"I'd like that," said Willenbrock. "Any time. Give me a ring. You have my number."

"I think it's better if you call me."

Because he seemed surprised, she added: "I'd just like it better that way."

Willenbrock was back in his office shortly before closing time. Jurek filled him in on the afternoon's business and handed him the completed forms. Then he looked at a car Jurek had agreed to take; the owner was coming back the next day to close the sale. Afterward Jurek gave Willenbrock two slips of paper with names and phone numbers, saying that a beautiful woman had come by and asked for him. A very beautiful woman. She had left a note. And a man had phoned who wanted Willenbrock to call him back. Willenbrock looked at the woman's note and let out a satisfied whistle. Then he took the other slip and read the name out loud.

"Berner." He thought for a moment and then started to laugh.

"A colleague," he said. "From the old days."

Jurek nodded, though he didn't recognize the name and scarcely knew anything about his boss's life before the car business.

"See you tomorrow," Jurek said as he left.

Paperwork kept Willenbrock busy for another half hour, after which he spent a long time on the phone. When he finished, he packed all the records and car keys in a black briefcase. Before leaving the trailer he switched on the alarm.

2

Willenbrock lived just north of town in one of the subdivisions that had sprung up in the last two years—twelve identical three-story homes. Each had a garden bordered by evergreen hedges, which, though just a couple of feet high, were designed to grow into tall, dense screens that would, in time, more clearly separate the houses. The access road into the small development was still unpaved; Willenbrock had to drive slowly so his wheels wouldn't kick up the sandy earth. However, once he reached the cluster of new buildings—recently landscaped with fast-growing, spindly conifers—a ribbon of smooth asphalt wound from one driveway to the next, its dark surface streaked with sand from the tires. Willenbrock pulled up to the driveway gate and watched with satisfaction as it opened automatically. He entered the house through the basement, put down his briefcase, and looked into the living room: the TV was on, and he could see the table set for dinner. He heard some noise coming from the kitchen, where he found his wife, who greeted him without interrupting her cooking. Sitting down on one of the chairs, he looked at her back, her behind, her legs. My God, he thought, why do I do it? I've got the sexiest girl here at home and I still can't stop chasing after every skirt I lay eyes on. But what can you do, everybody's programmed one way or another, it all boils down to genes, you just have to live with it. Willenbrock stepped behind his wife and gently breathed on her neck and hair, then reached up under her dress to stroke her buttocks and cautiously grope at her crotch.

"You'll never learn how to seduce a woman, will you?" she said calmly, without pushing him away. "Go wash your hands and come eat."

He tried kissing her, but she had lifted a pot off the stove and turned around carrying it, so he had to step back.

During dinner they talked about the boutique. She said she was thinking of giving it up, the shop wasn't bringing in enough. Willenbrock told her not to worry, that every business had its slow spells. His wife objected and said she didn't like living off him. She wanted to stand on her own feet; she hated being so dependent.

"It's humiliating," she said, "when a person my age can't take care of herself."

"It's new, Susanne, and new experiences are what make life so wonderful," Willenbrock replied, patting her on the hand. She sat still and let him make the gesture, but stared at him so hard he asked: "What's the matter?"

"You *like* it, don't you?" she said. "You enjoy having me dependent on you. You like the fact that I have to keep asking you for money."

"Don't be silly."

He picked up a tomato, cut it into slices, and slowly sprinkled them with salt.

"Want some?" he asked, offering his plate with the tomato. She went on staring at him without responding.

"Maybe. Maybe you're right," he said, disconcerted by her silence. "Maybe I really don't mind. I've always thought it was because the money didn't mean anything to me, never really has. But maybe there's something else I haven't quite figured out. I don't know. I just like being able to help you. Is that so terrible? In the past, men used to fight for their women, march off to certain death, even kill themselves on their account. Covering a few of your bills doesn't come close."

"I'm tried of it," she said, "and I hate it."

Willenbrock nodded, resigned, taking care not to contradict her. He thought about his grandfather, who had muttered a kind of chant whenever his wife got angry with him: It doesn't take much to keep a man happy, but no matter what you give a woman, she's never satisfied. Shower her with money one day, or dress her in furs, the next day she's back at it, snarling away like nothing ever happened.

After dinner they took a walk down the newly laid sidewalk that wound around the development to a small stand of trees. Willenbrock told his wife about the painter, but since he couldn't remember the man's name they couldn't figure out whether Susanne had heard of him. She asked whether he'd paid the man a fair price or if he'd conned him out of his car for next to nothing, and Willenbrock laughed out loud and told her she had the completely wrong idea about the used-car business and didn't need to worry about his clients: it was their choice to sell or not, he didn't force them to do anything they didn't want. Then he hugged her and asked about her mother, whom she had phoned that afternoon, but he didn't really listen to her answer—just kept nodding with sympathy and concern.

In the small shopping center that connected the new development to an older neighborhood of concrete-slab tenements, they stopped in front of a brightly lit café nestled amid a grocery, a dry cleaner's, and a store that sold toys, children's clothing, and newspapers. The place was empty except for a young couple sitting at one of the tables and a woman standing behind the bar. She was reading a newspaper, her head propped on her elbows. The vacant café looked depressing; but Willenbrock asked his wife to go inside with him anyway.

"Just for one glass," he said.

After they sat down, the woman came out from behind the bar and placed two oversized menus on the table. She recommended the day's special—fresh pike—but Willenbrock explained that they had already eaten. He ordered a glass of wine and a beer; the woman nodded, resigned, and took back the menus.

The couple at the next table were particularly loud. The man was trying to talk the woman into flying to Hong Kong with him for four days, but she didn't want to give up that many workouts. He tried explaining why now was the perfect time to go to Hong Kong, the last chance before the crown colony was to be returned to China.

"To China?" the girl asked, horrified. "Why China? You mean they're Chinese?"

The question threw the young man off balance. "Yes. At least I think so. Anyway, a lot of them are."

"You think I want to go hang out with a bunch of Chinese?"

she exclaimed in disgust. "Why don't you take some other girl?"

The young man tried to change her mind. He offered to pay her way, but the girl wouldn't budge.

"What's so great about Hong Kong, anyway? Nobody in his right mind goes there."

"Herbert says it's really exciting. Even better than New York."

"Herbert, huh? Where does he get these things? He's the one who talked you into that country house in Denmark. And that turned out to be a total loser, didn't it? Anyway, nobody from the gym's going to Hong Kong. They've all got better things planned."

"No, this really is special. Next year it won't even be there anymore, it'll just be China."

"So go on and take Pamela—except you'll have to buy two seats just for her," said the girl, laughing so hard she nearly fell off her chair.

Then they talked about the fitness center where the girl worked out several hours every day except Sunday. The young man tried getting her to switch to his gym so they could see each other more often, plus they could get a good deal on a joint membership, but she just laughed and told him he was jealous because the owner of her gym had twice given her a ride home.

"You're not even listening to me," Susanne said, reaching for her husband's hand. He looked at her and nodded his head. "It's true. All I've been thinking about the whole evening is going to bed with you."

"And you still have no idea how to go about it. You'd be

happy if women came with a switch you could flip to turn them on whenever you felt like it."

"That would certainly make things easier."

Willenbrock called the waitress, who was working on her crossword puzzle at the bar, and paid. On his way out he eyed the young couple, making no attempt to be discreet. The girl was quite pretty and remarkably slender. Her eyes were bright blue; her dirty-blond hair was cut to fall in layers over her tanned neck. A black lace blouse barely covered her breasts and was opened at the bottom to reveal her narrow waist. The young man had a nearly classic physique; his hair was light blond and carefully groomed. He wore a tight T-shirt to accentuate his broad shoulders and powerful upper arms. When he caught Willenbrock staring he straightened up abruptly, scanned Willenbrock from head to toe, and let out a sneer of disgust.

At home Willenbrock pulled Susanne into the bedroom despite some reluctance on her part. While both undressed he wondered why he was so aroused, just hours after having sex with Rita. Whenever he went to bed with another woman, he afterwards felt an urgent desire to sleep with his wife the moment he was back in her presence. He figured that sleeping around served to stimulate him sexually. As he peeled off his clothes, he surreptitiously searched his body for any telltale signs of the afternoon, all the while reasoning with himself that this craving for his wife's body after other sexual liaisons actually meant that he must have some sort of predisposition toward monogamy. Deep down I'm a pretty loyal guy, he told himself; these little affairs don't mean a thing; in fact, what they really do is prove how utterly fixated

I am on Susanne—no sooner do I leave another woman's bed but I'm filled with desire for my wife, a desire that's both passionate and tender, I want to caress her, I want to sleep with her, I want to lie next to her.

Although this train of thought took Willenbrock somewhat by surprise, it struck him as entirely plausible, and he was all the more pleased with himself when he didn't find any scratches or toothmarks on his body. He lay naked on the bed and watched his wife, who, as always, was self-conscious about undressing in front of him. She slipped off her underwear and quickly ducked under the covers. He stroked her hair and let his hand slide along her body and grasp at her buttocks.

"Wait," she said, "I'm cold. First you have to warm me up."

An hour later they were both in their bathrobes, washing dishes in the kitchen. Susanne asked him some more about the painter whose car he had bought that morning, and Willenbrock related the details of their conversation. Suddenly he remembered the slip of paper Jurek had given him. He glanced at the clock and told Susanne he had to call someone he used to work with. He went into the bedroom, retrieved the number from his jacket, which was lying on the floor, and sat down in the hall beside the telephone.

"This is Bernd Willenbrock," he said when a woman answered. "I'm sorry to be calling so late. I'm returning your husband's call."

The woman had him repeat his name and then asked him to wait. When Berner picked up, Willenbrock again excused himself for calling so late. Berner said he was happy to have a chance to chat after so many years—before their old firm went bankrupt, the two men had worked in the same research-and-development department. They caught up on what they'd been doing since then, and how they were now earning their bread, as Willenbrock put it. When the conversation began to bore him, Willenbrock suggested they get together some time. Berner agreed and was about to say good-bye when Willenbrock asked if there was anything else Berner had wanted to tell him. Berner sighed and said that with all their talking he'd nearly forgotten the most important thing: Did Willenbrock remember a Dr. Feuerbach? Willenbrock said that he did and asked what their old colleague was doing and whether he, too, had gone into a new line of work.

"I don't know," said Berner. "All I know is I never want to see him again." He stopped and waited for a reaction, but Willenbrock was already wishing he hadn't said anything; he was even regretting having called Berner at all. He had given in to a moment of sentimentality: the name had brought back memories, and for a moment he'd felt an urge to speak with his old colleague, even though he had had little to do with Berner back then, and in all the years of working together they had barely exchanged more than a few words. Yet if Berner had been of scant interest to him years ago and meant nothing to him today, why had he called the man, and why was he now making small talk with him?

"I never want to see him again," Berner repeated, once more waiting for a response, but Willenbrock only rubbed his stomach to break the tedium, and said nothing. In a way it's really nice, he thought, not having any more contact with all these people. That's the way to do it—every few years just strike the tents, burn the bridges, and make a fresh start. It's fun to meet new people, talk with them, learn about their lives and their opinions, discover the unique world that every person has to offer. And it can be even more fun to move on when there's nothing new left to find out. Sooner or later you get to that point with everybody, your best buddies as well as your girlfriends. I should just hang up right now, without saying another word, Willenbrock thought.

"He filed reports on all of us," said Berner right at that moment.

Missed my chance, thought Willenbrock, now he's back at it.

"Did you hear what I just said?" asked Berner.

"Who?" inquired Willenbrock.

"Our dear colleague Dr. Feuerbach. He told the management all sorts of things about us. When we cleaned out the main office we found a whole file stuffed with his reports. It's thanks to him that neither of us got to go to England. That was twelve or thirteen years ago, you remember? We were supposed to go to Leeds to check out the automated production line at that machine tool factory? It was all set, the factory had just arranged our visas if I remember right. And then the trip was suddenly called off and nobody ever told us why. Just like that, out of the blue. You mean you honestly don't remember?"

"Of course I remember," said Willenbrock, still bored.

"Well, it turns out it was that bastard Feuerbach. He passed on whatever he could about us. What we said in the cafeteria, all our stupid jokes, any little dig or wisecrack we made to pass the time. He wrote about your trip to Prague, when you secretly met with your sister and her husband. That's the reason you didn't get to go to England. And with me it was a little affair I must have told him about. So the next thing you know we were labeled unreliable—security risks. It was all in the file; I took it home. You can have a look if you want. Pretty disgusting stuff."

Willenbrock started to snicker, and Berner asked what there was to laugh about.

"Oh, you know, I always figured it was something like that. That's all," said Willenbrock. At the same time he thought: No, I'm lying, that's not all, but why should I tell you, Berner? Why should I tell you that not only did I figure it was something like that, I was certain someone had denounced me, except I wasn't thinking about Feuerbach, that's the only real surprise, the truth is I thought it was you, old friend. That's right, you, Berner, don't ask me why, but you always irked me somehow, which is probably the only reason I suspected you. I couldn't stand you, there was always something a little slimy about you, you know, and there still is, which is why I thought it was you, why I went out of my way to avoid you. Evidently I was wrong. Maybe it was Feuerbach, he always struck me as friendly enough, at any rate he knew his stuff and was a lot more fun to talk to than a slimeball like you. Okay, so I was wrong, but does that mean I have to talk with you about it now?

"That's all? That's all it means to you?" asked Berner, since Willenbrock didn't say anything else.

Willenbrock just nodded, lost in his thoughts, and the voice on the other end repeated, annoyed: "That's all? You have nothing else to say?"

"I don't know. What do you expect me to say? You want to waylay him somewhere and beat him up? Would that make you feel better?"

Berner breathed audibly. Then he said: "Do I have it right that this doesn't interest you? That you couldn't care less?"

"I wouldn't put it quite that way. But it's all so long ago. Besides, our dear Dr. Feuerbach can't touch me anymore. I'm on my own now, there isn't any boss to inform about me. The whole ugly business is over and done with. That's why it doesn't bother me. Not anymore. You see what I mean?"

"Not really. I don't think I do, Bernd. To me that seems like a very strange reaction."

"Well, that's the way I feel. What did you expect me to say? Look, I'm grateful to you for telling me about Feuerbach, but what am I supposed to do about it now? So he talked about us more than he should have—probably about some of the others as well. But we knew he was filing reports on the personnel. We know he was writing things down, even if we never saw what he was saying. What are you going to do? Report the man to the authorities?"

"No, I don't want to do that."

"Good, so what, then? What do you expect me to do?"

"I don't know. That's not my point. I just wanted you to know. About Feuerbach. I thought you'd be interested. I'm sorry I bothered you, I apologize for taking your time."

"Why are you so ticked off? What's the problem?"

"There's no problem. I thought I was doing you a favor. I was wrong. I'm sorry. Let's just end the conversation, all right?"

"All right," Willenbrock agreed. He held the receiver without saying anything else and waited for Berner to hang up. When the line went dead he spoke into the mouthpiece: "Asshole." Then he placed the phone back on the shelf.

He went into his study, put the note with Berner's phone number in a little wooden box on his desk, and switched off the light. A second later he turned the light back on, opened the box, took out the piece of paper, crumpled it up, and threw it in the wastebasket. Hanging on the opposite wall was a large, yellowing photo of a young man standing beside a glider, grinning into the camera with childish pride. Willenbrock gave the picture an encouraging wink, then left the study.

"My God, that was a long call, especially for you. What's going on?"

"Nothing. Nothing really. Someone from my old work. He told me what he's up to and I told him what I'm doing. That was it. I was afraid he was trying to get hold of me because he'd heard I had my own business and was looking for a job, but luckily that wasn't the case. Just a lot of old shoptalk and sentimental bullshit. Nothing important."

"Talking about the good old days?"

"Right, the good old days, that's right."

"Are you planning to see him? You can invite him over if you like. I've never met any of your colleagues from the old days. I don't really know any of your friends. You've always kept them hidden from me. Why don't you invite him over? I'll make a nice dinner."

"Berner's not a friend. He's slimy. You'd be bored out of your wits, and so would I."

He tugged at the belt of her robe. The knot came undone,

the black cotton cloth embroidered with Japanese characters slid apart, exposing a narrow strip of her belly.

"Ah," he whispered, "what have we here?"

Stroking her stomach with one hand, he hung his other arm across her shoulders and led her back into the bedroom.

3

The following week seven cars were stolen from Willenbrock's lot in one night, and the police were unable to uncover any meaningful evidence. The two officers who answered the call performed a routine inspection of the property, doing little more than strolling around and asking Willenbrock a few questions, so that he had the distinct impression they weren't taking the case very seriously. He complained about the lax investigation and was instantly rebuked. The policemen assured him that the break-in and theft would be pursued with all the resources and manpower appropriate to an incident with no personal injury, either until the case was solved or, failing that, until it was shelved. While they understood Willenbrock's indignation, he needed to keep things in perspective. Unfortunately, such offenses were reported all too frequently, but they couldn't be allowed to tie up the entire police force and keep it from attending to more urgent tasks. Willenbrock asked whether greater resources and manpower would have been committed if Jurek or himself, or both of them, had been beaten half to death. The younger officer, who had introduced himself as "Inspector," merely looked up from his notepad and, without reacting to Willenbrock's sarcasm, assured him that the appropriate response would have been made.

Using a small laptop, the officers took statements from Jurek and Willenbrock, then asked some questions that Willenbrock found offensive and which upset him so much that he asked the policemen if they suspected him of stealing his own cars. The younger officer explained in a bored, indifferent tone that they were duty-bound to consider all possible angles, neither ruling anything out nor accusing anyone before all the facts were in. The policemen took the title papers for the stolen cars and said they'd phone within the next few days to set up another meeting. Then they got in their car without saying goodbye.

As he watched them drive away, Willenbrock felt guilty. For some reason he couldn't explain, the officers had made him feel as if he really was being accused, as if he were on trial, not truly free but merely released on his own recognizance. The older officer's request that he remain available over the next few weeks sounded in retrospect like a demand, practically an order not to leave the city. He felt his anger building, and it did not subside when he realized that it was actually directed against himself. Still fuming, he ordered Jurek to walk around the lot with him and search the cars for signs of tampering, and in a tone laced with threat asked why there were only two customers waiting that morning instead of the usual crowd.

Jurek cocked his head, squinted one eye, and muttered: "What's wrong, boss? What's the problem?"

"I just had seven cars stolen off the lot. Seven cars vanish overnight without a trace."

"And you think Jurek has his hands in it somewhere?"

"No, I don't, but the police suspect us both. They don't trust you *or* me."

"Police are idiots. German polizei or Polish policja—all the same, all idiots."

"You're probably right, Jurek."

"I don't care what the police say. But what do *you* say? What about it, boss? Jurek's hands are clean? You trust me? Or should we say goodbye now and each man go his own way? Maybe that would be better, boss."

He held up his oil-stained hands.

"Who said anything about goodbye, Jurek? I'm just telling you what the police think. They suspect the cars weren't really stolen and that you and I are in cahoots with some gang to swindle the insurance company."

The Pole said nothing and merely looked at him skeptically, his head cocked, his hands still raised.

"It's all right, Jurek. Okay? I don't suspect you. Is that better?"

The Pole slowly lowered his hands and sniffed audibly. Then he gave his head an almost imperceptible shake and mumbled to himself: "I don't like this, boss. No, I don't like this one bit."

"Come, let's go see what we have. Check the locks, the doors, the window seals, you know. I want to know if they messed with any of the other cars. Somehow they managed to get inside the gate—they're bound to have left some bit of evidence. After all, they didn't have any keys. At least not mine."

"And not from me, boss."

"I didn't say that. Don't get me any more riled up than I am, Jurek. I'm mad enough as it is. Come on."

Over the next few days he spoke several times with the insurance agent, a very young inspector with mid-length hair and a carefully trimmed goatee. The man explained that unless Willenbrock implemented better security, the company would have to impose a considerably higher premium. Willenbrock wanted specific recommendations, and the impeccably dressed representative laid out a proposal, stressing over and over that it was only one of many possibilities and that he was by no means dictating what Willenbrock had to do. Willenbrock explained that he had already made some inquiries and that the cost of hiring a security firm was too high for his small, or at most medium-sized, business, and that he didn't want to hire a night watchman, since one man—presumably an older retiree—could hardly be expected to fend off a gang of seven, and Willenbrock didn't want to be responsible for the death of a pensioner.

"Seven?" asked the inspector suspiciously. "How do you know there were seven?"

"Of course, there could have been more," said Willenbrock, "but it takes at least seven crooks to drive away with seven cars."

"Right," said the young man, turning red. "I wasn't thinking of that."

"I know what you were thinking."

Willenbrock spoke with three other insurance agents over the next few days. He saw no reason to conceal his motive for switching companies, since he presumed they all exchanged information anyway. Unable to find anything acceptable, he decided to let his present coverage lapse and not take out any expensive new policy. Each evening he and Jurek secured the cars by removing critical ignition parts, aware that this painstaking work was at best makeshift protection against further theft.

"We'll just have to trust in God," said Willenbrock, with no great conviction—more as a reflex, as if to hedge his bets, mouthing words he did not fully believe and invoking a superstition he was reluctant to forgo, just in case it did prove effective and failure to do so might possibly invite disaster. He was not devout, did not belong to any church, but he still had some vestige of religion, some vague inclination he had never felt compelled to redefine. His pronouncement was more a rote reaction than the expression of any tangible belief, but, like the involuntary habit of crossing oneself, it pointed to the last discernible remnants of a childhood faith.

Jurek looked up. He gave Willenbrock a disapproving look, then bent once more over one of the car engines and, using both hands, set about loosening a spark plug boot.

4

In mid-November the weather suddenly turned cold. An early-morning frost coated the autumn-gold leaves, light snow covered the roofs and treetops, and the sidewalks were dotted with damp, greasy stains. Overnight, short skirts and linen jackets gave way to thick winter coats and puffy anoraks. By the next day the snow was gone, the streets and roofs were wet, the leaves had lost their autumn glow; what foliage remained was frost burned and dirty. Many branches had no leaves at all and at once seemed bare and ugly. The snow had gone, but the thick coats were there to stay, along with the cold and the unpleasant damp. The season had changed and now was showing its other face.

Every two hours Willenbrock tipped a bucketful of coal and cordwood into the small stove, cursing beneath his breath that he didn't yet own the lot he was using: all he had was a short-term lease and the vague promise of preferred treatment in the event the property came up for sale. He had hired a lawyer to pursue the possible purchase, but as long as the lot's legal status remained unresolved, he couldn't build a showroom with a real office and a proper workshop. For five years he'd had to make do with a trailer and other temporary arrangements, and the more successful his business grew, the more resentful he became. Still, he didn't look for a better site, since the present one seemed fine, and he was worried that a change of location might dent his success. Nor was he prepared to make any large investment, in light of the tenuous legal situation, at least for now. So he had no choice but to wait for the officials at the Federal Trust Agency to make their decision regarding the status of the lot, let himself be consoled by his lawyer, and remit an excessive share of his profits to the Ministry of Finance instead of investing it in his business. Resigned to this dreary state of affairs, he looked forward to the day when he could buy the property and begin construction, but for the moment he was exasperated and unable to summon the energy to make even the slightest improvements. His frustration peaked whenever he thought about the pending legal issue, or whenever the makeshift nature of his office brought it to mind.

People continued to visit the lot every morning to look over the cars and ask about prices. Most of the prospective clients were men, underdressed for the time of year and the sudden cold, though now and then a woman showed up, usually the companion of one of the male buyers. The customers almost always came very early and would be waiting at the gate when Jurek arrived to open. The few who came during the day tended to be locals who strolled around the lot, asked a few questions, and disappeared. Now and then someone ventured in to see about selling a car; they would feign shock at Willenbrock's offer but then, after brief consideration, accept it, either because they needed the money or because they wanted to dispose of their vehicle quickly.

At first Willenbrock wondered why the serious buyers

showed up exclusively in the early morning, but Jurek explained that they came to Berlin on the night train from the East and waited in the cafés at the train station until the lot opened for business.

In the last week of November, Krylov reappeared—a small, red-haired Russian who always wore a suit and a loud, garish tie. He was accompanied by the usual pack of young men he kept on hand to do his bidding, and whose willingness to oblige their employer verged on the obsequious.

When Jurek caught sight of the Russian, he turned without a word, walked to the trailer, and called his boss. On his first visit, Krylov had refused to negotiate with Jurek: he considered the Pole's command of German inadequate and insisted on dealing directly with the owner. That had led to friction between Jurek and Willenbrock: Jurek felt humiliated and suggested that Krylov was refusing to deal with him because he was Polish. The Russian had listened to the complaint in silence, then resumed his conversation with Willenbrock as if nothing had been said, as if Jurek weren't there, whereupon Willenbrock had reprimanded his employee in front of the client. Since then, Jurek avoided the Russian entirely, refusing to acknowledge him in any way. Whenever Krylov showed up, Jurek would tell his boss and instantly vanish beneath the hood of a car.

Willenbrock shook hands with Krylov and his entourage and invited them to warm up inside his office with a cup of coffee or some brandy, which Krylov politely declined. Willenbrock quickly fetched his coat from the office, then led the man to several parked cars roped off behind the trailer.

"How many do you need today, Herr Direktor?" he asked.

"Krylov pointed to his men and said: "Three. This time, only three."

"What make, what year, what price?" asked Willenbrock.

"We'll see."

Krylov opened one of the cars, sat inside, and gripped the steering wheel.

"How much?" he asked.

Willenbrock named a figure. Krylov cast a glance at the odometer and made a face, so Willenbrock added: "But we can talk about it."

"Yes, of course we can talk about it," said the Russian as he climbed out. "After all, we're civilized men, right?"

He continued, now and then opening a door to look inside a particular car or take a seat at the wheel, while Willenbrock trailed behind, along with Krylov's four escorts. Half an hour later he had made his choices, and they all went back to the trailer so Willenbrock could fill out the papers.

"The cars are okay?" asked Krylov.

"Absolutely. As always. You have my word, and I'll give you a written guarantee as well. Do you want to take them for a test drive?"

"Your word is enough, my friend."

Willenbrock stood up and asked the Russians to wait a moment. He went outside and called Jurek, told him which cars had been bought and asked him to get them ready. Then he returned to the trailer and again assured Krylov that all the vehicles were in order. Krylov nodded his approval. Willenbrock once more offered coffee or brandy—"Have a drop" was how he put it—and this time Krylov accepted. The Russian watched as Willenbrock took out a bottle and six glasses, waited for his host to fill the first two, and then took the bottle from Willenbrock's hand, poured a few drops for his men and handed them their drinks. Willenbrock passed around a box of cookies; each guest took one, ate it, and drained his glass.

"How are things back home? Mother Russia's getting some bad press these days. If you believe the papers, Moscow's one big den of thieves. Drugs, prostitution, organized crime, murders—it's enough to scare people away from your beautiful city. That can't be good for business, or for the tourists."

"Never trust what you read in the papers, my friend. Journalists need a good story, that's how they earn their living. They'll make up whatever their papers want to print if they have to. Believe me, things are no different today than under Stalin, and they were no different under Stalin than under the tsar. Moscow hasn't changed a bit, except that the poor have gotten a little poorer and the rich a little richer, like everywhere else in the world. As for prostitution, my God, that's no worse now either. Although it's true: the girls in Moscow these days are uglier than they used to be. All the pretty ones have gone to Western Europe. You know, it's heartbreaking, but the flower of Russian whoredom is walking the streets of Paris and Berlin. It's the same with the ballet. My God, I have tears in my eyes just thinking about the Bolshoi. Nowadays *anybody* can get a ticket. Anytime they want. The ballet even has to advertise—they never had to do that before. Ads for the Bolshoi—that's the true Russian tragedy."

Krylov picked up the bottle, poured some more brandy for

Willenbrock and himself, then carefully clinked his glass against Willenbrock's.

"Our great country is sending its best ballet dancers and whores to Western Europe, while we have to make do with second-rate goods. In my time it was different. Moscow came first. But the people in power today are selling off the heart and soul of Russia. A bunch of idiots and criminals, if you ask me. And if there's a problem in Moscow with gangsters and organized crime, it's because of them. Sadly, our politicians aren't cultured and educated like your German ones. We're stuck with crooks who can't manage a thing except stuffing their own pocketbooks."

Willenbrock laughed out loud: "That's an awfully rosy picture you have of our politicians. And here I thought you knew better. Where'd you come up with ideas like that?"

Krylov had once worked for a bureau within the Soviet government that covered Western Europe, and had made several trips to West Germany in the old days. After the breakup of the Soviet Union, he had been dismissed from his post; for two years he'd earned his living by helping German firms set up branches in Russia. Then he started his own business, which he described as an "innovative trading company," registered in St. Petersburg, Munich, and Milan. On his first visit to the lot he had handed Willenbrock his business card, which listed him as director of the Russian Venture Group—a small service firm, he explained to Willenbrock, designed to guide foreign investors through the jungle of Russian bureaucracy, to lead them out of the great Russian swamp. Among all the possible doors, he could always find the right one, and, just like a hero in a fairy tale, he knew exactly how to make it open. That was what he had to offer.

"And patience," he added. "I have the patience you Western Europeans have lost. To do business in Russia you need patience. *That's* what I sell. And it brings in a pretty penny."

Willenbrock had been impressed at their first encounter. He admired the Russian's self-assurance and resolve, and since he guessed Krylov might well become a regular client, he had immediately offered him a generous volume discount, which Krylov accepted: since then he had returned to Willenbrock's lot every two or three months, each time purchasing several cars, which he paid for on the spot, in cash.

"Russia is only great in war," Krylov continued, "and under an iron tsar. We don't take well to freedom. We were molded by Asia, not Europe. We protected you from the Asiatics and in the process became Asiatics ourselves. We sacrificed everything for the Europeans, laying down our lives to save Vienna and Paris from the Mongol hordes. We paid a high price, and Europe has no intention of paying us back. Today if you want to get good work out of a Russian, you have to whip him. We don't enjoy work like the Germans, who want everything neat and tidy."

The four men behind Krylov appeared to be following the conversation attentively, but they said nothing. Willenbrock didn't know whether they understood German and were truly listening or whether they were merely trained to wait for their cue. They looked like new recruits determined to anticipate every command and doing their best to keep a low profile. Maybe Krylov beats them, thought Willenbrock.

"That's a pretty idealistic notion you have about us Germans, Herr Direktor. As far as I know, Russia's had its share of iron tsars and whips, and I doubt if people were much happier."

"What does happiness have to do with it? In my day we had order and bread and work enough for everyone. That means a lot—something our people are finally beginning to appreciate."

"Sure, but you also had the gulag and a few other things people didn't especially appreciate. Stalin wasn't exactly a saint."

"No, but he did study to be a priest—people like that are always out to save the world. And don't forget, there was a war on, so for us Stalin was like an angel sent by God. You can't win wars if you put too high a value on every single life. The road to victory is paved with corpses—and plenty of Europeans have understood this, too, from the Great Elector to the Grand Inquisitor, from Hitler to Napoleon."

"You know, Herr Direktor, to listen to you makes me think you might be a little homesick for the good old days. But I'm willing to bet that even you are better off now than when you worked for the government."

"Of course I am, if you mean that I'm making more money. A lot more, in fact. Or that I own several cars and luxury homes and apartments in different cities. In the old days I wouldn't have dared dream of all that. I'm doing great . . . as long as I don't think too much about what these crooks have done to Russia. Such a proud country, and now look at it: one gigantic political ruin. I'm not European, you know, I'm a Russian—with all the silly likes and dislikes and awful sentimentality that even Pushkin complained about. I can't stand seeing my country so humiliated. I take its wounded pride personally. For us it's like how you Germans felt about Versailles. And right now we're waiting for a Russian Hitler to show up and put an end to it. Just one more, my friend."

Willenbrock refilled Krylov's glass and, pointing toward the four silent men, looked at him questioningly.

Krylov shook his head. "No, they still have a long way to drive. Eight hundred kilometers and two borders. Tonight they'll get their vodka, a bottle apiece."

He turned around to the four men on the sofa, who sat up still straighter. Their faces became even more docile as they waited for their leader to speak. But Krylov only nodded and returned to Willenbrock.

"And you, my friend?" he asked, after they had clinked and drained their glasses, chasing the brandy with a cookie. "You are content?"

Willenbrock nodded.

"That's what's so admirable about you Germans, you always land on your feet. Some people, like the English and Americans, live for the future, and others are stuck in the past, like the French and us Russians. But you Germans always keep your eyes fixed on the present. In both wars you were superior. You only lost because you were outnumbered. Then when the fighting was over and everything was in ruins, you saw your chance. You were the star pupils in both of the winning systems and you built yourselves back up better than any other nation. You turned defeat into a golden opportunity. We, on the other hand, have always lived in the past. The only Russians who really know how to live in the present are our glorious gangsters—our mafia, as you call them. You know, they're all devout Orthodox. They never say a word against the Holy Church, never lift a finger against tradition, but don't think they'll let a thousand years of Russian culture keep them from their shady dealings. Who knows, they may be our best bet. You Western Europeans were raised gently, but relentlessly, on the Enlightenment and capitalism, and North America was shaped by its settlers, with one hand on the plow and a loaded Winchester in the other. Maybe our gangsters will show us how to cope with the present without sneering at the past. Until now we've never managed to do that except in war—in war and in art, glory be to Pushkin, Tchaikovsky, and all the Russian generals. Maybe our mafia can teach us how to cope with everyday life when we're at peace."

While Krylov was speaking, Willenbrock capped the bottle, took it off the table, and stowed it in his desk. He wasn't used to drinking so early in the morning and was afraid Krylov might force another glass on him, which he would have a hard time declining, since refusal might be read as rejection. By discreetly removing the bottle he hoped to avoid another round of pouring and clinking glasses. He enjoyed hearing Krylov go on, and was tempted to ask his friend if he'd expressed the same views when he worked for the Soviet government, but in the end he kept quiet, partly not to annoy Krylov, and partly because he wasn't all that interested in the answer.

"Not a very sunny forecast," he said, and looked at Krylov's men, who were still sitting on the sofa like watchful Dobermans, never taking their eyes off their master. He bundled up the papers he had filled out and pushed them across the table. Krylov flipped through them carelessly, then said something to one of his escorts. The man reached inside his leather jacket and pulled out a well-worn black fabric case, which he handed to Krylov, who first counted the bills, then took several out and laid them on the table. Willenbrock spread them apart with his finger, scooped up the whole pile, and, without counting the money, placed it in his box. "Not a very sunny forecast for your beautiful country," he repeated as he did so.

He locked the box inside his desk and slowly got up, with the idea of ending the conversation. Krylov, however, stayed in his seat, playing with his empty glass. "How so, my friend?" he asked ironically. "You're doing well. I'm doing well. Everything is moving ahead again. We're both in business. Where's the problem?"

Willenbrock was caught off guard.

"I thought—" he began, but Krylov cut him off.

"Don't worry about Russia. She's been through a lot, but she'll never die, because the tsar can never die. Just don't you Europeans provoke her. That would be ill advised. We may not know how to live, but we know how to fight, and we know how to die. Like the song says: 'The Russian, he knows how to conquer.' "

Krylov laughed. He put his glass on the desk and shoved it over to Willenbrock. "One more for the road, my friend, and to our next meeting."

Willenbrock brought out the bottle and filled both glasses. He clinked one against the other and handed it to the Russian.

"In that case," he said, "here's to us, and to Russia. Your strength, your energy, and your will to live."

Krylov laughed again. "Actually, all that's a myth cooked up by our priests and poets. Let's drink to good old phlegmatic Russia, and to fatalism—that's something we have in abundance, that's what's allowed us to survive so long. The only energetic people in Russia were the German immigrants and the Jews. That's why neither has been too popular, you understand—they work too hard, they're too successful. How about drinking to our Russian mafia?"

Willenbrock sipped at his glass and quickly set it down inside his desk drawer. Krylov stood up, and his four escorts immediately did the same. Quietly issuing instructions, Krylov handed out three sets of keys and papers. Willenbrock walked his guests outside.

Jurek was right outside the trailer; he had opened the hood of a car and was busy changing sparkplugs. When the Russians came down the small staircase, he stiffened. As they passed, he exchanged glances with each—saying nothing, apparently indifferent. Willenbrock tried to break the hostile silence with a few casual words, but Jurek only nodded.

The sun had broken through the clouds and burned off the frost that had coated the cartops and windshields. A few isolated, wrinkled, dark-brown leaves still hung in the trees. When the men reached the first of the newly purchased vehicles, Willenbrock reviewed its features one more time. Krylov looked at Willenbrock and cocked his head, as if he were listening intently. Then he smiled and said: "Russia, Poland, the whole of Eastern Europe is good business for you, Herr Willenbrock."

"I can't complain," Willenbrock grinned.

Krylov spotted a bit of ash on his coat collar and slapped at it several times with his glove. When the collar was clean, he inspected his pants and shoes and then pulled on his gloves.

"I'm glad to hear that. I like doing business with happy people. Some people are always content and others are never satisfied, and the latter are very, very trying. To be avoided at all costs."

One of the young Russians had climbed inside a car and started the motor; the others watched as he flipped on all the buttons and switches.

"That's one thing we agree on completely," said Willenbrock. "I've always made out all right, even in the old days. And I've always been pretty content."

"That's what I mean."

"But, some things are just better than they used to be, that's all. Life is easier. I don't want to step on any toes, but the old system wasn't so great. Forgive me for saying so, but the old guys who ran our countries were idiots. I don't understand how an intelligent person like you managed to get on with them."

"Different times, my friend. You have to know how to make your way, even when things are tough. Especially then. When times are good any fool can get along. It takes a crisis to show if a nation or a man has real culture."

"Maybe you're right. But I'm not sad it's over. Life's more exciting. Sometimes a little too exciting."

Willenbrock stopped.

"What do you mean, my friend? Did something happen?"

"I was robbed. Last month some people broke into the lot and stole seven cars."

"That's a nuisance. Were they my countrymen?"

"I don't know. The police couldn't find anything. Though I can't say they made much of an effort."

"Seven cars—is that bad for you, my friend? I take it you're insured? Anyway, what's seven cars for a man like you? You wouldn't call that a crisis?"

"It just annoyed me, that's all."

"That I understand. Things like that are annoying. You'll have to figure something out. Put a stop to it. Otherwise they'll come back for more."

"I've already got something worked out."

"Then everything's in order, right, my German friend?"

Willenbrock wondered whether to tell Krylov about the telephone call that, to his surprise, had been weighing on him for weeks. He paused for so long that Krylov sensed something and looked him in the eye.

"It's silly. Evidently someone I used to work with made some trouble for me back then. Denounced me. I just found out who it was. The whole thing's disgusting. But thank God it's over."

"And what do you plan to do? What are you going to do with this person?"

"I don't know. I haven't decided. What would you do?"

"Ah, you Germans. Always going by the book. Always needing an official. I've heard you even have laws regulating bribery and slush funds. That's wonderful. Even criminals have to follow the rules! That's why I love you Germans. If God were German, imagine how orderly the world would be. There'd be a law for every problem: all we'd have to do is look it up. If God were German, Adam and Eve would never have sinned, since everything in Paradise would have gone by the book, too. But then, what kind of paradise would that have been? Probably only you Germans would have felt at home."

"What would you do in my shoes?"

"I wouldn't brood over it, my friend, that's for sure. I'd act and then put it out of my mind."

"Act how, exactly?"

Krylov looked at him and thought a moment. Then he called over the fourth man—his driver—and said something to him. The young man turned very red and seemed to be declining a request, but Krylov kept at it. Then the others perked up and started joining in. It was the first time Willenbrock heard their voices—bright, brittle, and a little raw, but childishly naïve and good-natured. The young man went searching around the yard, bending over a few times to pick something up. When he came back he set down two bricks and placed an arm-thick piece of wood across them. He stepped onto the wood first with one foot, then slowly raised the other until he was standing on top, waving his arms to keep his balance and getting the feel of his weight on the board. Carefully and slowly he then stepped off the small structure. He crouched down and massaged his hands as he fixed his eyes on the piece of wood. With a quick glance at Krylov, he threw his hand up and brought it crashing down onto the board. He let out a muffled cry and the board shot across the yard, slammed against a tire, and dropped to the ground. The young man stood up, looked at Krylov, embarrassed, said something that sounded like an apology, and ran off to fetch the board. He set it back on the bricks, shifting it several times to make it stable. Then he took it off again, repositioned the bricks, replaced the wood and adjusted it. Sweat was beading on his forehead. Krylov spoke to him reassuringly, then was silent, and everyone focused on the young man as he crouched in front of the board, concentrating. Once again he threw up his hand and brought it crashing down onto the wood. Once again he let out a kind of moan, but this time the thick board shattered; the splintered pieces lay between the knocked-over bricks. The man rose and rubbed his hand without looking up. Krylov, visibly pleased, clapped him lightly on the shoulder.

"Bravo," said Willenbrock, applauding the young man. "Do they learn that in the army?"

"Sergei's the only one who can do it," answered Krylov, "and he learned it in his village. Wouldn't that be one way to take care of your problem?"

"That might be one way," laughed Willenbrock, "but I don't think it's for me. That's not how things are done here, it could cause trouble."

"Feel free to talk to me, my friend. After all, we're partners, I'd be happy to help."

He looked straight at Willenbrock and the German understood that Krylov was seriously offering Sergei's services. The idea amused him and scared him at the same time, and he hurried to decline.

"No, it's impossible," he said.

Suddenly he felt his throat go dry, his tongue seemed swollen and paralyzed, and he had trouble getting the words out. He swallowed several times, then repeated that he couldn't possibly accept. The entire conversation struck him as unreal; he had the feeling he was standing outside himself and listening to his own voice.

Krylov nodded.

"I thought as much," was all he said. They went on to the next car. One of the young men climbed in and started the motor. The whole thing's absurd, thought Willenbrock. He stole a glance at the young Russian who had chopped the board in two.

"You must be out of your mind, Direktor," he said, as they moved toward the third vehicle. "I mean, the whole idea's insane. What kind of a place do you think this is? This is a civilized country. When you start taking the law into your own hands, then you're cooking in the devil's kitchen. But don't get me wrong: I appreciate your offer, and I'm very grateful. But I'm afraid it's out of the question. I don't use force. I never have. It's a matter of principle for me."

"So what are you going to do?"

"I don't know. Maybe nothing. Probably I won't do anything and just try to forget about it."

"If you can live with that, then everything is fine. Just forget about my Sergei. You asked for my opinion, my friend, and I'm used to taking matters into my own hands. Here in Germany you have officials in the tiniest village making sure things are done according to the rules, you have thick stacks of laws covering every possibility. But Russia's a big place, much bigger than the U.S.A. In Russia you either stick up for yourself or you're lost."

Then he called to Sergei, and they both climbed into the car.

"We'll be in touch," he said to Willenbrock, then gave him

a friendly nod and turned on the radio. Willenbrock watched, lost in thought, as the cars drove away. Krylov's a madman, he told himself, and was startled to notice a vague sense of envy welling up inside him, clouding his unambiguous refusal.

Jurek came ambling over. "Good deal, boss?"

Willenbrock nodded, still gazing out where Krylov had disappeared.

"Look at him, back on top of the world. He's got it all figured out. That man will never go hungry, not him—no, he'll leave that to others. Same as in Poland. People like that always wind up on top."

"We're not going hungry either, Jurek. What is it about him that bothers you?"

"People like that always come out all right."

"Why shouldn't he? He's good at what he does, and people like that are always in demand. What's your problem, Jurek? You don't even have to talk to him—I'm the one who does all the business. And besides, we can't be choosy about our customers."

"Business with a criminal. They should have hanged him when they had the chance. But his kind managed to crawl away and hide in the cracks, and now they're creeping back out."

"What did he do to you?"

"I'd hoped they were done for when their government collapsed. But those people always end up on top."

"He's a good client. I need him. I hope he does come back—in fact I hope he keeps coming here again and again to buy my cars. And you need him, too, Jurek, if you expect me to pay your salary."

Jurek's lips moved but he didn't say anything. He went on wiping his fingers with the rag, then jerked his head back to get the hair out of his face.

"I'll go balance those wheels now, boss," he said, sullenly.

"Do that," said Willenbrock.

5

Krylov's visit unsettled and confused Willenbrock more than he expected. Over the next few days he caught himself drifting off at his desk, staring into space, pondering what the Russian had said and mulling over his offer. The whole idea's absurd, he told himself, outrageous and barbaric, and criminal to boot, a throwback to the law of the jungle. He'd recently read that phrase somewhere and couldn't get it out of his mind; the image it called up struck him as forceful and vivid. Reluctant as he was to admit it, he felt drawn to Krylov's simple, violent solution. He envied the Russian his ready views and rapid-fire decisions, so different from his own approach. He resolved to forget their conversation, to suppress Krylov's proposal, erase it from his mind; he kept telling himself that the idea wasn't even worth considering, that he couldn't care less about Feuerbach. It's all so stupid, he thought, and so far in the past it doesn't matter; there's no point in dredging it up, what's the use of siccing some thug on the creep? Who needs revenge? It all happened in another life. I'm not an engineer at a bankrupt calculator company anymore. I'm a successful used-car dealer with fabulous prospects, and if I had the time to worry about anything it should be Eastern Europe and whether it will go on being good for my business—open and stable enough so that my customers have some cash in their pockets, but not so prosperous that they'll start buying new cars and forget about me. I never lost any sleep over Feuerbach back then, and I don't see any reason to do so now. I didn't know about him before and I'm not interested in him today, at least not enough to waste another thought on him. I can't afford to allow myself to get caught up in a past I don't need, don't care about, and have no use for whatsoever.

Willenbrock was determined to forget Feuerbach and the whole disgusting episode. He could barely remember the man and had trouble picturing him: all that came to mind was a well-trimmed beard, a pair of red-framed glasses with thick lenses, and a few conversations about work that had been entertaining enough, or at least not completely boring. But he wasn't even sure he would recognize Feuerbach if he ran into him. He would never have given the man a second thought if Berner hadn't called and recounted the whole sad story. Willenbrock sensed his annoyance shifting: it wasn't Feuerbach but Berner who was to blame for this growing sense of resentment. He felt Berner had cajoled him into chasing a ghost, a specter from times long past and connections long forgotten. He cursed Berner and his annoying phone call. He tried to put him out of his mind, and shut his eyes hard to strengthen his resolve.

Having decided not to renew the policy on his cars and the office trailer, Willenbrock ran an ad for a night watchman in a neighborhood paper. The day it appeared, twenty-five mostly elderly men responded; another eight called over the next few days. Several promised to bring dogs—trained, ferocious watchdogs they claimed would stop any intruder. A few said they owned blank pistols. Two men, who sounded very young over the telephone, boasted that they had Russian army pistols, which they proposed to keep on the job at night, even though they didn't have permits. Willenbrock also heard from two security agencies that specialized in protecting buildings and industrial sites, offering the services of uniformed guards.

The response to his tiny ad amazed Willenbrock. He invited six of the applicants in for an interview, and spent over half an hour with the first two, describing what he expected and hearing their ideas about how they planned to guard his lot; one showed photo after photo of his dog. With the four other candidates Willenbrock got right to the point; he told them how much he could pay and asked them to offer some brief suggestions. Then he took his time making his decision; he waited until two days had gone by without any new applicants before calling one of the men, Fritz Pasewald, a fifty-eight-year-old mechanic who had been out of work for half a year. Willenbrock liked him because he was the only applicant who hadn't sat there meekly but had matter-of-factly and directly explained what he would do on the job and what he wanted from Willenbrock. But the actual reason he was choosing Pasewald, Willenbrock realized, was because the man showed none of the same submissive bitterness that marked the other applicants—a quality that made Willenbrock irritable, even aggressive.

The new watchman started that same evening. He arrived half an hour before Jurek locked up and waited with his German shepherd outside the trailer. Willenbrock stood on the stairs while Pasewald calmed and secured his dog, then asked his new employee to step inside. He had Pasewald fill out a tax form, gave it a quick look and stuck it in his briefcase. He showed him the coffeemaker and the cupboard where the dishes were stored. In case of emergency, Willenbrock explained, Pasewald shouldn't leave the office before phoning first the police and then him. He posted a number by the receiver and assured Pasewald that he always kept his cell phone close by and could be reached anytime, day or night. Then he asked about Pasewald's dog, how old it was and if it was a purebred, adding that he hoped the dog would soon learn he wasn't a burglar but rather his meal ticket. Then, as he did every evening, Willenbrock put the money, car papers, and keys in his briefcase. Pasewald suggested that he could do some bodywork now and then, since, as Willenbrock knew, he was a trained mechanic; naturally he had his welder's license.

"That's great," said Willenbrock, "but you should speak to Jurek about that. And wait a few days before you offer. Try to get to know him first. Jurek's a little sensitive—the proud Pole, you know. I don't want him to think I'm dissatisfied with his work."

"It's just a suggestion," replied Pasewald. "Anyway, I won't get bored. I've brought along plenty to read."

"What are you reading?" asked Willenbrock.

"My daughter keeps me supplied. She's studying at the university and is determined to educate her old man. She picks out the books, and whenever I finish one she makes me answer questions. Just like an exam."

"What kind of books does she assign?"

"Everything. History, the origins of the earth. If I answer all her questions right I get to read a novel as a reward. But she even tests me on the novels."

"Your daughter wants to turn you into a professor."

"That's exactly what I told her."

"Then you've found the perfect job here: you can read whatever your daughter gives you and get paid for it."

He stood up and held out his hand. "Welcome aboard. I'm sure it will all work out. And watch out for yourself, not just for my cars."

"Catcher will watch out for me," said Pasewald, and as Willenbrock seemed puzzled, he added: "Catcher, my dog."

"See you tomorrow morning. But now go talk nice to Catcher so he'll let me out of the office."

He grabbed his briefcase and opened the door for Pasewald.

"We've got a man watching the lot at night," he told his wife over dinner, "so from now on I'll be able to sleep better."

"Sleep better?" she said. "That's impossible. You already sleep like a dead man."

"Well, now I can sleep like a dead man without a care in the world. I just hired this man off the street. He used to be unemployed, and as of today I'm paying him so he can read books all night long. Makes me feel philanthropic—plus I can claim him as a business expense. Good news all around, don't you think, Susanne? I suppose I could have gone through the Federal Employment Agency, and that would have saved me money, but then I wouldn't have been able to choose. Besides, that would have meant a lot of paperwork."

"You sure know how to take care of yourself. Things always work out for you, don't they?"

"They do indeed. Because I want them to. Don't forget, I come from a small town full of whiners. My mother whined because my father stayed a simple production engineer and never got appointed to a university—he didn't even make it to department manager. My relatives whined because there were always other people so much more successful. My teachers whined because they had to waste their lives on kids they hated. The whole sweet town was always whining. But me? I laughed. I always laughed. Whenever someone tried to trip me up, I laughed. If I flunked an exam, I just laughed it off. I was always happy with myself and with the world. Then one day I noticed that my laughing made the whiners whine even more. That did it for me. I decided I would stay happy no matter what. And that's how you wound up with such a happy husband. Aren't you glad?"

"Yes, at least most of the time. Though you can be a bit smug now and then. Especially the way you always manage to use people for your own ends, take advantage of them."

"The advantage is always mutual, love. I'm not forcing anyone to work for me. Anyone who doesn't like it is free to leave. I just don't want to have to put up with any more whining. It reminds me too much of my childhood."

He took his glass and the beer bottle and stood up.

"I have to make a phone call," he said, "but we could go to the movies later if you want. Just give me ten minutes. By the way, Frau Tuchter called from the travel agency, she wanted to know if we'd like to go to Venice over Christmas. Five days away from all the usual Christmas sentimentality. How about it, Susanne?"

"We already promised my mother we'd spend Christmas with her. Besides, I want to go, I want to see her."

"And your charming brother as well. Another delightful family reunion. What about New Year's?"

"Okay, but no more than three days. I can't close the shop any longer than that."

"Why don't you take it easy and hire some help? I've told you a thousand times, there's no need for you to be a slave to your boutique."

"Please, don't start in again with your paying for someone to work for me. It's my store. I want to do it on my own."

"Right," nodded Willenbrock, "self-fulfillment and all that."

His wife made a face and shook her head in silence. When Willenbrock opened the door to the living room she said: "And besides, we have to make another trip out to the country before winter. I've still got a few flowerpots to bring in before it freezes, and I'd like to go through the garden again before the snow comes."

"We don't have to give up a whole weekend for that, and certainly not New Year's. I could just drive out there sometime and take care of things. But let me go make this call. I'll be ready in ten minutes."

He closed the door behind him and sat down by the telephone.

6

By mid-December Willenbrock had let his inventory shrink to eighteen cars, which he displayed on the lot, and one ten-year-old Mercedes in the roped-off area behind the trailer.

"The holidays are almost here," Jurek had explained to him two years before. "Then no one will be coming from my country. And with the Russians you have to wait till Twelfth Night."

At the time Willenbrock had considered closing down in the middle of December and taking four weeks' vacation, but Susanne had protested; she didn't intend to let his business considerations dictate how she should live her life. Besides, how could she close the boutique in the middle of the Christmas season? She might as well give it up. Willenbrock had dropped the idea; instead, he leased the greenhouse on the neighboring property. For years the building with its clouded windowpanes—a witness to a past century—had stood empty and abandoned amid some volunteer cabbages, a scattering of flowers, and the tall, wild plants that commonly cropped up on the vacant lots interspersed among all the new construction. Willenbrock had managed to obtain a five-year lease that he could terminate earlier in the event that he managed to secure possession of the property he was using and could start building. He replaced the old broken panes and had a work pit dug inside, which he shored up with railroad ties. As a further temporary fix, he covered the structure with double-sided insulation batting and installed two used cast-iron stoves for heating. This way Jurek could use the structure as a workshop, making minor repairs and painting the cars in any weather.

Now that the holidays had come again, there was little for him to do at work, so Willenbrock decided to take a day off and drive out to his country house in Bugewitz, near the Stettin Lagoon, opposite Usedom Island. The town was less than a kilometer from the old Kaminer drawbridge, the remains of which loomed in the sky. The hoists had functioned through the end of the war, so the island stayed connected to the rail network despite the heavy shipping traffic. The iron structure towered above the flat land like a gloomy, rusty giant. It reminded Willenbrock of his childhood, his model train set.

The property lay on the edge of a forest, and since it was part of a nature preserve, there was a ban on new construction, so the Willenbrocks had reason to expect that the peace and quiet would be maintained, along with their open view, broken only by orchards and forests.

He had told his wife he was making the trip with a customer who had complained about a car; he wanted to look into the complaint and if necessary put it right. Susanne was surprised he wanted to devote a whole day to one client, instead of simply turning the car over to Jurek, but Willenbrock explained that complaints were bad for business, and besides, he could use the opportunity to drive out to Bugewitz, check on the house and garden, and make things ready for the winter.

What he neglected to tell her, though, was that it was he who had called the customer, and not vice versa. She was a university student and had just passed her driving exam. He had recommended a certain ten-year-old car and, after chatting with her for a while, came down in price.

He always made time for unaccompanied women who showed up on the lot to buy a car or sell the one they had. They were invariably young and offered a welcome change of pace, a rare and pleasant spot of color in the gray monotony of his mostly male and shabbily dressed clientele. Willenbrock would turn on the charm, joke and flirt, assess the woman's reactions to him, and sound out his prospects at winning her over—and not just as a customer. Whenever a woman interested him sexually, he tested the limits by pushing them, becoming forward merely to see what his chances were, to probe how far he could go. Some of the women protested immediately when he spoke to them too suggestively, reacting indignantly to the least personal remark, while others even allowed him to put his arm around their hips. After the transaction was finalized, he would ask for the phone number of any woman he wanted to see again, claiming he needed it for his records. Two weeks later he would call up and try to arrange a date.

He asked the university student how she was getting along with her car. She told him that, in fact, she regretted buying it. She had no driving experience and knew nothing about motors, gears, and clutches. She confessed that she would climb out of the car shaking, even after a very short drive, and so she practically never used it, except when there was no other choice and the streets were relatively empty. Willenbrock offered to help. He suggested they take the car out for a day's drive and assured her that afterward she would be a perfect driver. Taken aback, she asked how he could spare so much time, to which he responded that he really couldn't, but was always prepared to help his best clients. He told her to pick the day and he would pick the route, since he wanted her to get practice not only in the city but also on country roads and on the autobahn. If he chose the destination he could combine business with pleasure. The girl agreed and said that Tuesdays were best because it was always easy for her to get away. He told her he'd meet her in front of her apartment the following Tuesday, at nine on the dot.

"I didn't think you'd come," was how she greeted him.

"Turns out I have to go up to the Lagoon anyway," Willenbrock replied, "so it's no great sacrifice on my part. Now, where's our wondermobile?"

She showed him the car. When they climbed in, the girl got flustered and embarrassed trying to start the engine, but Willenbrock calmed her down. "I'm not your driving instructor and I'm not a policeman, Fräulein Retzlaff. Let's just have a good time, there's no rush. And don't worry if you do make a mistake. I'm not going to tear your head off. Try again."

They took the autobahn over to Prenzlau and then followed the major thoroughfares east out of town. Willenbrock did most of the talking, as the girl had to concentrate on driving, and spoke mostly in monosyllables. He repeatedly praised her technique to make her feel secure. When they passed a country inn he asked her to turn around and pull into the parking lot. He invited her to lunch; even though they were the only guests they had to wait a long time to be served. She talked about the university, where she studied entomology.

"Does that mean anything to you?" she asked.

"Insects?" ventured Willenbrock, uncertainly.

The girl nodded appreciatively.

"So you actually study those miserable little gnats?"

"More or less."

"Why? I have screens all over my house just to keep them out. What's the point of studying them? And what will you do once you have your degree?"

"I don't know. I just study what interests me. Because I'm curious. Insects are one of the most exciting populations on the planet. They're a lot older than we are. They have an infinite variety of species. Every imago—that's the insect in its final form—is a miracle of perfection, unbelievably beautiful. More beautiful and more impressive than any other life form, including humans."

"But, seriously, what can you do with a degree in bugs and butterflies? What do your professors say? Do they have some practical course telling you how this wonderful field can help you earn a living?"

"No. Actually there's not much you can do with it at all."

"Doesn't that worry you?"

"Nobody in my class knows what they'll do after they graduate. We're all trying to stay in school as long as we can." She laughed.

"What's there to laugh about? Sooner or later you'll need some money, don't you think?"

"Sooner or later, sure. Then I'll find a job," she answered, unconcerned—"something to keep my head above water and pay the rent. And finance my car, of course."

"You got a good deal on that car, Margot. I hope you realized I could have gotten a lot more for it. It's a good car, a very good car."

"I like the car, and I appreciate it. I also appreciate your giving up your day for me."

"It's all part of the customer satisfaction program."

"Including the meal? Are you this generous with all your customers?"

"That's a special service reserved for beautiful women," he said, and reached for her hand. She looked at him briefly and waited several seconds before removing it to pick up her glass of water.

After the meal they drove through Anklam to Buggenhagen; they walked along the Peenestrom and looked across the river at the island. The girl felt cold; Willenbrock offered his jacket. He wanted to take a little walk through the fens, but she insisted on heading back as soon as possible. She didn't have the right shoes for a tramp in the wet grass and the damp forest floor, and besides, she was still cold.

"In just a minute you'll be able to warm up, Margot. The house is heated. I phoned in an hour ago from the restaurant to turn on the heater. By the time we get there it'll be warm as a bathtub."

"You turned on the heater by phoning in?" the girl asked, amazed.

"That's right." Willenbrock laughed. "Like I told you, I used to be an engineer. I still like to play with gadgets. I love spending money on them—I guess I'm easily seduced. Every year I go to the computer and electronics fair, but these days it's purely a hobby. My car's loaded with all sorts of electronic toys, too, stuff I don't really need, of course."

"Were you always like that?"

"Absolutely. In school I had the biggest electric train set of anyone. It took up our whole attic; I had trains running on three levels. I had a rail hoist that I built myself which I could use to lift or lower a locomotive plus one car. I doubt even the Bundesbahn has that anymore. It was a little like the bridge I showed you. Are you interested in that sort of thing? In technology?"

"No, I'm happy if my car runs and I can manage to send a fax."

"That's what I thought. On the other hand, you know all there is to know about insects."

"No I don't. Nobody knows all there is to know about insects. We don't even know all the species. But bugs and butterflies bore you, right?"

Willenbrock laughed. "I'm afraid so. I don't understand the first thing about them. Come on, let's go to my place. You can warm up there."

They got back in the car and Willenbrock directed the young woman along the country lanes and cinder-slab roads to his property.

It was an old farmhouse, built of clinker brick on a stone base. The roof and windows had been rebuilt. The cowshed and the huge barn, which together with the main house formed a rectangular farmstead, were still being restored. A wooden scaffold was set up over the door to the cowshed, and the empty window frames were hung with tarpaulins. In front of the barn was a stack of fitted wooden rafters, covered by some old doors that had been taken off their hinges; next to that were two palettes of roof tiles wrapped in plastic. Without saying anything, Willenbrock led the way through the yard and up the small flight of steps to the main house. He unlocked three locks with separate keys.

"A hundred and thirty years old," he said. "A hundred thirty-four, to be exact. Solidly built, too—over several generations."

He opened the door and quickly stepped inside to activate a switch hidden behind the stairs.

"The security system," he told the girl. "I have to turn it off or there'd be a hell of a racket. When you don't spend a lot of time in a house, you have to invest in things like that."

"Besides, you like all this electronic stuff."

"I love it. Take a look around, check out all the rooms. I'll be ready in ten minutes, I just have to straighten up a little and bring some things inside. Shall we have another coffee before we head back?"

"I'll make the coffee. Just tell me where to find everything. Is that the kitchen, through there?"

"That's right. But watch out, there are two mousetraps lying around somewhere. The little beasts always show up in the fall. They treat the place as if it's been in their family since 1862—and come to think of it, it probably has."

He climbed up to the second floor. The girl opened the kitchen door and admired the well-furnished room; she was impressed. Then she found cups and coffee and put some water on to boil. She opened the doors to the other rooms on the ground floor, but just looked at them without going inside. Then she set the table in the kitchen, brewed the coffee, and sat down next to the warm heater.

"I see you found everything," said Willenbrock, coming into the kitchen and washing his hands at the sink. "And it's warm in here, too. Feeling a little better?"

"It's great. The house was warm from the moment we stepped in."

"Long live technology. And, of course, your bugs and butterflies as well, Margot."

"I like your house, Herr Willenbrock. It's like a little palace."

"No, just an old manor house. But please call me Bernd, we don't have to be so formal."

"I guess you can make a lot of money in the used-car business."

He looked around at the furnishings, then nodded. "Yes, if you buy and sell the right cars for the right price, you can actually do pretty well. But not if you give them away like I did with yours."

He sat down next to her, let her pour his coffee, and stared at her so intently she turned red. With one finger he cautiously stroked the back of her hand.

"Do we have to go back right away or do you have a little time, Margot?"

"I think it's better if we go."

He nodded in agreement.

"You drive well. You drive very well. You'll make out fine with the car."

"You're a good instructor, Bernd. At the driving school I was a nervous wreck."

"Why? You're a good driver. So, did you take a look around?"

"Yes. Very impressive. Almost too fancy for a weekend house."

"Would you like to see the upstairs?"

"What's up there? The bedroom? I don't have to see that. I'm sure it's equally impressive."

"I don't have any mirrors on the ceiling, if that's what you mean."

"Do you live here alone? Are you married?"

"Yes, and quite happily, too."

"In that case we'd better be going. Your wife will be waiting for you."

"No," he said. He took her hand, held it up to his mouth, and kissed it.

"What's that supposed to mean?" the girl asked, annoyed, and jerked her hand back. "You think I owe you for the ride? Or did you think I'd be so impressed with your little dacha that I'd jump into bed with you?"

"Relax, Margot, there's no reason to get angry. I just kissed your hand, that's all. A polite little gesture. A touch of the old chivalry, a quaint German custom—didn't you learn that in school?"

"Let's go, Herr Willenbrock. Don't think I'm so stupid as to fall for that. Please, you're old enough to be my father."

"Ow—that was cruel. Below the belt."

"When you're done with your coffee I'll wash the dishes. We don't need to run the dishwasher for these two little cups."

"I would. I make it a point to avoid doing anything I can have a machine do for me. That's freedom, Margot. I use my money to buy time. Time I'd otherwise have to waste doing things I don't like or that bore me. The money frees me. It lets me buy time for living—and that's the only value it has for me."

"If time for living is what you're after, you should stop smoking."

"That kind of thinking's a little too simplistic for my taste. But you're right, I'm not very consistent. If you really don't mind washing up, I'll take another look at the cowshed."

He stood up and drained the coffee cup, gave her a quick nod, and went out. The student washed the dishes and dried them carefully before putting them back in the cupboard. She turned on the radio and stood by the kitchen window, where she watched Willenbrock fix something on the scaffold before he disappeared into the cowshed. When he came back he stood in the door to the kitchen and asked if she was ready to leave.

"I'm sorry," she answered, "I'm afraid I overreacted earlier. I must have sounded like a schoolgirl."

"Maybe you were afraid you'd fallen into the clutches of a rapist."

"I'm sorry. Please forgive me."

"No problem," he said.

She was standing in front of him; suddenly he put his arm

around her hips, pulled her to him, and kissed her. She attempted to push him back, but he held her fast and pressed her to him, so that their faces were only inches away from each other. They looked at each other in silence, without moving, without the slightest sign of emotion.

"Let go of me," she said.

He dropped his hands.

"Ready to go?" he asked.

"In a second," she answered, "I'd still like to see the upstairs. If that's all right."

He stepped aside to let her pass, pointed to the stairs, and said: "Please, after you."

She walked slowly up the broad, curved staircase, looking at the framed portraits of farm couples in traditional Pomeranian dress as she went. Downstairs he latched the door to the house and followed her with measured steps, stopping when she did.

"Nice," she said. She viewed the upper level with large, lingering eyes. In the bedroom, Willenbrock showed her the wardrobe he had built, with doors that opened at the press of a button. He stood beside her, his hands in his pockets.

"Why did you call me? Why did you drive out here with me? To give me a driving lesson?"

"I wanted to see you, Margot."

"Didn't you say you were married?"

"Yes, I am."

"And your wife?"

"I wanted to see you. Is that a crime? I liked you. As soon as I saw you. It was like thunder and lightning when you walked onto my car lot. I can't help it. You are unbelievably beautiful, Margot."

"I don't know. I don't even know why I came out here, or why I went driving with you in the first place."

"I don't know either. But it's beautiful, it's beautiful being with you."

"I'm not going to sleep with you, Bernd. Just to make that clear."

"That's fine. Who said anything about sleeping with me? I'm just happy to spend the day with you. Would you like to see the shed and the barn? They're not fixed up yet, I still have a couple years of work to do."

"No, I don't want to. Tell me the truth, why did you call me?"

"What can I say? I think I'm a little in love. But I know—I'm old enough to be your father."

"I didn't mean it like that, Bernd."

"Whether you meant it or not, it's the truth. My God you're beautiful."

"Stop it, you're embarrassing me."

"Can I ask you a favor, Margot? I'd like to kiss you, just on the cheek, if you'll let me."

"I don't know. What is it you're after, Bernd?"

"One kiss, just on the cheek. But if you don't want me to, I'll understand, Margot. Butterflies and insects aren't supposed to be touched, they're too delicate."

"Please, Bernd. I don't know. I'm all confused."

"Would you like to leave? Shall we head back?"

"No. Not yet."

"I'm going to kiss you now, Margot. Just once, very gently, very tenderly. The way you kiss a butterfly."

He went slowly up to her and kissed her on the cheek. She

turned her face toward his and he placed his hand on her neck and drew her to him.

In Berlin they said goodbye on the street. The young woman thanked him for being patient with her driving.

"If you have any more problems with the car just give me a call," he said, kissing her on the cheek.

"I didn't call you. You called me. Or have you forgotten?"

"And I'm glad I did, Margot. I'll call you again sometime. We had a nice trip, didn't we?"

"Very nice," was all she said, "but it's better if you don't call me anymore. I have a very jealous boyfriend. It was nice, let's leave it just like that."

She waved to a young man leaning out a window on the fourth floor, locked the car door, crossed the street, and walked to her building. Willenbrock watched her disappear inside. Then he lit a cigarette; the two men stared at each other, and Willenbrock sauntered back to his car, feeling pleased.

7

Two days before Christmas, Willenbrock handed Jurek an envelope.

"Your Christmas bonus," he said. "I'll see you after New Year's. Get some rest, and say hello to your wife for me. What's your boy up to, anyway? Is she managing okay with him, or is he still acting crazy?"

"He doesn't listen to a word she says," Jurek answered, "and his friends are no good. Nothing but hooligans."

"Come on! How old is he—thirteen, fourteen? They're not hooligans, they're just kids. Didn't we raise a little hell when we were their age."

"He's seventeen. Believe me, these kids are hooligans. The problem is his father's not around. But what am I supposed to do? I can't make enough in Poznan to support us."

"Talk to him, he's got a head on his shoulders. He's knows you have to be here to work. Tell him he has to take over as the man of the family, look out for his mother. You'll have some time at home, you can explain things to him. And buy him something really nice. A computer—that'll keep him busy. Get his mind on other matters."

"He already has a computer. He has everything. I buy him whatever a kid his age could want, but it's no help."

"A difficult age," said Willenbrock, at a loss. "In any case, I hope you have a nice Christmas. And don't hit him—that won't help either."

"It won't help, it won't hurt. A happy Christmas to you, too, boss. Many blessings."

After Jurek said goodbye, Willenbrock went into his office and cleaned up. He'd brought along an extra briefcase so he could pack more papers than usual and work at home over the holiday.

Shortly before five, when Willenbrock switched on the outside light, Pasewald showed up to begin his watch. Willenbrock also gave him an envelope with some money. Pasewald looked surprised, so he explained: "I realize you haven't been here long enough to be officially entitled to a bonus, but you've got to celebrate Christmas too, right?"

He asked Pasewald if he'd like a television in the office, and offered to bring in a small portable one, but the watchman declined. He watched too much TV at home; here he just wanted to read the books his daughter had picked out for him.

Willenbrock understood and nodded. "Over the holidays you don't have to spend all night here. Just look in two or three times. Even burglars take time off at Christmas. I wouldn't want to keep you from your family."

Pasewald turned down the offer. "My grandchildren are still little. I see them in the afternoon; by evening they're already asleep. And my wife likes to go to bed early. She doesn't mind if I'm not at home."

Willenbrock picked up both briefcases. "Well, have a merry Christmas. I'll see you again on January third. I might drop in once before then. If anything comes up, you have my phone number."

He stowed the briefcases in his trunk and drove off. He stopped in at a jeweler's to pick up the necklace he'd ordered for his wife. He had already paid for it and was on his way out when he turned back and quickly chose two pieces from the display case—a ring and a brooch—and had them wrapped in fancy paper for Susanne's mother and sister. Next he drove to Alexanderplatz, parked his car in front of police headquarters, and went into an electronics store to buy more presents and a few little things for himself. After he called his wife from the car to tell her he was still running errands in the city and would be home a little late, he stepped out to look over the presents in the trunk and see if he'd forgotten anyone. Then he got back in the car and made some more phone calls. Half an hour later he was sitting in the lobby of the hotel at the Gendarmenmarkt; he ordered an espresso and leafed through a newspaper as he watched the waitresses and guests. When a red-haired woman wearing a fur hat and a long black coat walked in, he stood up. He kissed her on the cheek, led her to his table and took her coat, which he draped over one of the chairs.

"I'm really glad to see you, Frau Doktor."

"Are you insane?" she said. "What's so urgent that you had me called out of a faculty meeting? The last one of the year, no less."

"You look good, Charlotte. Very elegant."

"You mean that's why you called me? To tell me that! And right when they're deciding the allocations for next year, too—do you know how important that is?"

"It's nice of you to come, Charlotte. I just had to see you, that's all."

"You really have lost your mind. I can't believe you. I race out like a lunatic just to come and drink coffee with you? Tell me it's not true. You said it was a matter of life and death."

"It is. I thought I'd die if I didn't get to see you."

"Terrific. I'll have one cup of coffee and that's it. Then I'm gone."

Willenbrock took her hand. "I didn't dare hope for anything more. I just had to see you again before the year ended."

"A little holiday anxiety? Afraid of the big family reunion?"

"Of course," he said. He called a waiter and ordered coffee and a bottle of champagne.

Half an hour later he retrieved the key to his room. Before they got in the elevator, he asked the waiter to follow with the opened bottle and serve them upstairs.

Willenbrock and Susanne spent Christmas at her mother's, in a village on the Weser River, south of Bremen in Lower Saxony. Originally from Thuringia, she had moved to the village after her husband died, to be with one of her sons. He owned a well-construction business that also specialized in ground inspections for new buildings. The mother lived in his house, but separate from the family, in a converted attic with its own entrance. Her isolation was made worse because even though she'd been living there for ten years, she was still considered a newcomer and an outsider in the village—someone to say hello to on the street and engage in a brief casual conversation, but not eligible for any closer acquaintance, to say nothing of friendship. And while her son lived under the same roof, he and his family seldom found time to do things with her, either to visit upstairs or invite her down.

Willenbrock and his wife stayed up in the attic. Susanne's brother had offered them the guest room on the second floor, but it was her mother who had invited them for Christmas, and since she had already made room for them, and Susanne didn't want to upset her, they complied with her wishes.

Aside from short walks around the village, everyone spent the days together in the house.

Willenbrock noticed that whenever the family had to come together—for meals, church, or exchanging gifts—they always dispersed again as quickly as possible. The two children played in the living room, which was all done up for Christmas, but retreated to their own rooms the minute the grown-ups came in. The three women—Susanne, her mother, and Christine, her sister-in-law—spent the whole day in the large kitchen. When they weren't fixing meals or washing dishes they'd sit at the kitchen table and chat. Willenbrock felt a little bitter about being left to the mercy of Fred, his brother-in-law. Fred had been running his own business for twenty years, and since he was successful and a family man, as he put it, he was always giving his sister's husband helpful advice and passing on lessons drawn from his own experience. He would go so far as to turn off the TV in the middle of a sports program Willenbrock was watching, declaring that the show wasn't interesting, then force Willenbrock to join him in his study, where he'd launch into a lecture or expound a list of useful tips. Trying to avoid an argument, Willenbrock would focus intently on his cigarette and let the flood of words wash over him. Struggling to keep the lengthening gray ash intact, he would watch the glowing tip smolder its way up the white paper. Then, at the very last moment, when the bent and brittle column of burned tobacco came perilously close to falling, he would tap it into the ashtray.

Fred was explaining how to deal with banks—who to talk to and who to avoid.

"Always speak with the boss, or at least with his deputy. You have to arrange it so that whenever you walk in, whoever sees you immediately tells the manager. After all, they live off your money; they're paid from the interest on your account. I trust you've got a nice little sum tucked away, so you should behave accordingly. Act as if you suspect them, check up on them, and above all make sure they know you're in contact with other banks. You have to keep them guessing. That way they'll work especially hard for you. Also, make a point of inviting the manager to meet you in your office. That makes an impression, even if it never happens."

He asked about Willenbrock's investment strategy and whether he had a financial advisor. Willenbrock stubbed out his cigarette, looked at his brother-in-law, and appeared to be thinking. Then he got up, walked over to the dark-brown sideboard, and ran his fingers along the hand-carved columns.

"Eighteen hundred and twenty," said Fred. "One of my wife's family heirlooms. Today it's worth a fortune."

He joined Willenbrock by the sideboard, opened the upper-right door, reached in, and pressed a hidden button located under a shelf. A narrow compartment popped open inside the door frame, a secret cubicle. Full of pride, Fred turned to his brother-in-law and looked at him expectantly.

"You know, it has four of these compartments. They're all well hidden and operate perfectly. Good German workmanship. It'll last for centuries."

"I know," said Willenbrock, "you've already shown it to me twice before."

"It really is a fantastic piece. People have offered me huge sums for it. So what's the story? Is your advisor any good?"

"Sure. He's a great guy. Not bad at team handball, either. We play in the same league. The forty-five-plus group, of course."

"That's not good, Bernd. You shouldn't get too chummy with your advisor. How can you talk straight to him if he's your sports buddy?"

Willenbrock nodded thoughtfully and replied: "Tell me, do you cheat on your wife?"

"Come again? What do you mean?"

"I mean, do you sleep with other women or just with your wife? You know, monogamous or swinger?"

Fred looked automatically at the closed door, then asked, indignant: "What kind of question is that? We're sitting here talking and suddenly you come up with something like that."

"It just popped into my mind, that's all."

"Not a very appropriate subject for a family gathering. Especially at Christmas. You've got some pretty strange ideas. I don't ask you whether you cheat on my sister."

"If you did I'd tell you."

"I don't want to know. Enough, let's change the subject."

Willenbrock's mother-in-law came in carrying cake on a platter and looked at them closely. "Have you two been fighting again? You only see each other once a year, can't you manage to get along?"

"We weren't fighting," said Willenbrock. His brother-in-law nodded and added: "We were talking about business, Mother."

"Not at Christmas, children. Come on in the living room. The table's all set for cake and coffee."

Three days later Willenbrock and his wife flew from Hamburg to Venice. They had booked a suite in a small, three-storied pensione in Cannaregio that seemed to be staffed by a single person; at any rate they always saw the same little old man morning and evening, pushing his way past them on the stairs, carrying breakfast trays or fresh towels. Every time they ran into him he asked if everything was to their satisfaction, then always added that even if the weather was lousy today it would be sunny tomorrow, according to the TV forecast. Their two rooms were narrow and sparsely furnished, and the breakfast was so meager that after the first day they decided to eat out. In Berlin Willenbrock had suggested to Susanne that they stay at a four-star hotel, but she'd insisted on this little pensione. She hated luxury establishments, which struck her as absolutely identical the world over, so that when you stepped into the lobby or the elevator or your room, you had the feeling you'd been there before. Even though each of these places had its own uniquely lavish decor, they somehow looked alike, completely interchangeable. The result was that she lost all sense of the city she was visiting; she couldn't escape a feeling of déjà vu, which made the cities seem interchangeable as well. Consequently she preferred staying in smaller pensiones, where the cramped space and frugal offerings felt more authentic, more local. Low-priced pensiones, public transportation, inexpensive restaurants frequented by the locals, and taxi drivers who either jabbered away or drove in silence—these were what distinguished one city from another, what gave her a sense of its character as much as famous museums and monuments. This is what she needed to experience to get a feel for a place, to understand what made a given city tick. She had adopted this point of view years before, having come across it in a novel by one of her favorite authors. Since then she always took it as her guiding principle when arranging vacations. So when Willenbrock suggested they move to a hotel on the Lido or the Grand Canal, she refused; but as he was familiar with, and even amused by, his wife's opinions, he readily gave in, although he did prefer the expensive hotels. He saw no reason why getting to know local ways and customs meant having to renounce the luxuries he appreciated.

They spent three days wandering around a rainy, gray Venice, making every effort to avoid the most touristed places. They explored the outlying districts, visited restaurants and cafés full of Venetian fishermen and tradesmen; they spent hours observing the goings-on, listening to conversations, watching the hand gestures, enjoying the spectacle as if it had been staged just for them.

They set aside half a day for the island cemetery of San Michele. Susanne had brought her camera; she took pictures of the plaques and gravestones that interested her, and copied down some of the inscriptions she found especially moving. At first Willenbrock wandered with her through the cemetery, but after an hour he sat down on the stairs by the exit and made phone calls until she came back, exhausted and happy, and they caught the ferry to Murano.

On their last day they took a gondola all around the canals.

Willenbrock found it boring, and he didn't like being stared at by the tourists on the bridges, but Susanne had insisted. For her the gondolier was the local equivalent of a taxi driver, and she conversed with him throughout the trip in a jumble of German, Italian, and English that had a grammar all its own. Willenbrock enjoyed listening to the two go at it, and feigned interest just so he could add to the confusion by tossing in bits of Polish and Russian, though neither Susanne nor the gondolier let that distract them. Susanne simply ignored his remarks, and the gondolier, a short, powerful man in his fifties, didn't even seem to notice that some new, totally unknown languages had entered the conversation.

The next day Willenbrock paid for the room; he found the old man making his rounds with a stack of towels, which he draped over his shoulder to write out the bill. At Susanne's request Willenbrock gave him a sizable tip; the man thanked him profusely and accompanied them out to the street, still carrying the towels, to point the way to the nearest landing, though this was hardly necessary.

They arrived in Berlin late that afternoon. Dropping off their luggage at home, they drove into town in separate cars—Susanne to her boutique, to take down the vacation sign, check the mail, and prepare for the next day, and Willenbrock to his lot, where he looked over the vehicles before sitting down in the trailer. He read his mail, opened a package of electronic parts he had ordered, and made phone calls until Pasewald showed up with his dog. He listened to Pasewald's report on the past several days and then drove straight to his gym in the Hansastrasse. He showed his card to the girl at the desk, took a locker key, and went into the dressing room. Minutes later he was inside the gym, saying hello to his teammates, who were already playing. He had their captain, Dieter, assign him to a team, and spent an hour running across the floor, sweating and panting, chasing the ball and scoring goals. After showering they all went for a beer to a nearby pub run by an Italian. They analyzed the game, described their respective New Years' celebrations, and talked about business. All but two of the men, who both worked in the same bank, were small business owners.

Genser, who dealt in computers and Russian-language software, was attempting to tell a story about being robbed in a hotel. He frequently traveled to Eastern Europe, and talked a lot about his experiences in Moscow, Petersburg, and Kiev—hair-raising night rides through empty streets, and contract negotiations suddenly interrupted by armed men silently assembling behind their Russian boss while he went on doing business, smiling and stubborn, without so much as batting an eye.

One night, said Genser, when his teammates were finally ready to listen, he was awakened in his hotel room by the sound of someone rummaging through his things. When he realized Genser was awake, the intruder signaled him to stay in bed and keep still. The man then calmly went on searching through Genser's belongings, and, once he was done, walked out the door. As soon as the man had left, Genser turned on the light and phoned the desk. Two gentlemen from the hotel management showed up, tried to calm him down, and asked what had been taken. They reproached him for not locking his room, but he insisted that he had been very careful to lock the door, whereupon the two men pointed out that there were no visible traces of a break-in and that Genser's own key was still in the lock where Genser had obviously left it. They asked him not to report the incident; the hotel would reimburse him for whatever had been stolen. Genser told them he really hoped he'd run into the burglar one more time, just so he could ask the man how he'd gotten in the room: Genser distinctly remembered leaving the hotel bar, taking the elevator to his floor, opening his door, and carefully locking it behind him. He'd even given the doorknob a good shake to make sure the bolt was properly engaged. He had shaken it so hard, in fact, that his ring had caught on the knob and scraped a little skin off his finger. So the suggestion that he had neglected to lock his door was hardly possible. Two days later a waiter told Genser that he wasn't the only guest that night who'd had uninvited callers come in through a locked door, but the man asked Genser not to tell anyone that he had mentioned this. The management had forbidden all employees to say anything about the burglaries.

Genser's teammates enjoyed listening to his story and tried to figure out how the burglars had managed to break in. Before the conversation moved on to other subjects, Genser told about another incident that had happened in Moscow when he was staying with a girlfriend. She owned a fifth-floor apartment; a burglar had broken into the kitchen by climbing up the fire escape, and entered the room where Genser and his friend were sleeping. They both woke up. His friend had put her hand on his chest to calm him down; later she said she'd been afraid he might get up or scream. She signaled to him to stay still. The man's a pro, an addict, she whispered in Genser's ear, he just needs a few bills for his next fix, he won't do anything as long as he doesn't feel threatened, but one false move and he wouldn't hesitate to use his knife. The intruder shined his flashlight over their bed for a second. He had noticed they were both awake and was checking to make sure they weren't doing anything. Slowly and carefully he opened the wardrobe and the drawers, searching one after the other, constantly checking with his flashlight to see that they were staying quietly in bed. Through half-closed eyes, Genser and his girlfriend watched the intruder subject the bedroom to a thorough search; the man picked up Genser's jacket, took out his wallet, emptied it of its cash, then put it back in the pocket. When the beam of light fell on them, they shut their eyes tight and scarcely dared breathe. After what seemed an eternity—Genser guessed it lasted about ten minutes—the burglar left the room, went back to the kitchen, and climbed out the window. When all they could see through the open door were the fingertips of the man's black gloves clinging to the windowsill, Genser's friend took her hand off his chest and asked him to wait another few seconds before turning on the light. Then they both got up; she went to call the police, and he went to the toilet because he had nearly shit himself. The police showed up six hours later and took their statement with routine indifference. Since neither Genser nor his girlfriend could describe the intruder, and since he had worn gloves, the police explained there was practically no chance of catching the man; they merely advised the girlfriend to get better security and put bars on her windows. They were much more interested in Genser: they grilled his girlfriend about their relationship, how often he stayed with her, asked where he was from and what he did for a living. When he explained his work to them, they wanted to know whether he could get them discounts on computers for their children. That made Genser mad, but his girlfriend told him to keep quiet. Since then, he told his friends, whenever he traveled to Russia he always stayed in hotels, though as they could see, even that wasn't always safe.

"Good God!" said one man, and Willenbrock asked Genser whether the attacks hadn't scared him enough to consider selling his software someplace else.

Genser waved off the question. "You're not safe anywhere," he said. "The same thing could happen to you here, today, on your way home. And anytime I get frightened, all I have to do is look at my bank balance for consolation. Whenever you go digging for gold, you have to expect some danger, and there's plenty of gold there, let me tell you. Whenever you have a country falling apart like that, the money comes bubbling to the surface."

"Where's anybody safe these days?" said Gerd, Willenbrock's financial advisor, a stocky, balding man. "We all know about Moscow and New York, that you can't take the subway at night or walk through a park after dark. But it's plenty dangerous here at home, where nobody worries about getting attacked and everybody's completely oblivious. You're never ready for it, and that's the real threat."

Genser nodded in agreement. He was pleased that his stories had been so well received. Willenbrock called the waiter, paid, and finished his beer. He waited for everyone else to pay and they left the pub together.

Monday morning Willenbrock arrived at his lot and found Jurek standing in the pit; he had set a car on blocks inside the old greenhouse and was covered with oil. Willenbrock asked about his holidays, how his family was getting along, but Jurek kept his answers curt, then explained that it was a waste of money to open up so soon, their customers wouldn't start showing up for at least another week, and there was nothing he had to do to the cars that couldn't wait a few days. At home he had the apartment to paint, the rabbits to butcher, and the roof to fix before the snows came. His wife couldn't do everything herself, and one week wasn't enough for him to finish all the jobs he'd put off for a whole year. His boy wouldn't touch a shovel unless somebody was standing over him telling him what to do. Willenbrock let Jurek grumble, then asked him to give the Opel a new paint job during the next few days; it had been sitting there four months without a buyer.

"Paint it red, Jurek, and you'll see, somebody'll go for it."

Jurek muttered something and applied himself to replacing the brackets in a tailpipe assembly. Willenbrock went off to the trailer and sorted through the papers he had brought from home, placing some on the bookshelf and filing others in his desk. At nine he wandered out into the yard. There were no customers in sight; he walked the few steps to the gate and opened it, to show the city that the holidays were over and that he was open for business.

Over the next two weeks he was offered six vehicles. Four men accepted what he bid; each took cash and told Willenbrock he was getting a good deal, which he happily confirmed. The other two negotiated briefly and drove off when

Willenbrock refused to pay more. One of them was carrying a price guide prepared by the automobile club; he showed it to Willenbrock and pointed out what he considered the accepted price range. Willenbrock just laughed, whereupon the man promised to report his unprofessional business conduct to the authorities. Willenbrock wished him luck and even held the door open to encourage the man to be on his way.

8

Willenbrock had received some mail from one of the political parties inviting him to a public meeting on the development of the district where his lot was located. His first reaction was to throw everything away—the "personalized" letter, the pamphlets, the accompanying literature—but an hour later he remembered seeing something and fished the invitation back out of the trash. He smoothed the paper and carefully reread the text. The speaker's name, Frieder Geissler, seemed familiar, though Willenbrock couldn't say exactly why. Then it dawned on him: Geissler was the name of his former research group manager, and he wondered whether this was the same man. Geissler, too, must have lost his job, and at his age had probably had a hard time finding another. Maybe he was working for this party to make ends meet. He'd never seemed all that political; Willenbrock had no idea what his views were and couldn't say whether he'd had an affiliation with any particular party. They'd never actually discussed politics—maybe keeping politics out of the workplace was one of Geissler's great unsung achievements. At any rate, Willenbrock couldn't remember anything remotely political ever coming up at any of their meetings; Geissler always kept a tight rein on the group and refused to tolerate private conversations. It was a little strange, Willenbrock thought, but on the other hand, Geissler had a reputation as a workaholic, so nobody was surprised at his zeal, his stubborn insistence on following procedure, or his reprimands if he came into a room and caught someone telling a joke or showing off some new acquisition. He certainly gave the appearance of a compulsive worker, but maybe that was just his way of keeping out of trouble with the management. Seeing that name on the invitation made Willenbrock curious. He tacked the announcement on his bulletin board and decided to attend, just to see if this Geissler was indeed his old boss.

On the last Tuesday in January he drove to the address listed, a restaurant not far from the entrance to the autobahn. He went alone—Susanne had simply laughed at the thought that he, of all people, had decided to go to a town hall meeting. He told her he wanted to get a look at the people who had the power to make decisions that affected him, his business, his whole life.

The meeting had already begun when Willenbrock walked into the banquet room at the back of the restaurant. Four men and a woman, presumably party representatives, were sitting behind two tables that had been shoved together and draped with a yellow cloth. The audience was scattered among other tables throughout the room; except for two couples, everyone was sitting alone. Willenbrock sat down at an empty table near the podium and sized up the people around him, who seemed to be listening without much interest. He saw two familiar faces—the owner of a construction company and a hauling contractor—and nodded to them.

Then he turned toward the panel. A man with blow-dried hair and a loud flowery tie was discussing renaming two streets in the district, and complaining that representatives from other parties were hampering their party's initiative and thereby impeding the democratization of the city. He spoke about old and new thinking, about backward-looking representatives, who, unfortunately, were also to be found among their coalition partners, and about his party's uncompromising determination to build a better future. And right next to him was Willenbrock's former boss. Geissler nodded to Willenbrock several times and even gave a discreet wave when Willenbrock did not respond.

To Geissler's right was the only woman on the panel, and seated next to her was the same Willi Feuerbach who'd been the subject of Berner's phone call a few months back. Willenbrock, surprised to find him there, couldn't help staring. He was amused that two of his old colleagues had evidently become politicians, or something of the sort. Maybe, he told himself, these parties exist just to collect anybody who's fallen through the cracks, a refuge for all those who've gotten the short end in life and can't accept their insignificance. Feuerbach had also nodded when he noticed Willenbrock's sullen, stern gaze fixed on him.

The speaker finished and opened the floor to questions. Since no one seemed eager to say anything, he asked for suggestions, complaints, or proposals, and stressed that democracy could only be achieved if they all worked together, that it demanded every citizen's active participation. He looked encouragingly around the room, but the bored listeners just sat there, and averted their eyes whenever the speaker looked their way. The speaker then took a small pile of index cards from the table in front of him, leafed through them, and once more looked out at the room, hoping for some response. He stated how much he admired the East Germans for their diligence and their determination to rebuild—not only today but also in the past. Especially in the past, since they'd been so much worse off than their counterparts in the West, and had achieved so much with so little help and without any up-to-date technology. He confessed that he didn't know if he himself would have had the courage or strength to weather the hardships they had endured over the years, if fate had landed him in the eastern part of their common country after the war.

"What could the average guy do, the little man worried about his job, his home, his family?" he said to the half-empty room. "The answer, of course, is nothing, except to get along with the people in charge," he added as he scanned the tables.

"With the people who had been put in power over you," he went on, after a brief rhetorical pause, "I don't know what I would have done, whether I, too, might not have joined one of the official parties, just to be left in peace, to get on with my life, to keep my family safe and my children out of harm's way."

He nodded to his colleague sitting next to him, who was peering enthusiastically at the audience throughout the speech.

"Where could you turn? To what government agency, what secret service . . . when none was truly democratic?" he asked, apparently quite pleased with himself.

Willenbrock gave a start and looked at the speaker in amused bewilderment. He took a pencil out of his jacket pocket, found an envelope in another pocket, and jotted down what he'd just heard. The speaker saw Willenbrock writing, and looked directly at him as he again asked if anyone had anything to say. Willenbrock felt the man's gaze but did not look up; he took his time writing down the sentence before calmly and coolly putting the envelope and pencil back in his pocket.

When it was clear that no one was going to speak, the man concluded by saying he assumed his platform had the support of the assembled citizenry, and that he would devote himself energetically and selflessly to see that the will and wishes of the people were fulfilled.

The woman on the panel thanked the speaker and called on her colleague, Frieder Geissler, district superintendent of urban development and environmental protection, to say a few words about the progress made in connecting the outlying subdivisions to the main sewer system. Geissler spoke briefly, reading from a paper, since he had so many figures to convey. After his presentation, several listeners—including the hauling contractor—raised their hands, and a heated debate erupted about the high cost of connection fees and sewer bills. When Geissler finally insisted that they would simply have to accept the figures he had just presented, the hauling contractor threw a fit. He leaped to his feet, took two steps toward the podium, and roared so loud that everyone was momentarily scared into silence. But since he had nothing to say beyond repeating the same assertions over and over, he soon just walked out, slamming the door behind him. For a moment the room was completely still. Willenbrock watched the stupefied members of the panel. The woman whispered something to her colleague, who merely shrugged his shoulders in return. At that point the man closest to Willenbrock stood up and left without a word, followed by one of the two couples. Now there were only seven people remaining, and the party representatives quietly consulted among themselves.

Finally the first speaker took the floor once again and moved to table the discussion in favor of a later public hearing on the controversial subject. He promised to present all legitimate objections to the district office and do what he could to see that the existing plans were reviewed and revised. Satisfied, he turned expectantly to his colleagues and sat down.

The woman thanked him. She said that their party always valued this type of frank exchange with constituents. Then she yielded to another functionary, a small, pockmarked man in charge of youth, education, and culture.

The small man rose and adjusted the paper in front of him. Before he began speaking, another listener got up and left the room. When the door closed behind him, one more man stood up and followed. The woman presiding over the meeting looked irritated and concerned. As soon as the room had quieted down, the speaker began his presentation. He read some statistics and a resolution that had been adopted by his department.

After yet another person left the room, the man with the wide tie interrupted the speaker and asked the remaining listeners if they had any objections or requests. He and his colleagues would be happy, he assured the gathering, to modify the agenda, even on the spur of the moment, since the party was truly committed to close interaction with the citizens. He looked around in silence, then asked the pockmarked man whether he wished to continue with his presentation. The man had been left standing behind the table, at a loss; he shrugged his shoulders and said that as far as he was concerned he could easily discuss the future of the adult education center some other time.

Before the panel could come to an agreement, the second couple fumbled with their coats and departed in silence. Willenbrock leaned back in his chair, amused, observing the five people at the table and the only other person left in the audience, an older woman. Frieder Geissler stood up and spoke to the man with the loud tie, who was apparently their superior or the local party chief. As Geissler had turned his back to the room, Willenbrock concluded the meeting was over and got up to leave. The men and woman at the table suddenly looked at him. Willenbrock felt uncomfortable; for a moment he wondered whether to sit back down. He glanced at the older woman, but she showed no sign of getting up. She seemed to be patiently waiting for the meeting to go on, and kept smiling up at the committee. Somebody's wife, thought Willenbrock; she's probably married to one of the panelists, she's just waiting for her husband to finish; so she and I are the only ones to stick it out this long—at least she has a reason, but what the hell am I doing hanging around here?

Their expectant expressions annoyed him; he groped in his jacket pocket for a cigarette and took his time lighting it. Without looking back at the speakers, he reached for his leather jacket, which he put on as he headed for the exit.

Suddenly Geissler called out his first name. The familiar voice, that same old slightly carping tone his boss had always used to summon him, instantly brought back memories. He could smell the musty offices and the freshly waxed corridors, the long production rooms, where women in white aprons sat under dusty neon tubes assembling machine parts, and he could hear the steady metallic clanging echoing through the factory grounds and the office building.

Willenbrock stopped and turned around. Geissler was coming toward him, arm outstretched; he reached for Willenbrock's hand, shook it, time and again saying how surprised and happy he was to see him. Willenbrock pressed his lips together and gave an embarrassed nod. He freed his hand from Geissler's grasp and fended off the torrent of questions with a series of laconic responses: "Fine . . . I'm doing great . . . fantastic. I have a used-car dealership. No, I don't need any help, thanks. Top of the tax brackets, if you know what I mean."

Geissler was surprised and suddenly fell silent.

"But thanks just the same," said Willenbrock. He saw that Geissler was taken aback by his response. The man had probably been expecting him to pour out his sorrows; maybe that's what he got from all the others who used to work for him and had primed himself for a similar litany from Willenbrock. Or else he disapproved of the used-car business and was disappointed to learn the lengths to which an educated man had to go to earn a living.

"I'm really glad to see you," Geissler said once more. "Do you live in this district? Are you a member of my party?" Before Willenbrock could reply, he added, "No I guess not, or I'd know it. After all, I know all the members personally. But

I hope you're sympathetic to our platform. I've always thought very highly of you—you know that, don't you, Bernd?"

Willenbrock shook his head. "I'm only here by chance. I've never been interested in parties and politics. It's a lot for me just to vote every four or five years. Work, family—it takes all my time. And if I have fifteen free minutes, I don't want to spend it sitting in some smoky back room."

Geissler's face registered disapproval. He seemed on the verge of saying something but decided against it and merely asked: "Did you see that Willi Feuerbach's here, too?" He nodded toward the table. "He's been in the party for two years. Before that he kept a pretty low profile, too—politically, I mean."

The woman at the next table got up, walked to the front, and sat down beside the pockmarked man.

"Do you have some time?" Geissler asked. "Can I buy you a beer? I've just got to finish a couple things here, but then the three of us could all go somewhere."

"To talk about the good old days?"

"Just a thought. We haven't seen each other in ages. After all, we did use to work together."

"Sure thing, boss."

"Wait right here. Just two minutes, Bernd."

Geissler turned around and Willenbrock stood by the door, undecided, recalling his unpleasant phone conversation with Berner. Fifteen minutes later he was sitting with Geissler and Feuerbach in the front of the restaurant. He listened to the two rehash the meeting, how badly it had turned out. Willenbrock sipped at his beer and watched them. These two guys are from another life, he thought. How nice to be done with all of that. They bored me back then and they bore me now, and neither one of them realizes how annoying they are to everyone else. He observed Feuerbach and asked himself why he ever let himself be talked into joining them.

"Must be pretty tough, this party work. You two don't exactly look happy," he said during a lull in the conversation.

Geissler gave a forced smile. "Well, these things take time. Time and effort," he said, "but at least we're trying. We need people. People who are willing to get involved. People who care about what's best for everyone, and aren't just out for themselves. Democracy doesn't work unless people are ready to take responsibility."

He spoke so emphatically and so seriously that Willenbrock had the impression he actually believed what he was saying.

"By joining your party, you mean?"

"That's one way, yes."

"I'll think about it," said Willenbrock. "I promise," he added, when he noticed Geissler's look of disbelief. "And how are you getting along, Willi? You're in the party, too?"

"But just an ordinary member. I'm working at the Buch Clinic. They needed an engineer for their equipment."

"Who knows, there might be a career in politics for you yet. You might climb the ranks and make it pretty high in your party." Willenbrock paused briefly before casually tossing out: "By the way, Berner called me up recently. You remember Berner. We talked for a long time. He had a lot to tell me."

Willenbrock looked alternately at Geissler and Feuerbach with feigned absentmindedness. He saw they were both uncomfortable, and waited.

"Berner. Right," said Geissler, looking at Feuerbach with displeasure. "I can imagine what he had to say. He phoned me, too. With these wild accusations against Willi and a few others from the old group. Between us, Bernd, he didn't have much good to say about you, either. He sounded a little paranoid, as if he had a persecution complex. My God, the things he came up with. I had a long talk with Willi about it, and so did our local committee. There's no doubt Willi made a few mistakes. He was too gullible, too trusting. Probably a little careless, too, our Willi. Said some things he shouldn't have. But he definitely wasn't guilty of anything, they didn't establish any blame. He didn't even get a reprimand."

Feuerbach had turned crimson as Geissler spoke. He fiddled with his glasses, adjusting them over and over, and opened his eyes wide, as if trying to work out a speck of dust. Willenbrock watched him; it was unpleasant to see the man so embarrassed he was practically squirming in his seat. Now he regretted having mentioned Berner's call; he regretted having come here at all. He saw Feuerbach's gaze roam uncomfortably around the table without finding a place to rest; he had the feeling he was witnessing some obscene denuding. He saw Geissler looking at him expectantly and said: "Well, that settles that. Here I thought I finally knew who to blame for my bad luck, my old misfortune, so to speak. The way Berner put it, the firm considered me a security risk. No trips abroad, not even to Prague or Moscow. No international congresses—all because Bernd Willenbrock had been branded a security risk."

Geissler opened his mouth in indignation and drew in a large breath. "Are you saying it was Willi's fault you never got to travel?"

"I don't know. Somebody said something about me, and that was it. You know how it worked. Some people were allowed to travel, they had contacts, kept up with the latest developments, stayed informed, while I was lucky if I got an occasional look at a technical journal from the West."

"That was the cross we had to bear. All of us suffered."

"Some more than others, Frieder. And Berner told me that my particular cross came courtesy of our colleague Dr. Feuerbach."

Geissler took another deep breath, turned to Feuerbach, and told him to say something. "We're talking about you, Willi. Don't you have anything to say?"

Feuerbach looked up in agony. "I'm sick and tired of the whole business."

He closed his eyes for a few seconds while the others waited in silence, then said: "Berner's right. I owe you an apology, Bernd. It was only later I found out they stopped you from going to London because of my report. But that wasn't my intention, you have to believe me. I was our group's union rep, you know that. One of my duties was to give a yearly assessment of all my coworkers. Everybody knew that was part of my job, including you. I may have been careless, I'm sure I didn't think things through like I should have. But I never meant to blacklist anybody. And I can't do anything about the fact that they put my reports to other uses."

He looked Willenbrock in the eye and held his gaze until Willenbrock asked: "So should we just pretend it never happened?"

Willenbrock looked at Feuerbach invitingly and tried to grin, but he felt awkward. You poor dog, he thought, what is it you want to say now? What *can* you say? You got caught, and now you're squirming. I'm sick and tired of the whole business, too, believe me. But it would be better if you didn't say anything, I don't want to hear any explanations or excuses, you stuck your hand in the shit and you got splattered, old buddy. You've been found out, and now you're sitting here all sheepish like some two-bit shoplifter who's been caught in the act. Just don't make excuses, because I don't want to hear them, and besides, I have no intention of letting you off the hook. I'm sorry, but there's no fence to mend here. I'm not about to forgive you, that's just the way life goes, and if you keep whimpering and looking at me like a dog begging for a bone I swear I'll walk out and let you two party big shots convene another meeting. So let's just drop it, okay, especially the apologies and all that crap. I'm sorry, but you can't undo anything and I don't plan on forgetting it either, so the best thing we can do is keep away from each other for the rest of our lives. I should have gotten up and walked out the minute I saw you up there. But just quit this kicked-dog routine, it makes me sick to my stomach. I'd rather hear you deny everything. Go ahead—say you didn't do it, lie like a rug, what do I care? I don't trust you anyway. You're just a little asshole and you always were. The truth is, my friend, I never could stand you or Berner, this is just one more strike against you. So I'm simply going to forget you. I'll get up in a second and think of something to say, but it sure as hell won't be "See you soon" or "Let's keep in touch." Then I'll head over to the bar and pay—I don't need either of you picking up my tab, that would turn the beer in my stomach. So just give me the chance to make my exit, give us all the chance for me to leave with no more explanations and no more excuses. That's the last thing I'll ever ask you for, my big-mouth friend, and don't beg for forgiveness because I shit on forgiveness.

Willenbrock finished his beer, put down the empty glass, pushed it to the middle of the table, waved for the waiter, and said: "It was nice seeing you and talking about old times. But I'm in a rush, I have to go now."

He stood up and put on his leather jacket.

"If either one of you wants to buy or sell a used car, my firm is always at your disposal."

Geissler seemed annoyed. "I thought we'd have a chance to talk, Bernd. I have the feeling that there's so much left unsaid between the two of you. You really ought to sit down together."

"Unsaid? Between Willi and me? I don't think so. At least not on my part. And as for Willi, he preferred talking to other people, and he said more than enough. Ciao, gents."

He nodded to Geissler, turned to the waiter standing next to him, and paid. Then he quickly left the restaurant and walked to his car. He started the engine, pushed for windshield-washer solution, and let the wipers swish across the glass several times. He tilted the rearview mirror to look at his face.

"My God," he said out loud, "what was the point of that?"

Then he readjusted the mirror and drove off.

He told his wife about the meeting. Willenbrock said they'd promised him and the other two people there that in the future they'd do everything different and better.

"Two of my old coworkers were there, including Geissler, my old boss. He's now some party bigwig spouting the usual nonsense. Afterward I had a beer with the two of them and we rehashed some old stuff."

"Then at least you had a pleasant evening. I shoveled snow for an hour. Not a job for women, at least not according to our neighbor Dr. Wittgen."

"The old guy next door?"

"He's a real gentleman, very charming."

Willenbrock looked at his wife, amused. "Are you trying to tell me something, Susanne? Is there something you'd like to confess? A real gentleman? Charming? Should I go fetch the pistols?"

"He was a big help."

"I'm sorry about the snow. I would have taken care of it in the morning. Don't be annoyed. Believe me, I would have preferred shoveling snow for two hours to seeing those guys."

He sat down next to her and stroked her arm. With his free hand he reached for the TV remote, turned it on, and surfed the channels. When he found the one with wrestling he lowered the volume, picked up the telephone, and dialed a number. His wife extricated her arm and left the room. Willenbrock spoke to Gerd, his tax consultant, about the upcoming match—without for a moment taking his eyes off the huge men in their masks, who were each trying to frighten their opponents and impress the audience with their shouts and threatening stances.

9

On the first Wednesday in March, Willenbrock drove to his lot like he did every morning. The gate was wide open: ever since he'd hired Pasewald, the slatted steel panels were opened every day at eight o'clock, so Willenbrock and Jurek could drive straight in. Willenbrock parked behind the trailer, got out, and locked his car. Something was different; he could sense it. He looked around but didn't notice anything out of the ordinary. Still, he hesitated, reluctant to go inside without first checking the vehicles on the lot—everything seemed to be in order. On the stairs to his office he suddenly realized what was bothering him: Pasewald's dog, Catcher, wasn't there to greet him. Maybe the dog's sick, or maybe Pasewald left him at home, he thought, but he raced up the small staircase anyway and flung open the door. He found Pasewald tied to the armchair with electrical tape and extension cords; the desk and cabinets were open, the floor was littered with papers and debris. Willenbrock hurried over to the watchman, carefully pulled the tape off his mouth and his small goatee, cut the remaining tape, and began untying the extension cords.

"Where's Catcher?" asked Pasewald. "Where's my dog?"

Willenbrock tried to get him to explain what had happened, but the watchman just kept asking about the dog. As soon as his feet were free, Pasewald jumped up and ran toward the door. By the exit he had to catch his breath, holding on to one of the open cabinets to steady himself. Then he dashed outside, Willenbrock right on his heels. Pasewald called out for his dog. They found Catcher by the fence, dead. The dog's muzzle was clenching a nightstick, his teeth were sunk into the wood; his skull looked like it might have been fractured, but there were only a few drops of blood in his dark fur. Pasewald sat down beside his dog on the damp ground and stroked its fur over and over.

"Tell me, Fritz," Willenbrock asked again. "What happened last night?"

He tried to help the man up, but Pasewald shook off his hand, then looked up at Willenbrock and said: "They killed Catcher."

He said it plainly and tonelessly, as if all he had registered was the death of his dog.

Willenbrock gently brushed his shoulder. "Get up, Fritz, you'll catch cold. Please come in the office."

The watchman still didn't react; he continued stroking his dog's stiff, frozen fur. Willenbrock turned around and went back to the trailer. He tried dialing out but the phone wasn't working. He pulled on the wire: it had been torn from the jack. Taking out his cell phone, he called the police and reported what he had found. The dispatcher promised to send a car right over. Willenbrock started picking up the papers scattered on the floor and putting them in order. Now and then he looked out the window at Pasewald; he saw the man pick up his dog, carry it to his car, and lay the body in the trunk. When Pasewald finally came in, he sat down on the couch, repeating that they had killed his dog, his Catcher. Willenbrock walked over and placed his hand on Pasewald's shoulder, but said nothing, and then returned to his cleaning.

Half an hour later a car pulled up; two policemen got out and headed for the trailer. Willenbrock saw them through the window. He recognized one of them from the earlier incident, when several vehicles had been stolen six months before—this officer was one of the two who had come out to investigate. The man had annoyed Willenbrock, who'd felt he was suspected of stealing his own cars.

Willenbrock opened the door and invited the policemen in. He described how he had arrived at the lot and found the night watchman tied up, and that the watchdog had been killed. Then the police questioned Pasewald, who stuttered as he gave a halting account of what had happened during the night.

At around two in the morning the dog started barking, which wasn't particularly unusual, since people often walked past the lot at night and sometimes provoked him. But then Pasewald had heard a loud howling sound that was very unusual, so he grabbed his flashlight and stick and left the trailer. All of a sudden he was attacked by three young men he guessed to be barely in their twenties.

"Were they wearing masks?" one of the officers asked.

Pasewald shook his head.

"You mean you got a look at them? You could recognize them if you saw them again?"

"Of course. I'll never forget them as long as I live."

The three had jumped him; one was wielding an odd-looking short stick. Pasewald called for his dog and grabbed at the stick to ward off the blow; that same instant he felt a terrible shock and blacked out. He didn't know how long he was on the ground unconscious; he only came to when one of the men kicked him. The three men made him get up and go with them into the office.

"Were they speaking German?" the policeman asked. "Were they Germans or were they foreigners?"

Pasewald looked at the officer for a second as if he hadn't understood the question. "They were German," he said finally. "Dumb German kids."

In the office they threatened to use the electric prod again unless he handed over the keys to the cars. He told them that the boss took all the keys and papers home every evening and that he didn't have anything or know anything, he was just the night watchman. He asked them about his dog and they laughed. Then they tied him to the chair and ransacked the office, dumping everything on the floor. After that, they left. He heard them try several times to start one of the cars, with no success. Half an hour later they came back and asked about his own car. Pasewald had left his keys in the ignition; evidently the thieves hadn't gotten to his old car. So he told them he didn't have one, that he came by bus. Before they left they gagged him and once more held the electric stick against his arm. This time he didn't black out, either because he was sitting down or because he was prepared for the shock, but his whole body went into a spasm, causing him to bite his tongue. And that's how Herr Willenbrock, his employer, had discovered him. He found his dog this morning: Catcher was dead, they had killed him.

The policemen took down a description of the men and then questioned Willenbrock and examined the damage in the trailer. They explained it was pointless to search for fingerprints inside; they'd look over the cars that had been tampered with and see if they could find something usable there. They weren't interested in seeing the dead dog, though Pasewald asked them three times. They said he should go home and get some sleep. The officer who had recorded Pasewald's statement on his laptop told him that he'd eventually need to sign the report, but they could take care of that later, first he should take his dead dog home. He noted Pasewald's address and suggested he go straight to a hospital and get checked out.

Together, the four men left the office. Willenbrock walked Pasewald to his car and told him to take the next night off and regain his strength, but Pasewald insisted he'd be back at work, although without his dog. Willenbrock put his hand on Pasewald's arm and said he was very sorry about Catcher; he'd gotten used to the dog and would miss him. Pasewald nodded and got in his car.

After Pasewald left, Willenbrock returned to the policemen. Together with Jurek, who since he'd arrived had stood beside them without speaking, they examined the parked cars, trying all the doors. Three vehicles had been broken into. The policemen retrieved a case from their car and began searching the three vehicles for fingerprints. Willenbrock went into the office and called Gerd; he told him about the break-in and assault, and said he was sorry but he'd have to miss tonight's practice. Then he phoned his wife's boutique, but hung up without saying a word when he heard her answer. He didn't want to tell her about this new break-in; he didn't want to upset her. Instead he called the phone repair service, reported the damage to the line, and requested that they fix it as soon as possible. After that he went out to Jurek and asked whether he'd be able to fix all the cars himself or would some have to go to a garage. Jurek pointed to the policemen, who were still working on one of the cars, pressing strips of tape on the doors and on the steering wheel.

"They're not done yet, boss," he said, "I have to wait till they're finished."

Willenbrock nodded. "As soon as they leave, check the damage. At least now we don't have to waste time on any insurance agents. Another reason to stay uninsured, Jurek."

Willenbrock went into the trailer, picked the rest of the papers off the floor, sat down at his desk, and began putting them in order. One of the shelves had lost its support; he hammered the bracket back and nailed it in place. The policemen knocked on the door and came inside. They gave him a statement to sign and started to leave.

"So what happens now? What are you planning to do this time?" asked Willenbrock.

"We'll open an official investigation, Herr Willenbrock," said the policeman, not failing to notice Willenbrock's sarcastic tone. "And for your information, we always follow standard procedure. We also solve more cases than you think. But the papers never report that, they only write about the ones that get bungled."

"So there's a chance you might actually catch these guys sometime soon?"

"We'll do all we can."

"That's reassuring. Anyway, this time you don't have to bother checking *me* out. There's no chance of insurance fraud, since I no longer have insurance. After the last robbery, which somehow never got solved and which you suspected I might have had a hand in, I had to drop my insurance, the premiums went up so much. With the taxes I have to pay, it's one or the other, taxes or insurance, and I don't exactly have a choice, do I? I have to keep shelling out my hard-earned money so you can go on solving all these crimes that never make it into the papers. Bottom line: I'm now uninsured."

"That's your decision," the policeman said, unmoved. "It's up to you whether you insure yourself or not. And for the record, Herr Willenbrock, we weren't singling you out back then. We were only doing our job, which is to look at every case from all possible angles. Which is exactly what we're going to do this time, too, regardless of how the injured party treats us."

"Have I offended you?"

"We'll be on our way, Herr Willenbrock. In any event, you'll be hearing from us."

They went to their car, loaded up the trunk, and drove off.

Willenbrock stood at the open door of the trailer and watched them go. He felt the police were harassing him. By comparison, as far as he was concerned, the break-in itself was no more than an annoying setback. He was sorry for Pasewald and felt responsible for what had happened to him; after all, he had hired the man and given him a dangerous assignment. And he felt bad about the dog. Apart from that, though, he wasn't so upset about the actual damage to the cars or the mess in his office—he considered it more a nuisance than anything else. The police investigation and all their questions were just as bad. He felt that both the burglars and the police had gone too far; they'd crossed a line, invaded his space, trespassed on his privacy. He felt exposed, stripped naked. He wanted a shot of brandy and opened the cupboard; all three bottles were missing. Evidently his night visitors had found something after all.

Willenbrock went outside to Jurek, who reported that he could fix the cars by himself, but that it would cost a few hundred since he had to put in new locks. One door was badly banged up and might need replacing, but first he'd see what he could find at the junk yard.

Willenbrock nodded. "I'm counting on you, Jurek. The whole thing's pretty sickening."

"You're right, boss. People like that should be shot. Shot dead. I wouldn't work as night watchman unless I had a real weapon."

"Jurek! What are you saying? You'd really shoot those guys? You heard him—they were kids."

"If they steal all you have, boss, then I'm out of work. And then what?"

"But to shoot them, just like that? You don't really mean it."

The Pole bent over the car door and went on twisting away at a screw without speaking. Willenbrock looked at him; he was amazed how worked up Jurek was.

"My son's been with the police for two days now," said Jurek suddenly.

"With the police?" asked Willenbrock, surprised. "What do you know? But at least these days it's a steady job. One of the few with a future. Did *you* get him to join?"

"That's not what I mean. Władek's not working there. He's in jail. He stole a car with two of his friends. He's become a criminal. Just like the guys who broke in here. Not a kid, but a hooligan, a thief."

Jurek struck at the lock with his bare fist, as if he wanted to bang it out of its housing, and shook his head back and forth in despair.

"I'm sorry," said Willenbrock. "Do you need some time off? You want to go home?"

"What for?" Jurek grumbled. "I have to earn money. I have to feed my family, pay the fine. Why go home? There's no work for me there. The boy's in good hands with the police. They'll give him a good hiding, no problem. Maybe that way he'll come to his senses."

"Maybe. Anyway, he's probably better off with them than with you."

"Yes, boss."

"You're too impatient with your Władek."

"You know, boss, they ought to take thieves like that and chop off their hands. Like in Turkey or Arabia."

"Are you out of your mind, Jurek? For God's sake, what kind of medieval idea is this?"

"Cut off the hand that steals from another."

"Your own son? You really want them to chop off his hand? You want him to be a cripple? A cripple for his whole life, because of one stupid mistake?"

"Better go without a hand than live with sin, boss. Better

make it to paradise with just one hand than wind up in hell with two."

Willenbrock looked at the Pole and thought a moment. "But your own son?" he asked, and when Jurek didn't respond, he laughed out loud and added: "Of course, if you're talking about eternity, I guess one hand isn't too high a price. But it does make life a little tougher here on earth."

He waited by the car, looking on a moment as Jurek worked, then asked: "And what about Pasewald, what should I do about him? Insurance is worthless; the police don't help; and a night watchman doesn't do the trick, either. What should I do, Jurek?"

Jurek had removed the lock and was using a tiny flashlight to assess the damage to its seating. He tried the key, held the lock up against the sky to see inside, then looked at Willenbrock.

"Back home, you make arrangements. Two friends of mine made arrangements. You pay, boss, you understand?"

"Who do they pay? The mafia?"

"Where do you think I live, boss? No, not the mafia. Not that big an operation. Just a few local crooks. But they let my friends get by. That's all."

"You think that's all right, Jurek? You of all people?"

"I didn't say it's right. You asked me what to do, so I told you what my friends do, how they take care of things. There's nothing right about it at all, but what in this world is right?"

He tossed the lock onto a rag. "Ask Pasewald, boss. Let him say if he wants to stay here at night. And buy him a gun."

Jurek took a cardboard box out of his tool case, ripped it open, and shook out a new lock, which he placed next to the one he had removed, and carefully compared the two. Willenbrock turned away quietly and went to his office. He sat at his desk, turned on his computer, and reached for the telephone.

Later that afternoon he told Jurek to take off early, that he would stay and wait for Pasewald. If the night watchman didn't show, which is what he hoped, he would lock up and trust the lot to the good Lord, which seemed the best protection available. Jurek, who didn't like to hear the Lord's name taken in vain, merely nodded and changed out of his work clothes.

Pasewald showed up at seven on the dot, his hand and head bandaged. Willenbrock asked what the doctor had said.

"Everything checked out okay," said Pasewald.

"And your dog?"

"I'm going to bury him," answered the watchman. "In my garden." He seemed embarrassed. Willenbrock felt there was something Pasewald wanted to get off his chest, and looked at him in anticipation.

"I'm sorry," Pasewald hesitated. "I've let you down. I don't know if you want me to stay on. It'll be a while before I can afford a new dog. But you know there's not much I can do against an attack like that, especially against a whole gang."

"I'll pay for a new dog. Go find a good one, you're the expert. I'll pay whatever it costs. And don't say you let me down, Fritz, that's nonsense. What worries me is that I can't sleep soundly with you here by yourself. Next time things might turn out even worse."

"Don't worry about me. I'm old enough to look after myself. As you can see, I'm not one for playing the hero. I just made a mistake, I shouldn't have run outside. I should have locked myself in and called the police right away. Maybe then nothing would have happened to the cars. And my Catcher would still be alive."

"The whole thing makes me uneasy, Fritz. I have no intention of letting you go, far from it, but I'd understand if you decided to quit."

"I know I'm not much help, but I like the work. I'd rather be here than at home."

Willenbrock nodded, picked up his briefcase, and said goodbye. He got in his car and was almost off the lot when Pasewald came running out.

"One more thing. I didn't tell my wife what happened—I just said that the dog was run over by a car. I don't want her to know. Otherwise she wouldn't be able to sleep while I'm here. You know how women are always scared, always worrying about everything."

"I'm worried about you, too, Fritz," said Willenbrock, then pushed a button to roll up the window and drove away.

Two days later he told Jurek over lunch that he needed to go to the bank that afternoon and look up a client afterward. Jurek took the information in silently, spooning his canned soup.

"What have you heard from your son?"

The Pole didn't answer.

"What does your wife say?"

"She just grumbles," he said indifferently. "Every day I phone her and every day she gives me the same complaints."

"Does she have anyone who can help out? A neighbor? Or the church?"

"The neighbors are jealous because I work in Germany.

And the church isn't the same as it was. It used to be against the regime, everybody helped each other, no problem. These days the church is on the other side. Now that it has power, they don't need us. The priests don't listen to us anymore. I'd even consider leaving if it wasn't a sin."

"Tell me if you need to go home. We can work something out."

"No, boss. Not necessary."

Jurek put down his spoon, pushed his plate away, and crossed himself. His fingernails were black from oil and grease. He tapped a cigarette out of a squashed pack he kept in his shirt pocket.

"We used to be brave, proud, and poor," he said, lighting the cigarette, which flared up since some of the tobacco had crumbled out. "But these days we're just poor. What's there to be proud of? I'm happy I work for a German. That's what I'm proud of, boss. And *this* coming from a Pole—that's almost a sin, too."

"Things'll change, Jurek. There'll be other times."

"Yeah. Sure. I know. I just hope I don't have to live through them as well."

"You're a little nuts, Jurek, you know that?" said Willenbrock, standing up and putting on his jacket. "I should be back in two or three hours. Don't forget to unplug the kettle when you're done."

"My son's a criminal, boss. He's in jail, and not because he said something against the state or passed out leaflets like we used to."

"Times have changed, Jurek. He's just a stupid kid, and they'll give him a good hiding, right?"

The Pole said nothing, but put out his cigarette, stood up, and brewed some tea. Willenbrock left the office. At the bank he consulted with an investment advisor and asked her to buy some bonds for him. Back in his car, he looked over the bank's brochures, then took his telephone from his pocket and tapped in a number. When he heard a man pick up, he disconnected without speaking. He searched for a number in his address book and tried again. The woman who answered was surprised to hear his voice. Willenbrock apologized for his long silence, said something about working without a break, and asked whether he was still welcome.

"I miss you," he said cheerfully. "I want to see you."

He let her finish reproaching him and repeated how much he'd been thinking about her. Then he cut her off to say she didn't have to tell him everything over the phone, he'd be right over and she could bawl him out to her heart's content in person. He slipped the cell phone in his leather jacket, started the car, and drove to the old museum. At the parking meter he paused for a moment, undecided, then put in enough coins for two hours. He walked to an apartment house along the Spree. A couple with a German shepherd was sitting in front of the entrance, blocking his way. Both were wearing dirty, olive-green jackets and had hair dyed bright red and yellow. Willenbrock paused a second for them to make way. They asked him for five marks; he gave them one, tossing the coin onto their duffle bag. They looked at the coin without picking it up and called him a cheapskate, but pulled their feet back far enough to let him pass. He went to an apartment on the third floor, rang the bell, stepped back, and unwrapped the roses he had brought. A young woman with blond hair in a high pile opened the door, silently looked him up and down, then examined the flowers. She was wearing leggings and a loose, washed-out sweater.

"I see one rose is already drooping," she said in lieu of greeting him.

"That one's me," said Willenbrock. "It wilted when you yelled at me on the phone. Are you going to let me in?"

The woman looked at him sullenly.

"I don't have much time," she said. "I'm on the night shift and just got up. Your phone call got me out of bed. And the place is a mess. But, all right, fine, come on in. Just for a coffee."

Willenbrock pressed the bouquet in her hand and stepped in. She sat him down in the living room and went to the kitchen. The place looked different; she must have bought new furniture or rearranged things, he couldn't tell. In any case, Willenbrock didn't remember the room like this. For a moment he sat there, undecided, then went to the kitchen.

"Can I help, Barbara?" he asked, and stroked her shoulder. She handed him some cups and made the coffee. She took out one plate, placed two slices of toast on it, then set it on a tray along with the coffeepot and sugar bowl and went to the living room. He followed her.

"I'm sorry, but I haven't had breakfast yet," she said. She poured coffee into both cups and began eating her toast.

"Bon appetit," he said, and continued: "I'm sure you won't believe me, but I've thought about you every day. I've missed you so much, Barbara. Literally every day."

"You're right, I don't believe you," she said.

She broke off a piece of bread and shoved it in her mouth while stirring several spoonfuls of sugar into her cup.

"Why should I? You haven't called once in six months. Half a year. Somehow I don't have the impression you've been pining away for me."

He ran his finger along the pattern of the tablecloth. "It's true, it's been a long time since I called, I know. But I've been thinking about you all the time."

"Did it ever occur to you I might have gotten married again? Or that I might have a boyfriend? A lot can happen in half a year, you know."

"That's true. So, are you married? Do you have a boyfriend?"

She didn't answer, just poured herself more coffee and stirred several more spoonfuls of sugar into the cup.

The sad, drawn-out tooting of a ship's horn broke the moment of silence.

"It wouldn't matter to me," said Willenbrock, reaching for her hand.

"It would to me," she said, pulling her hand away.

Willenbrock wanted to explain why he hadn't managed to call for so long. He told her about the break-ins and the stolen cars, the conversations with Krylov and his advice, the futile calls to the police and the hassle with the insurance company. Barbara let him go on without showing any interest in what he was saying. She brought another slice of toast from the kitchen and, while he kept talking, started applying her makeup with the help of a pocket mirror. When she was done, she carefully put the compact and brush in her bag, finished her coffee, and got up.

"Excuse me for interrupting, but I have to go now," she said. "I'm sorry, I won't be able to hear the end of your story."

Willenbrock was surprised. He looked at his watch and stammered awkwardly: "Here I'm going on about things that probably don't interest you in the least. I just wanted to tell you why I hadn't called for so long."

"And you did. So now let's go, please."

Willenbrock stayed in his seat, defiantly. "You have to have a little time to spare for me. Ten minutes, Barbara. We haven't seen each other in ages."

"You've been here almost an hour—that's all the time I had. You told me what was on your mind. And now I have to go."

She went into the hall and opened a closet. She took off her sweater, stuffed it in one of the compartments and, wearing only her leggings, picked out a dress. She held it up in front of the hall mirror, catching his gaze in the reflection. Indifferent to his presence, she draped the dress across the back of a chair, took off her leggings, adjusted her panties and pulled on the dress. She slipped into some high-heeled shoes and an overcoat. Then she opened her apartment door and waited for Willenbrock. In front of the building he tried to kiss her goodbye, but she turned her head away so that his lips barely grazed her cheek.

"I hope we'll see each other again."

"Of course," she said coolly. Then she smiled at him brightly and added: "Don't call us, we'll call you."

She strutted off, head held high, without once looking back. In his car Willenbrock tried to contain his anger. He had made a stupid mistake, going on about his own troubles and the problems with his business, which didn't interest anybody except himself. He felt he'd acted like a child. He'd gone to Barbara's hoping to sleep with her and she'd let him in, which had seemed like a good sign, considering her mood. And then he'd talked about the break-ins and rambled on like some stupid schoolboy. Instead of spending the afternoon in bed with her, he'd bored her with his problems, going on about things that weren't so terrible and didn't even bother him all that much. He felt like a fool. She was right to kick him out like that. He'd have to work hard to fix this one; a bouquet of roses wouldn't do it this time. As he drove past the Molkenmarkt he saw Barbara talking with a young man. He could see her face, she looked lively and jovial. All he could see of the man was his back. He was immediately jealous of this stranger; it annoyed him that Barbara was evidently attracted to the man, that he was making her laugh, that the two were clearly having a good time. "You idiot," he said to himself, half out loud, as he watched them through the window. He didn't move until the driver behind him honked several times.

10

At the beginning of April, Susanne phoned him at work. The moment he heard her voice he knew something was wrong, because she never called the office—she hadn't even seemed to want to know much about the two break-ins, and when he mentioned the attack on Pasewald, all she said, and with a tone of reproach, was that he had to expect things like that in his line of work.

"Bad news?" he asked, when she said hello.

"Mama died."

He could hear she was crying.

"I'll be right over, love."

He told Jurek what had happened and went to see Susanne.

The funeral took place a week later, on a Saturday. They drove out to Susanne's brother's Friday evening. When they got there, Fred and his sister embraced, then studied each other in silence.

"It's better this way," Fred finally said. "Better for her. After the stroke, things went downhill fast. At the end she was barely able to breathe."

He touched his sister's cheek, then led her into the house. Willenbrock followed with the suitcase and the gigantic wreath he had bought over Susanne's objection; she had just wanted a simple bouquet. This time they were back in the guest room. The attic apartment where Susanne's mother had lived had already been cleared; the workers were scheduled to come during the next few days and hang new wallpaper, so that the teenage daughter could move in.

Over supper Fred described their mother's last days and hours and talked about plans for the funeral. Afterward he and Willenbrock went for a beer at the local pub, to discuss the catering arrangements with the proprietor. Fred shook hands with everyone there. Willenbrock noticed that the men in the pub were respectful to the point of being obsequious.

Once they'd sat down and ordered, Fred leaned toward Willenbrock and said, "I don't want Susanne to know about this, but the last days with Mother were horrible. Her mind was completely confused; she didn't know who we were and ran around the house all day looking for something, don't ask me what. She turned on all the lights and appliances and went through our closets and drawers. I was really scared that she might burn the house down while we were sleeping. And we had to make sure she didn't run out into the street, or something just as bad could have happened. You know how the people around here gossip, they'll jump on anything. You can imagine what they'd do with a crazy old lady. Anyway, Susanne doesn't know any of this, and I don't want her to find out. She was very attached to Mother—of course the two of you didn't have to take care of her. Anyway, I'm glad she's fine. And us, too, for that matter."

A waiter brought their beer; they clinked glasses. Then Fred talked about his drilling company, which had just gone through a long and aggravating audit, and gave his brother-in-law advice on dealing with the tax people. A waitress brought another round; as she served the beer she casually rested her hand on Fred's shoulder for support. Willenbrock smiled at her. After she left he interrupted his brother-in-law's monologue to ask if he was having an affair with the girl.

Fred made a face and said: "Do you ever think about anything else? I'm a married man."

"I realize that," replied Willenbrock. "I was just asking about that waitress. She's pretty." He followed the girl with his eyes, then turned back to his brother-in-law. "Or is that kind of thing impossible here? Everybody keeps an eye on everybody else, right? No secrets?"

Fred Herlauf grew indignant: "I'm a married man, and tomorrow morning we're laying my mother in her grave, and nothing else is any of your goddamn business."

"Okay, fine. Our wives are waiting, let's finish our beer and go home."

Fred called the waitress, paid, and moved toward the door. Willenbrock stood up and reached for his jacket. The waitress asked if he wanted to settle his bill. Willenbrock, who had assumed his brother-in-law was picking up his tab as well, apologized to the girl and gave her the money. The two men walked home in silence and sat down in the living room for half an hour with their wives and the Herlaufs' teenage daughter.

"Was there a problem?" asked Susanne.

Willenbrock shook his head and Fred said: "Problem? No, no problem. I just sometimes wonder whether your husband's in his right mind."

"I sometimes wonder the same thing," said Susanne, "but then maybe men really are assembled differently. Most of them have at least a couple of screws loose."

Half the village came to the funeral. Very few had ever even spoken two words to the deceased, but going to a funeral was the neighborly thing to do, especially considering that Fred Herlauf was the biggest employer around and for several years had served as honorary mayor. Besides, it was a Saturday. The minister began his eulogy with a poem by Rilke, then spoke of how the departed had found a haven in the love of her children and grandchildren, where she would always remain. He mentioned Fred's name three times in his short address, each time glancing up at Susanne's brother, whereupon the guests turned their heads as well, much to Willenbrock's amusement. After the coffin was lowered into the ground and one of Fred's employees had placed a bronze dish filled with earth next to it, Willenbrock stepped back to let his wife stand beside her brother and his wife and children. He didn't like the idea of total strangers extending their condolences, so he waited off to the side, watching the line of people slowly inch forward, until the last of the mourners had shaken hands with the family. Then he joined Susanne and the Herlaufs, and they all went to the pub, along with several of Fred's friends and acquaintances.

A table had been set for forty people in the banquet hall, an annex off the main room. Because Susanne had taken a seat next to her brother and the minister had sat down on her right, Willenbrock found himself on the other side of the table, between a corpulent, red-faced bald-headed man and a thin girl in a dark woolen dress. He introduced himself to his neighbors.

"Family?" asked the bald man.

Willenbrock nodded.

"My condolences," said the man, quickly and indifferently. Then he turned to speak to another bald man seated diagonally across the table. Without asking, the waiters placed a mug of beer in front of each of the men and coffee cups in front of the women and set three large tin coffeepots in the middle of the table. Then they brought out large platters of boiled beef, roast pork, boiled potatoes, and sauerkraut. Willenbrock tried to start a conversation with the young girl next to him, but she scarcely spoke. Every time he asked her a question she thought long and hard before finally answering "I don't know."

"How can you not know whether you knew the lady who just passed away?" he asked, puzzled, and gave her an encouraging look. The girl just averted her eyes bashfully and said, after a few moments: "I don't know."

When everyone had eaten, Fred tapped his spoon against his glass, stood up, and thanked the minister for his words at the gravesite, and his wife for her selfless care of his dear departed mother. Then he thanked everyone for coming and said that anyone who wanted brandy or a liqueur should simply tell the staff. He sat back down and had the waiters pass around a wooden box of cigars and two packs of cigarettes. As the guests resumed their talk, the babble of voices grew louder; only Willenbrock and Susanne sat there quietly in the middle of the crowd, since no one spoke to them. They didn't say anything, just listened to the ongoing conversations, which were getting merrier and merrier. Later the guests got up and stood around in groups, talking about the recent election, various illnesses, and a Dutchman who'd sold one family a gigantic cutlery set that he claimed to have brought into the country to show at a trade fair and now was forced to sell for far under value, since the high customs duties meant he couldn't take it back to Holland.

Fred Herlauf was standing with four heavyset men, all smoking cigars and talking loudly; suddenly they burst out laughing. As Willenbrock headed their way, he heard one of them—a small, very fat man with squinty eyes—say: "My secretary complained about *her* pay, too. I told her that, like every other girl in the world, she was sitting on a nice little piece of property and she should put it to work for her."

The five men roared with laughter. Fred waved Willenbrock over and introduced him to the others, telling them he ran a used-car business in Berlin. Then Fred said: "You know what Horst just told me? Let's see if you Berliners are really as smart as you pretend. Do you know why society hasn't done anything about the fact that women have been oppressed for three thousand years?"

"No, why?" said Willenbrock.

"Because why mess up something that works?—and once again they burst out laughing. Willenbrock only grimaced.

He looked around for his wife, nodded to his brother-in-law, then walked off to join Susanne. He heard Fred whispering, presumably about him. The four men laughed some more; when Willenbrock turned around, he saw they were all watching him.

Late in the afternoon the waiters brought out an assortment of cakes; Fred closed things down just before five. The guests took their time leaving, lingering to shake hands with one another and say a few words goodbye.

Fred stayed at the table while his wife went home with the two children and Susanne. He asked for the bill and drank an herbal brandy with Willenbrock and the proprietor.

At home Fred wanted to talk with Susanne and Bernd about the inheritance, but Willenbrock asked to be excused as it was a matter between brother and sister. He left the living room and lay down on his bed. By the time Susanne came in he'd fallen asleep. She woke him up just in time for supper. He asked how the conversation had gone, what her mother had left, and whether they'd come to an agreement. Susanne said that all she'd wanted was her mother's ring and an old brooch, as well as a photo album that had been carefully maintained and labeled. She and her brother had agreed that everything else—the furniture and the money—should go to Fred's children. Susanne showed him the jewelry and the album; Willenbrock viewed them with minimal interest.

"The main thing is that you didn't argue," he said. Then he got up, splashed some cold water on his face, and accompanied Susanne downstairs.

That evening they played Scrabble with the kids. Fred quickly excused himself, saying that he had some work to do in his study. Willenbrock had the feeling Fred was leaving because of him, but he didn't say anything, and the women only exchanged a silent, meaningful glance. When they went to bed, Fred was still sitting at his computer; he barely looked up when they said good night.

The next morning, just after breakfast, they packed to leave.

"Now we'll see each other even less," said Fred's wife, Christine.

"Why don't you come out to our place sometime?" Susanne asked. "It's been ages since you visited. You haven't even seen the new house."

Fred only nodded, set their suitcase in the trunk, hugged his sister, and shook hands with Willenbrock. He was back inside before the car had left the driveway.

Until they reached the autobahn, Susanne kept the road atlas spread out on her knees, giving her husband directions. Then she clapped the book shut, stowed it in the glove compartment, looked out the window, and said: "What is it with you and my brother? Why can't the two of you get along?"

Willenbrock thought for a moment and said, without taking his eyes off the road: "I don't know. I don't have anything against him. He just bores me, that's all. Your brother's the kind of guy who wants to eat steak but then gets upset that he can't shit out the money he spent on it."

"We grew up poor. He built this all up by himself," his wife objected.

"So what!" answered Willenbrock. "You can't live by taking revenge on your life."

At work there was a lot to do, as there was every spring. It was the busiest season of the year: more people came to sell their cars, and almost every morning buyers from Eastern Europe were lined up outside waiting for the gate to be opened. Willenbrock suggested that Jurek send a few cars to a nearby garage to be repaired, but he declined.

"No problem. I'm better and cheaper, boss," he said. Jurek worked overtime every evening, inspecting the vehicles, changing parts, painting and polishing.

Pasewald, who had meanwhile acquired a new dog, a boxer that was still young and frisky, didn't have to come in before nine, since Jurek had so much to do. Willenbrock occasionally stayed on as well, just so he didn't always end up leaving before Jurek—doing paperwork in the office rather than at home, or else busying himself with parts he'd ordered for an electronic security system for the country house in Bugewitz.

Once again he and Susanne began driving out to the country on Saturdays after closing time. There Willenbrock resumed his work on the roof, cut down the trees he hadn't gotten to in the fall, cleared the field, and worked with his wife fixing up the little herb garden. In the evenings they sat by the fire, reading, Susanne engrossed in popular novels while Willenbrock leafed through airplane books, read biographies of pilots, or pored over albums of vintage machines and magazines showing the latest models.

The first week of May his lawyer called to say he would finally be able to purchase the lot, and since the conditional building permit was still valid, he could start on a new showroom in a few weeks. Eager to begin, Willenbrock immediately phoned Martens, an architect friend he had consulted over two years before. Martens' office had already prepared all the necessary documents and drawings. Because Willenbrock intended to stay open during construction and planned to be at the lot every day, they agreed that Martens would serve as the nominal project supervisor, while Willenbrock would oversee the work onsite and would keep the architect informed. Martens had taken bids from several construction firms and chose one he'd worked with four times previously. Willenbrock said to give them the go-ahead; he was anxious to have his new showroom before the year was out. Then he called a real estate agency and had himself put through to a Herr Trichter. He asked whether he could still take out an eight-month lease on the property adjacent to his dealership, and whether the terms were still the same as when he first inquired. When he was assured they were, Willenbrock requested a contract be drawn up, effective immediately. Then he found Jurek in the former greenhouse and asked him what changes they would need to make in the yard. Within a week he had a fence built around the adjacent property, with a new entrance gate. He had a power line laid and then moved his trailer and all the cars to the newly rented lot.

A few days later they broke ground. An excavator shoveled out earth for the foundation, a smaller digger cut trenches for the waterlines, sewage pipes, and cables. From his trailer window, Willenbrock watched the progress of the construction. He had had Martens give him a schedule and a list of all the tasks Willenbrock was to supervise and report on. Several times a day Willenbrock went outside to check on the construction workers. When it came time to pour the foundation, he stayed on site the whole day, only going over to the temporary lot when Jurek called him to close a deal, fill out a contract, or pay out or take in money. Willenbrock enjoyed the construction; he was happy, and pleased at the rapid progress. In front of the workers he acted suspicious and dissatisfied, and was always running around, tape measure in hand, asking questions when anything seemed unclear or not quite right, and demanding meticulous explanations. But the truth was he felt elated, and that feeling triumphed over whatever minor difficulties cropped up or the mistakes he uncovered and insisted be fixed at once. Five years earlier, when their new home was being built, he had been similarly happy at first; as the work went on, however, the problems began to snowball: two of the contractors he was using went bankrupt, which delayed progress on the interior and caused a great deal of frustration. But he'd learned from experience, and hoped that this time he'd covered all the angles. He loved to talk about the construction; whenever customers asked, Willenbrock would explain the plans, and had they requested it, he would gladly have shown them around the site.

Almost every evening he updated Susanne on the building and tried to convince her to come by after work some day or on a weekend, so he could show her how everything was shaping up, but she declined. She was tired when she came home in the evening, and on weekends she wanted to get out to the country as quickly as possible. Her boutique still wasn't turning a profit. She frequently had to run out on business errands, which meant closing the shop, sometimes for hours, so she finally relented and hired a young woman as part-time help.

Krylov, who had been to Willenbrock's lot twice that year, offered to supply him with materials at prices far below the normal German rate. Willenbrock asked whether the Russian wares were top quality—he couldn't risk getting sued if something happened and it turned out he'd bought defective goods under the table. Krylov merely laughed and assured

Willenbrock that his stock was exclusively German and always top-of-the-line. After clearing it with Martens, Willenbrock placed an order with Krylov for enough polished granite to cover the whole showroom floor.

"But I'll need receipts," Willenbrock said. "One for the bank, and one for the tax people. No matter how good the stone is, I have to be able to show a receipt."

"Of course," Krylov nodded, "of course you need a receipt—I know the Germans. A bona fide receipt runs three hundred marks, you can't get one for less, and I don't make a penny off that. But maybe you'd prefer to take care of the receipt yourself? It might be cheaper."

"No thanks. You obviously have better connections in my country than I do, Herr Direktor. So since I'm taking your granite I'll take your receipt as well. May I ask how you're able to sell the stone at that price—fifty percent below the going rate?"

"Of course you can ask, my friend. But do you really want to hear the answer?"

"Is it stone meant for Russia?"

Krylov shook his head. "My dear German friend, let's just say that the world of commerce is full of marvels."

11

During the night of July 27, Willenbrock was woken by a quiet creaking. That morning he and Susanne had driven out to their place in the country. He had cut the grass with a tractor mower until late in the afternoon; then they had gone to the woods to look for the first mushrooms—boletes and chanterelles. They ended up taking the car because much of the forest was under water; someone had apparently broken open a dam. For weeks people in the village had been talking about nothing else. They complained about the environmentalists, who had long been arguing that the moors, which had been drained, should be restored to their original state; many suspected them of having breached the dam. Others pointed to a local construction firm, suggesting that they might have done it to get the business—a new dam had been on the books for years. But since that company was the only employer in the area, the locals kept their speculations to themselves, leaving the more vocal objections to the newcomers and weekenders. Led by a long-haired musician, protestors posted signs, collected signatures, and set up roadblocks to get the press to pay attention to the ecological crime.

After dinner Susanne and Willenbrock sat in front of the

fireplace; she talked and watched the flames, while he leafed through a catalogue of solar-powered gear. He was planning to finish the roof on the barn and cover the entire surface with solar panels that would supply all their energy. Around eleven they went to bed in the downstairs bedroom, since the one upstairs was hot and stuffy, and quickly fell asleep.

When he woke up, Willenbrock needed a moment to get his bearings. But the second he registered the noise—a muffled shuffling coming from the next room—he was wide-awake. He cautiously put his hand out to check whether Susanne was lying next to him, or if she had gotten up and was now tiptoeing through the sitting room on her way to the toilet. Even before his fingers touched her, however, he knew that the hushed sounds coming from next door couldn't be his wife; nor was it a mouse or some other small animal. At that point he realized someone else was in the house, in the sitting room right next to the bedroom. He hadn't turned on the alarm; he only did that when they went back to Berlin. Lying in bed, he listened intently, thoughts racing through his head. He remembered one of Genser's close calls and how he had said that professionals never hurt you unless they felt threatened. But he was doubtful that the burglar in the next room was a professional. Most likely it was a young man from a neighboring village who was out of work, or else an illegal immigrant who needed some quick money and a car to get him from the border zone into the heart of the country. He was probably hungry, too, and foraging for food. Willenbrock had no idea what the intruder might do when he came into the bedroom and found them there, whether the man had enough sangfroid just to keep an eye on them and not attack, assuming they stayed in bed and didn't move. He decided he couldn't risk it. The man might be armed, and if he turned aggressive and chose to attack them anyway, they would be utterly defenseless.

Willenbrock gently brushed his wife's face; she sleepily turned away. He carefully stroked her cheek until she woke up with an almost inaudible sigh.

"Quiet, be very quiet."

He had placed his hand on her shoulder and could feel her suddenly start to shake.

"Stay still," he whispered in her ear.

As quietly as possible, he slowly peeled off the bedcovers, stood up, and went to the door. He took hold of the handle and, little by little, for what seemed an infinitely long time, pressed it down without making a sound. His hand was damp with sweat and stuck to the handle. He cracked the door open and saw a man standing in front of the open display cabinet, one arm reaching deep inside it. The man must have heard Willenbrock or sensed him; he turned around, saw him, and immediately jumped back. In three bounds he had reached the kitchen on the other side of the sitting room. Willenbrock switched on the light and was about to give chase when the man came back brandishing an iron rod. Before Willenbrock could get out of the way, the man brought the rod down hard against his arm; it slid across his body and hit the floor with a bang. Willenbrock leaped back into the bedroom and threw his whole weight against the door to hold it shut. Meanwhile Susanne had gotten up and was standing by the bed in her nightgown, screaming.

"Out the window," he yelled. "I'll follow you."

The intruder pounded away at the door, which shook with every blow; it was on the verge of splintering. Willenbrock again told his wife to escape through the window but saw she was incapable of moving. She stood rooted to the floor, crying hysterically, her body convulsing. There was no way she was going to climb out the window; Willenbrock had to abandon his plan of jumping out after her and running to the next farmhouse for help or to call the police. The door panel was now split in two places—two long fractures in the wood. He couldn't ward off the attack much longer; the panel would break any second and he would get the full force of the iron rod. He looked at Susanne, then suddenly tore open the door and began roaring at the top of his lungs. Somehow he hoped the farmers in the village might hear him and come to his aid, although the nearest neighbor was on the other side of the field. The attacker, baffled by the unexpected charge, stepped back. He had been startled by Willenbrock's outburst and stood there holding the rod but didn't strike. Willenbrock kept roaring and glaring at the intruder. He saw the man's eyes flickering uneasily, darting around the room; the man was also panting heavily. He's scared, too, Willenbrock told himself. He's panicking. Willenbrock went on roaring, even though he was trembling with fear and nearly out of breath. Then the man renewed his attack, catching Willenbrock on the shoulder. Willenbrock sensed he had been hit, but it didn't hurt, and he realized he hadn't felt either blow. When the man again drew back his arm, Willenbrock tried to grab hold of the rod as it came crashing down, but missed, and the iron struck his wrist. Still, he didn't take his eyes off the intruder, nor did he stop roaring, even for a second. Now the man began to shout as well, something Willenbrock couldn't make out, since he kept on roaring as loud as he could. He heard another voice coming from the kitchen; it sounded worked up and insistent. He thought he heard Slavic-sounding words and feverishly tried to come up with some appropriate Russian expressions, which he shouted at random, regardless of their meaning. The man struck again, the iron rod clanged against the floor; Willenbrock looked around for something to stave off the blows, but the only thing in reach was a heavy armchair. Raising his left arm to shield his head, Willenbrock caught two more blows; by swinging the door around at the man he was able to ward off a third. The wood was beginning to give; Willenbrock tried roaring even louder. Now he distinctly heard the second man, whom he hadn't yet seen, yelling something that sounded like an order; Willenbrock was almost sure he was speaking Russian. Willenbrock noted that his attacker was nearly a head shorter than himself. The man with the rod called to the one in the kitchen, and Willenbrock sensed a moment of hesitation. Taking advantage of the opportunity, he lunged two steps forward, shouting and threatening despite the raised rod. The man backed off into the kitchen; Willenbrock slammed the door and then threw himself against it to secure the room he'd won. He braced himself with all his might. Two heavy blows came from the kitchen and left his body shaking, then all was quiet. Willenbrock stopped roaring and listened. He turned his head to tell his wife one more time that she should escape through the window, but before he got a word out, a knife came through the door panel, only barely missing his head. If he hadn't turned a second earlier to speak to

Susanne, the point would have sunk into his right cheek, since his entire body and head had been pressing against the door. Willenbrock froze, breathing heavily, and stared at the blade in front of his face. When it was pulled out, he shifted his position without taking pressure off the door, and placed his two hands against the massive wooden frame, which could better withstand both iron and knife. He heard voices behind the door; they sounded agitated; the words were fast and furious. Willenbrock now had no doubt they were Russian. Behind him, from inside the bedroom he heard his wife's steady whimpering. Willenbrock weighed what to do next, what was possible. Still pressing against the door, he looked around, but there was no suitable weapon in sight, not even a stool. He pretended to make a phone call and asked very loudly if he had reached the police. Then he said he had been attacked and made sure to use the word "hooligan" several times, since he remembered that Russian had a similar word. Sounding impatient, he insisted that the police come right away and repeated this sentence in Russian. Then he called out to his wife that the police would be there in a few minutes. He spoke loudly, overenunciating his words, partly so that the burglars would hear him and understand, and partly in the hope that the statement would calm Susanne down, despite the obvious absurdity of what he was saying. He heard steps; someone was running away, but then another blow rattled the frame, and the man who must have been standing just behind the door blurted out something Willenbrock couldn't decipher. The man repeated the sentence and then he, too, appeared to leave: Willenbrock heard someone racing out the kitchen and down the hall, his shoes echoing on the tiles. Ready to jump back at the slightest sound, Willenbrock carefully set his head low against the panel, to protect himself from another knife thrust. Then it dawned on him that he had nothing on but his pajama top, which barely reached his groin. He must have looked grotesque, or even comic, as he tried to chase back the intruder—a middle-aged man, half-naked, unarmed, roaring like mad. Willenbrock cautiously opened the door to the kitchen: the room was empty. The iron rod was lying on the floor. Willenbrock quickly snatched it up, shut the door again, and leaned against it, exhausted, trying to catch his breath.

"It's over," he called out to Susanne, "they're gone. We made it. We're all right."

He again put his ear to the door, alert for anything suspicious, afraid the burglars might have only retreated a little and were lying in wait, ready to attack as soon as he stepped outside.

His wife finally stopped whimpering. The house was now completely still. Willenbrock opened the door a crack, keeping a firm grip on the iron rod, and peeked inside the kitchen. He could hear his heart pounding. No one was there; the door to the hall was ajar. He waited a few seconds, then opened the door the rest of the way, sprang into the kitchen, and turned on the light. He took a quick look around, all the while gripping the iron with both hands and holding it in front of him, ready to strike. Then he went to the hall and switched on the light there. Both doors to the outside were wide open. He stepped to the windowsill in the kitchen, picked up the phone and dialed the police emergency number, barely glancing at the buttons so he could keep his eye on the sitting room, the brightly lit hall, and the doors open to the outside. He examined the iron rod; only now did he realize it was a brass-handled poker, like the ones he kept by the wood stove on the second floor. They almost beat you to death with your own poker, he thought. He pressed the phone against his ear and grew impatient because no one was picking up; then suddenly he noticed it wasn't ringing. He tapped the receiver switch several times, but there was no sound. He tugged on the cord; it was securely fastened to the wall; he couldn't see any damage. He hung up, gripped the poker more firmly, and crept back out into the hall. Keeping a constant lookout on all sides, he carefully climbed up the stairs. At the top, he opened the door to his little workroom and waited. Seeing no sign of movement, he reached around the doorjamb to turn on the light, then leapt in, brandishing the iron. No one. The room had been ransacked, his briefcase opened. He picked it up and immediately saw that his cell phone was missing. He quickly ran downstairs to the bedroom. He turned on the rest of the lights and opened every door in the house. Susanne was sitting on the bed in her nightgown, sobbing quietly.

"Get dressed," he said. "We have to go to the neighbor's. We have to get help, call the police."

He turned off the light in the bedroom so they couldn't be seen from the outside. He had Susanne hand him his clothes and placed them on the end of the bed, so he could stay by the open door and see into the next room while putting them on. He carefully set the poker on the bed within easy reach. Once he was dressed, he stood by the open door and waited for Susanne. As they left the bedroom together, he turned the light back on. In the hall they put on their coats; he took the heavy metal flashlight from the storage space next to the cellar door and switched on all the outside lights. From the porch he had a view of the entire yard; there was no one to be seen.

He signaled to his wife to wait a moment and went outside alone. He ran the flashlight across the grounds, carefully examining every corner, every potential hiding place, then let the beam glide across the neighboring meadow toward the forest.

"Come on," he said, without turning around, "we can go."

They walked very quickly, practically running; in one hand he held the flashlight, which he kept shining all around them, while in the other he kept a firm grip on the iron poker.

When the neighbor's dog started barking, Willenbrock felt safe. He now put the poker under the arm he was using to hold the flashlight and placed his other arm around Susanne, all the while saying: "It's fine now, calm down, we're all right, love."

At the gate he tried to distract the furiously yapping dog so he could press the doorbell without getting hurt. He rang several times, then shined his light around again. A window on the ground floor opened just a crack; their neighbor asked in a drowsy, grouchy voice who was there and what the racket was about.

"It's us, Heiner. We've been attacked," said Willenbrock, trying to make himself heard over the dog's barking.

"What's going on?" asked the neighbor, now wide-awake.

The window closed, a light went on in the room, the drawn curtains moved. Willenbrock and Susanne stood outside the gate, constantly scanning the grounds with the flashlight, waiting impatiently while the dog went on barking. Lights came on, first in the kitchen, next in the glassed-in porch, and then in the yard. Finally their neighbor Heiner appeared, a tall, strapping farmer with tousled red hair. He had put on some clothes and was wearing wooden clogs with no socks. He came to the fence.

"What did you say? What happened?"

He took the dog by the collar, opened the gate, waved them inside, and walked them up to the porch.

Willenbrock briefly described what had happened and explained that his phone was dead. Heiner tried his phone; he had no dial tone, either.

"Let's drive to the village," he said. "Susanne can stay here with Maria."

He went inside and came back with the keys.

"Go in the kitchen," he told Susanne. "Maria's awake, she'll be right down. And lock the door behind us."

He joined Willenbrock in the yard, calming the excited dog, and drove the car out of the garage. He had to chain the dog to open the gate and leave the yard. After they'd driven a few feet, Heiner shifted into reverse, backed up, locked the gate, and unchained the dog.

"It's safer that way," he said to Willenbrock. "You never know."

They drove slowly past Willenbrock's property. Lights were on in all the rooms. Without leaving the car, the two men searched the area, but didn't notice anything unusual.

In the village they rang at the apartment house where the

local policeman lived. They had to wait a long time before a surly voice came through the intercom.

"We need you," said Heiner. "Willenbrock's been attacked. Come down, and bring your weapon."

For a moment there was no answer. Then the policeman told them it wasn't his responsibility. They should call the emergency police, this was their jurisdiction, and they were properly equipped.

"Our phones are out, we can't call," said Heiner.

The policeman told them to use the public phone in the village square.

"What if they cut that line as well?" asked Heiner.

A crackling in the intercom indicated that the policeman had hung up. The two men looked at each other, stunned, and went back to the car. When they got in, the farmer said: "Always was a lazy asshole."

Heiner drove to the village square and stopped at the phone booth. Willenbrock searched his pockets for change, but didn't find any. He was about to ask Heiner when he remembered emergency calls didn't cost anything. He dialed the number; a man picked up after the first ring and asked what was the matter. Willenbrock reported the attack, making an effort to stay calm and logical. The official asked for Willenbrock's address and directions how to get there. He promised to send a patrol car right away. Willenbrock said he'd be waiting at his neighbor's, one house further down; the official made a note. As he spoke over the phone, Willenbrock kept the iron poker clamped under his arm.

"They'll be right over," he told Heiner. The farmer nodded.

They drove back. Heiner parked his car in the garage, went to the woodshed, and came back with a heavy chain and padlock to make his garage door more secure. He had briefly tied his dog again, and now set him loose.

The women looked out from the lit porch. Susanne had settled down a little and was trying to soothe her neighbor, who had become so upset that she was having chest pains. They all sat in the kitchen, and Willenbrock described how he had woken up and immediately sensed something threatening inside their house. He told the neighbors about the fight, the blows he had taken and his attempt to defend himself with the door. He pulled back his sleeves and rubbed the bruises on his arms, which had turned red and were beginning to ache. Every few minutes Heiner went to the living-room window, opened it, and looked out toward Willenbrock's place. When he saw a pair of headlights and a blinking blue dome light, he walked Willenbrock and Susanne to their house.

A patrol car was standing in front of the property; two policemen had climbed out and were searching the grounds with flashlights. They told Willenbrock to describe the attack, then went to their vehicle to phone.

"A detective squad is on the way," said one of the officers when they came back. They went through the house with the Willenbrocks and their neighbor, checking every room and shining their lights in all the corners, even in the small attic loft. The window screen in the upstairs living room had been slit open on one side; evidently the burglars—or at least one of them—had come in that way. Next to the fireplace lay a rusty corner post, evidently taken off an electric pasture fence. The four-piece fireplace set—sturdy iron rods with brass handles—was gone. Willenbrock couldn't spot any other damage. In his workroom he quickly looked through his briefcase, but nothing seemed to be missing apart from his cell phone and a small leather tool holder.

The men left all the lights on and went into the yard. The new iron door to the cowshed, which Willenbrock had had put in that spring, was bent along the bottom; the burglars had tried in vain to pry it open. His car stood inside, unscathed, among the piles of building materials, stones, rafters, and slats. Willenbrock tried all four doors, but they were locked. The police ran their lights over the stacks of lumber, then Willenbrock locked the shed, and they went to the barn, which was only closed off with sheets of plywood. Because there was no electricity, the men had to search the place with their flashlights. The officers asked Willenbrock whether anything was missing, whether anything looked different. Willenbrock said no. Susanne joined them; she was afraid to be in the house by herself. Willenbrock put his arm around her.

Outside in the grass they found a dirty old heavy jacket like the ones worn by construction workers. The police asked Willenbrock if it was his; he said it wasn't. He wanted to pick the jacket up, but the police asked him not to touch anything. A few paces further on they found a set of carving knives. Willenbrock had bought it two days earlier at a building-supply store; instead of putting it away, he had left it on the porch. The burglars must have taken the knives and either dropped or discarded them when they ran away.

A second car pulled up outside the gate; a woman and a man got out and came in the yard. The woman introduced herself as Detective Bühler, then pointed to her colleague and said merely: "My colleague."

Willenbrock invited them in. Their neighbor took his leave. Willenbrock saw him to the gate, thanked him once more for his help, and apologized for the night's disturbance.

"Don't worry, Bernd, that's what neighbors are for," said the farmer, waving him off. "Just take care of whatever you have to."

The four police officers sat around the table on the porch. Detective Bühler took out a small laptop, switched it on, and Willenbrock once again had to describe the attack while she wrote everything down. When he mentioned the blows with the iron poker and showed his upper arm, she asked whether he had called an ambulance. Willenbrock raised both arms, turned his hands, and wiggled his fingers.

"Nothing's broken," he said.

After the detective had taken his statement, they all went through every room of the house one more time and again searched the cowshed, barn, and meadow. Willenbrock unlocked everything for them, then went back inside to attempt to persuade his wife to lie down, but she waved him away. The officers returned with several plastic specimen bags they had used to collect the evidence recovered outside. One of them was carrying the three remaining iron pokers, which they had found in the garden. The policeman gave them to Willenbrock, since they couldn't find any usable fingerprints. The thick metal rods were noticeably bent, a result of the work they'd been put to. At the sight of the twisted metal, Willenbrock reached involuntarily for the bruises on his arms and shoulder; they were now hurting more and had swollen substantially.

In the back of the garden, a wide opening had been cut in the wire fence.

"It looks professional," said the detective. "They made sure they had an escape route before they broke into the house."

She guessed that the burglars had come into the garden sometime after dark and had cut the fence in case they were surprised and had to make a sudden getaway. They had then waited under one of the trees, as suggested by the hand towels found there, which the men evidently took off the clothesline to sit or lie on. After that they had watched for the lights to go off in the house, and then held back for at least another two hours before trying first to break into the locked cowshed where the car was parked. Since they couldn't pry open the heavy, well-secured iron door, they decided to break into the house, presumably to look for the keys to unlock the shed and start the car. They had noticed a window on the second floor that was open except for the screen. One of the men climbed onto the glass roof above the patio, as indicated by the garden chairs stacked on top of one another, and entered the house through the cut screen. Once inside, he traded his fencepost for a fire poker, went down to the ground floor, and opened the main door, using the key in the lock, to let in one or more accomplices. It was clear from the evidence that the perpetrators must have had pliers or wire-cutters, flashlights, truncheons, and crowbars. They'd cut the fence clean through, without leaving any traces. The detective suspected they had also cut the local phone line;

this could be verified in the morning. The men had left their truncheons by the fence and armed themselves with the corner posts. The burglar who had climbed through the window on the second story had left his post in the upstairs living room and taken all four fireplace irons, which he handed out to his accomplices as soon as he opened the door from the inside. The accomplices left their fence posts next to the house; it was worth noting that they hadn't just dropped them but carefully had laid them alongside the stone stairs, so as not to trip over them if they were surprised and had to make a run for it. Since four pokers and four posts had been used, one could assume that there had been four perpetrators. The detective praised Willenbrock; he had acted in exemplary fashion.

"What's wrong?" she asked. "Do you feel sick? Do you want to lie down?"

"It's just that when I look at those pokers I wonder whether my bones really did withstand all those blows. Maybe I should get myself X-rayed."

"You should. No question about it."

The detective asked a colleague from the patrol car to call the ambulance. The man got up and went to the car. Willenbrock asked whether someone could stay in the house until he came back from the hospital; he didn't want to leave his wife alone just now. The detective promised someone would wait for him.

"You've been a great help. Thank you. I feel a lot calmer," said Willenbrock.

"That's my job. But you really did do everything perfectly.

Exactly by the book. You have yourself to thank that it turned out as well as it did."

Willenbrock protested. "That's the second time you've said that, but if you don't mind my saying so, that's nonsense. I was just lucky that things went the way I thought they might. The man hitting me saw I was completely defenseless. It was the other guys, his accomplices, who were scared by my shouting. Even if they did run away because of my screaming, the only reason my attacker took off was because he saw them make a run for it. It could have turned out differently, very differently. When you're standing in front of a bunch of armed thugs wearing nothing but a pajama top, there isn't any right way to act. You simply have to do something, and it either ends up to be the right choice or dead wrong. I was just lucky."

"You didn't panic, Herr Willenbrock, that counts for a lot."

"That's not true. I *did* panic. Otherwise I would have collapsed on the floor at the first blow. Please stop telling me that I did everything right. There's no right way in a situation like that, even if your textbooks say there is. Everything could have turned out differently—not as well as it did, as you put it. I could be dead. Both of us could have been killed."

The two policemen from the patrol car sat at the table in silence, listening with interest and watching their colleagues from the criminal police do their job. They drank the coffee that Susanne had served them and listened to Willenbrock's statement with childlike curiosity. For them, the attack was a change of pace—not entirely unwelcome, most likely—from their usual night-duty routine.

The front door was open and from a distance they could hear faint music. The detective asked Willenbrock who might be making music at that hour; there couldn't be a discotheque anywhere nearby.

"That's Wickert, a musician from Berlin," said Willenbrock. "He often has guests. They sometimes party all night long."

The detective suggested they go see the musician, in case he or his guests had noticed something out of the ordinary. She asked Willenbrock to go with her; her colleague would stay in the house with Susanne. One of the two policemen offered to run them over to Wickert's, and the detective and Willenbrock climbed in the patrol car.

At Wickert's place several people were sitting around a bonfire, drinking wine; a few were playing instruments. When Willenbrock showed up with the two officers, they were greeted cheerfully, as if they were expected, but when they came closer and the guests saw the police uniforms, all conversation ceased and everybody stared at them. Three men quickly tossed their cigarettes into the bonfire and waved their hands in the air. A tall man with hair below his shoulders asked the policeman what he wanted and why he was on his property.

"Do you have a search permit?" he said in a slurred voice. Then he recognized his neighbor, shook his hand, and asked if they'd been too loud.

Willenbrock said they hadn't.

The detective quickly explained why they had come and asked whether anyone had seen any strangers or noticed anything unusual, but none of the guests had anything to say.

"Were they Russians?" asked the musician. "*Tovarishchi?*"

"Presumably," said Willenbrock.

"Go on with your party," said the detective, who grinned as she added: "And don't smoke so much. That stuff isn't good for you."

As they returned to the car, one of the musicians began singing, and others joined in until soon the whole company was belting out a Russian folk song, accompanied by two guitars and a violin.

"That's a cheerful neighbor you have," said the detective.

Willenbrock nodded.

Back at the house, the detective's colleague asked whether they'd learned anything. Detective Bühler shook her head and carefully sealed the evidence from the garden and the house in plastic bags.

When the ambulance finally arrived, Willenbrock said goodbye to his wife and walked out with the detective. The driver and a young doctor climbed out of the white van and wanted to know what had happened. Detective Bühler asked them to take Willenbrock to get X-rayed; the doctor jotted down something on his pad. When the detective mentioned the break-in, the doctor said that they had seen two men walking along the road toward Anklam, a detail that had caught their attention since they weren't used to seeing pedestrians there at three-thirty in the morning.

The detective turned back to the house, knocked on the windowpane, and waved the patrolmen outside. She quickly passed on the new information and told them to go and check out the two men on foot.

Willenbrock climbed in the back of the ambulance and sat down on the bench. The doctor asked if he wanted to lie down, Willenbrock said no. The two policemen took off before the ambulance driver managed to turn the van around on the narrow, unfinished lane. Five minutes later, on the way to Anklam, Willenbrock saw the police car parked by the edge of the road; the policemen had gotten out and were talking with two men, whom they kept in the beam of their flashlights. Willenbrock saw only the men's backs; neither one was very tall. The ambulance rushed past; he looked back through the window but couldn't see enough to try to identify the men.

At the clinic, the night-duty clerk showed Willenbrock the way to the X-ray section. He had to wait a long time until a doctor appeared, an older man who was yawning loudly, followed by a nurse. Willenbrock briefly recounted what had happened. The doctor listened with half-closed eyes, told the nurse what to X-ray, and then disappeared behind a door. Willenbrock followed the nurse into the X-ray room and took off his shirt. Afterward he was told to wait in the hall. He sat down on a bench and closed his eyes; he tried to sleep but the scene immediately came back to him, the fearful and desperately determined face of the young man hitting him.

The doctor reappeared and asked Willenbrock to step into his office. He clamped the X-rays onto the light box, explained the images to Willenbrock, and said that nothing was broken. The swelling would increase over the next few hours and would not subside for another few days or even weeks. Willenbrock should check in with his own physician, there was a possibility of periostitis, which could be painful. As the doctor stood by the light box, explaining the X-rays, his eyes remained half-closed, and Willenbrock had the impression he was talking in his sleep. At last he looked at Willenbrock, so that Willenbrock could actually see his eyes for a moment, but then the lids sank down again.

"Every week," the doctor went on, "we see a case like yours. They should build walls. Walls everywhere. It's impossible to stop all these people. A wall around Germany, around every country. And a few extra walls in Yugoslavia, Israel, and Northern Ireland. Then things would be quiet. After all, they keep wild beasts in cages, right?"

At that point he closed his eyes completely as if he were about to nod off in front of the light box, and left the room without another word. Willenbrock waited a few seconds, disoriented, then looked for the nurse and asked whether that was all and how he should get home, whether the ambulance would take him.

"The ambulance isn't responsible for taking people back home," the nurse replied, and went on writing.

"So how am I supposed to get back?" Willenbrock was tired and upset and felt miserable.

The nurse kept writing. Eventually she looked up, sighed, opened a drawer, filled out a transportation voucher and gave it to Willenbrock. She said he should have someone at reception call a taxi. Before he left she carped that the hospital had a limited number of vouchers and to fill them out meant extra work for her, but the patients never think about anybody except themselves.

Willenbrock had to wait for the guard at reception to return, either from making his rounds or a trip to the toilet. As he got in the taxi, the driver asked whether he was paying cash or had a voucher from the hospital. Once they were out of the city, the driver said he'd prefer if Willenbrock paid in cash and collected the reimbursement from the hospital himself—all these vouchers were a pain to process. Willenbrock explained that he didn't have any money on him. The taxi driver, annoyed, stopped talking. Willenbrock looked out the window; he didn't want to fall asleep, he was scared he'd dream about what had happened; he was too afraid to close his eyes. A weak light in the sky hinted at the coming sunrise; between the tall trees lining the road he could make out a narrow streak of color, a barely perceptible glow.

When the taxi reached the small rise just before Willenbrock's farmstead, the driver saw the police car and the brightly lit house; he asked Willenbrock what had happened.

"I was attacked," Willenbrock said, indifferently.

The driver whistled through his teeth, turned around, and said: "Welcome to the club."

As Willenbrock started to get out, the driver reached under his steering wheel and pulled out a pistol.

"Since then I always carry this."

"A little dangerous," said Willenbrock. "Those things can misfire, you know."

The driver stashed the pistol. "That's my insurance. It's very comforting."

The detective's colleague, whose name Willenbrock either hadn't understood or just never heard, had stayed by Susanne's side. Susanne asked about the results of the X-ray and told her husband that the police had arrested the two men on the highway. They had brought them back to the house and asked her to identify them while they were sitting in the back of the car. She had looked at the men but couldn't really give an opinion, since she hadn't actually seen any of the attackers. As she was explaining this, she looked at the policeman.

"We leave no stone unturned," he said.

The policeman got up and said that if everything was in order he'd like to go. Willenbrock thanked him and saw him out. Then he carefully locked the door and went with Susanne from room to room, turning off the lights. By the time they were in bed it was already dawn.

"I'm afraid," his wife said, when they'd had lain beside each other for some time. "I'm afraid to be in the house."

Willenbrock was silent. He didn't know what to say.

Around eleven they were awakened by a knock on the door. A patrol car was outside; a policeman asked Willenbrock and his wife to accompany them to the station. Some suspects had been taken into custody and the police wanted to set up a witness identification. Willenbrock asked if it was the two men from the highway, but the policeman couldn't say. He'd only been told to bring Herr and Frau Willenbrock in for an identification. Willenbrock explained that his wife hadn't actually seen any of the intruders and was therefore unable to help, but the policeman said he had been ordered to bring both of them to the station and asked them to please come along. Willenbrock was too tired to try convincing the man of the fact that it was pointless to involve Susanne. He asked him for a moment's patience and went back to the bedroom. He and Susanne washed up, got dressed, ate a day-old roll, and climbed in the police car.

The station was a large, three-story building with a courtyard in front packed with cars. The policeman accompanied them inside and reported their arrival to a colleague at the entrance. Together they climbed a staircase up to a hall where a man in uniform was already heading to meet them: he introduced himself as the on-duty officer and invited them into his office. He said that the two men in custody hadn't had anything on them, no missing objects from the Willenbrocks' house or any other personal effects. They didn't even have papers; they'd probably thrown everything away before they were seized. The officer had ordered a patrol car to search the arrest site, but the patrolmen hadn't turned up anything. In the meantime, however, he'd succeeded in determining the suspects' identities by checking their fingerprints against the database—Andrei and Artur Gatchev, brothers from Moscow with a very long record, though up to now only in their own country.

The officer asked the couple to look at the men in order to identify the night intruders.

"Or else to exonerate them," he added, laughing.

"There were four," said Willenbrock, "there were four men in my house. I only saw one, and just heard the voices of the others, two or three of them, speaking Russian."

"We've only caught two," said the officer.

"There must have been four," Willenbrock insisted. "There were four iron pokers, four irons to use for hitting. Why would the burglars arm themselves with two apiece? It doesn't make any sense. And it wouldn't be practical. Don't you think? Anyway, the detective thought there were four."

"Fine with me. But today we're looking at two. I hope that won't keep you from making the identifications."

He asked them to have a seat in the hall. Willenbrock assumed they would be taken to a room with a one-way mirror window, where the Russians would be shown in a lineup with some other men. That's how it was always done in the movies.

An official walked past, eyeing them curiously, proceeded to the back of the corridor, opened a door, and waved a man over, then opened a second door and brought out another young man. The policeman walked the two men back down the corridor, and Willenbrock understood that this was supposed to be the identification, that these were the brothers from Moscow picked up in the night. For a moment he felt a spasm in his heart. He looked at Susanne; she, too, had realized these were the suspects. She turned away so she wouldn't have to see them. Willenbrock stood up and went over to stop them from coming closer, to protect Susanne. Then the Russians, the policeman, and Willenbrock all stood in the hall looking at one another. The Russians were young, very young. The older one might have been twenty-five, his brother was at least five years younger. Both were short; Willenbrock and the policeman were each a head taller. The younger brother grinned at Willenbrock awkwardly. Willenbrock was sure that he had never seen him before and turned to the older one, who looked him in the eye without moving a muscle. The man seemed detached and bored.

Willenbrock felt his resentment toward the police growing. He hadn't wanted a direct, unprotected confrontation; he would never have agreed to it, he felt himself caught off guard. He didn't want to look the Russians in the eye—and most of all he didn't want them to see him.

Yet now they were standing face-to-face, and it was too late, and pointless, to protest. He shot an angry glance at the policeman, who was waiting to lock the suspects back up, then stared at the older of the two Russians. He tried to remember, but couldn't say for sure. Everything was so different. In the night he had seen a man standing in front of him wielding an iron rod, aggressive, scared, and in a panic—just like himself. Now he was looking at a calm, composed, skinny young man in police custody, who didn't seem the least bit threatening. On the contrary, he seemed helpless and in need of protection, slight as he was, shabbily dressed in cheap pants and a thin shirt.

Willenbrock was surprised how frail the man seemed. He tried to recall the scene, but couldn't really gauge the size of the man who had hit him—he seemed to remember the man was shorter than himself. And at the time he hadn't paid any attention to what the man was wearing.

Without saying a word, Willenbrock sat down close to Susanne, to shield her from their gaze. The official locked the two Russians back in their separate rooms, or cells, then asked the Willenbrocks to come to his office so he could take a statement. Susanne repeated that she couldn't identify anybody, since she had never seen the intruders, and Willenbrock explained that he wasn't entirely sure. It could have been the older brother, but he couldn't swear to it. He asked them to compare the fingerprints. The detectives had found some prints they were very pleased with, particularly on the glass roof over the patio. When the policeman asked again, Willenbrock repeated: "I'm not entirely sure. It could be him, but I wouldn't want to accuse the wrong person. Check the fingerprints."

The officer went into the next room to type up the statement.

Willenbrock asked his wife whether the two men were the same ones she had been shown while he was getting X-rayed. She couldn't say.

"They were sitting in the car. I could barely see them. And I didn't want to look at them, either. What for? I didn't see anybody. All I did was sit and scream. You had to do everything by yourself. I'm upset because I didn't help you at all."

"All either of us did was scream. That's exactly what the detective praised us for. Apparently it's the best thing to do if you're attacked. At least that's what she said."

Through the open door Willenbrock could make out the officer who, with some difficulty, was feeding a sheet of paper with several carbons into the typewriter. He lined them up, checked the paper, took them out again, turned over one of the carbons, and finally started pecking out his text, letter by letter.

"The keys," said Willenbrock, suddenly.

"What do you mean?"

"They have our house keys. They didn't get my car keys or my wallet—those were still on the clock where I left them. But they have the keys to our house in Berlin, and to the car lot. I put them in the display case and I'm sure they weren't there this morning. I'm positive. I saw they were missing when I went to the bathroom. I only noticed it in passing, but I'm sure the keys weren't there."

"What should we do? Tell the police, tell them."

"What good will that do? We have to get back to Berlin

right away. We have to change all the locks, if it isn't too late already. There were four men. Even if these are two of them, where are the others?"

"How would they get our address?"

"How would I know? But we have to get back to Berlin."

He got up, went into the next room and asked the hapless policeman, who was still at the typewriter, how long it would take. The officer promised they would be escorted home right away. Twenty minutes later he brought out a sheet of paper, asked them to read it through carefully and sign. Willenbrock stared at the sheet in disbelief; there were only eight lines. The officer had taken half an hour to type out eight lines. When he read through the text, Willenbrock protested. He demanded that the policeman write down what he had actually said. It wasn't true that he hadn't recognized the men; he just wasn't completely certain. There was a difference, and he asked that it be noted. Besides, he had requested that the fingerprints be compared, but there was no mention of that, either. And what's more, the Willenbrocks' name and address were misspelled—all that should be corrected, too. The policeman nodded. He took the paper, went into the next room, sat down at the typewriter, and put together a new bundle of forms and carbons. He carefully collated it, adjusted it several times, and fed it into the machine. He spent a long time hunting for each letter and kept staring intently at the paper before him and at the Willenbrocks' documents as he retyped the form.

Willenbrock became jittery. He stood up and began pacing the room. Susanne kept asking him to sit down, but he didn't respond. When the officer came back half an hour later with a new form, and Willenbrock was again dissatisfied with the way his statement had been recorded, he asked for a pen so he could correct the text himself. The officer told him that wasn't permitted. If he didn't feel he could sign this statement, then the officer would simply have to type out a new one.

"I have no time for this," Willenbrock said, irritated. "Do you think I can spend the whole day at your station? Today of all days?"

He accepted the pen from the officer and signed the statement. He asked to be driven home as soon as possible. The officer promised, but it was another fifteen minutes before a policeman appeared and called out his name.

On the way home Willenbrock held his wife's hand, which was still shaking slightly. The two policemen in front were strong, stocky men. The one on the passenger side was wearing sunglasses; he had rolled down his window and was leaning back, relaxed, his elbow cocked against the window frame. He was chewing gum and had shoved his cap back. The man's seen too many American movies, thought Willenbrock.

"What's going to happen with the two Russians you arrested?" he asked the policeman.

The driver said: "I don't know. They'll probably be deported. Taken to the border and handed over to our Polish colleagues. Then it's home to Russia."

"You mean they just deport them? That's all?"

"Yes."

"And the next day they're back here."

"Could be," the man agreed, "it's happened before. But then they'll be deported again. Those are the rules of the game."

"Why aren't they put in prison? After all, they did try to beat me to death. That's attempted manslaughter, which is a major felony as far as I know. You can't just deport criminals like that."

"It's not up to us to decide," the driver said, indifferently. "Our prisons are already full of our own people."

"German prisons only for Germans?" asked Willenbrock, annoyed.

Both policemen turned around for a brief moment. "Couldn't have put it better," the driver answered, deadpan.

Willenbrock searched the house for his key ring, but just as he suspected, it was gone. Susanne looked in her purse and was relieved when she pulled out her own set. He rushed her to leave and together they packed the wicker basket and their bags. Then he carefully locked the house. Before leaving the village, they made a quick detour to thank Heiner again for his help and to update him. Heiner listened carefully, while his wife kept shaking her head and saying to her husband that it could happen to them.

"No," Heiner declared, "it couldn't. Bernd doesn't have a dog. They wouldn't dare set foot on our property."

Passing by their place again on the way to Berlin, they saw Wickert, the musician, waving them over. He handed them several credit cards made out in Susanne's name, a telephone card, and a few wet pieces of paper he had come across while he was walking along the road, right where the Russians had been arrested, and where the police had ostensibly searched.

Susanne hadn't yet noticed they were missing. Then Wickert pulled a cell phone out of his pocket and asked if it was theirs; he had found it a few yards farther down. Willenbrock looked at it and said it was. They thanked the musician.

"Pretty bad night for you, huh?" Wickert asked. He had tied his hair back into a ponytail with a rubber band.

"Yes," said Willenbrock.

"We weren't exactly very neighborly last night, were we?" the musician went on, smiling awkwardly.

"That's okay," said Willenbrock. "You couldn't have known."

"That's true. We just saw the cops and we don't exactly like having them on our property. You understand. Voice of experience, you know."

"I understand," Willenbrock nodded.

"That Russian song right then wasn't the best choice either, was it? But we had no idea."

Willenbrock shrugged; he and Susanne climbed back in the car.

" 'Suliko.' That's what we were singing. You know, 'Suliko,' Stalin's favorite," the musician explained. "It's actually quite a beautiful song."

"If it was Stalin's favorite, then maybe my attackers liked it too," said Willenbrock. "You may have had a receptive audience after all."

Wickert was still embarrassed. "Well, let's say I owe you a song. Your choice. Whenever you want, I'll come and sing for you."

Willenbrock nodded encouragingly. "I'll let you know," he said, and started the engine.

12

They were back in the city by early afternoon. The house was untouched—no traces of forced entry or attempted break-in. Willenbrock and his wife went through all the rooms but found no sign of unwanted visitors.

He told Susanne he needed to drive out to the lot, but she didn't want to stay in the house alone. So he took the wicker basket and their bags out of the car, which was parked in front, and sat down in an armchair while Susanne unpacked. He suddenly felt very tired. Something had been destroyed, he thought, something's over: things will never be the way they were. He let his gaze wander through the room as if he might discover what he had lost. Retrieving the spare keys to his lot from his desk, he went outside to wait for Susanne.

They drove to the lot and pulled up next to the fence, from where they surveyed the parked cars and the trailer in the early twilight. Willenbrock opened the gate, walked up to his office, and looked in the window before going inside. Then he climbed the steps, turned the handle, and pushed at the door. The office was undisturbed. He and Susanne stayed until Pasewald showed up with his dog. All Willenbrock told the watchman was that his keys had disappeared; he asked Pasewald to secure the gate with an extra chain and promised to switch all the locks the next day, just to be safe. Pasewald asked whether he'd lost the keys or someone had stolen them. Willenbrock thought for a moment.

"The fact is they were stolen," he said. "But I don't think the thief has any way of knowing what they're for. There's probably no need for me to worry, but it's better to play it safe. Anyway, you better keep an especially sharp eye out tonight."

He looked at his wife, who was staring at him, bewildered. Back in the car he apologized to her and explained why he hadn't told Pasewald about the attack.

"I didn't want to upset him," he said. "Maybe we're just letting our imaginations get the better of us. And you finally got to see my new building. I hope you like it. But I know you're not interested, otherwise I would have shown you around."

"It's not a good day for that," she agreed. "But some other time I'd like to see it."

When they drove off, they saw Pasewald looping a thick chain through the iron bars of the gate. His dog kept running between his legs.

They went to bed early, since they hadn't slept much the night before, but it took them a long time to fall asleep despite the fact that both were worn out and exhausted. Willenbrock kept catching himself listening to noises coming from outside.

He woke up suddenly in the middle of the night. Straining to catch every sound, he kept very still. He realized Susanne was also awake, so he turned on the light. He looked at the clock; it was twelve after two.

"It's nothing," he said to his wife soothingly and caressed

her face. "It's just the exact same time as last night. Almost to the minute, I think. This is when I woke up yesterday, this is when the whole show began."

Susanne asked him to search the house with her, otherwise she wouldn't be able to get back to sleep. They went to the bathroom, put on their silk robes, checked the front door, then went through the house room by room, turning on all the lights. Willenbrock switched on the outside light and glanced through the window at the yard and garage.

When they were back in bed, Susanne said they should sell their country house. She'd never be able to spend another minute there in peace, she wouldn't be able to sleep there anymore, and she'd certainly never stay there alone—she was too afraid after what had happened. Willenbrock pointed out that she'd have to deal with the same feeling no matter where she was, that she'd never feel completely safe after an attack like that. Finally they agreed to wait half a year and then decide about the house.

"They destroyed something, a place inside me I thought was invulnerable," said Susanne, "a private space where I was absolutely secure. Now I'll never feel that way again, not in a big house or in a tiny apartment. That's what I can't forgive them. Ever. I feel like I've been stripped naked."

"I know," said Willenbrock, slowly, in the darkness. "Something's changed." After a pause he added: "Maybe, eventually, we'll be able to forget it. Maybe in time everything'll be the way it used to be."

His wife merely snorted dismissively and didn't answer.

Over the next few days they said nothing more about the break-in. They didn't mention it at all. They both seemed to be avoiding the subject, not even hinting or alluding to it, and as the next weekend approached, without consulting with each other they both made plans to stay in the city instead of driving out to their country house. They woke up, night after night, always at two o'clock. When Willenbrock felt his wife lying next to him, also unable to sleep, he reached for her hand and stroked it in silence. If she had to go to the bathroom, she asked him to get up, too. He would go ahead of her, turn on the lights, and wait for her. Susanne felt embarrassed and apologized. Then they would spend an hour lying awake in bed, trying to calm their frayed nerves so they could go back to sleep.

During this time he rang up Pasewald twice in the middle of the night because he would suddenly find himself worrying about the watchman and the car lot. The first time, the phone rang several minutes before Pasewald managed to answer. The watchman was surprised to get the call; he told his boss that everything was in order.

The second time Willenbrock regretted calling even before Pasewald could get to the phone, and for a moment he considered hanging up. When the watchman answered, Willenbrock asked about a red briefcase he had supposedly left on his desk, and apologized for the disturbance.

On Wednesday it started raining and didn't stop for a whole week. Late Friday morning the crane used to erect the columns and trusses was driven off the site. An engineer from the construction company came to inspect the building's progress. Willenbrock accompanied him on his rounds and listened silently as the man spoke with the workers and told them in no uncertain terms they needed to be more careful about covering the fresh concrete where the columns had been set.

"Your showroom's going to be magnificent," the engineer assured Willenbrock as he put the documents in their see-through sleeves back in his briefcase, "more like a show palace. You should put a line of chorus girls in there instead of all these old cars. Anyway, we're going to make sure you get the best."

He gave the workers an address and told them to report there after lunch.

"Why are you pulling them off the job—why aren't they staying here? And what happened to the crane?" asked Willenbrock.

"The columns are up. Next week we start on the roof. We don't need a crane for that, roof work's better done by hand. And it'll cost you less. By Wednesday we'll have the roof up. After that they hang the ceiling."

They watched the men put their tools away and drive off without saying goodbye.

"Why wait till Wednesday?"

The engineer looked up at the sky, skeptically. "Believe me, with this weather, it's better if we hold off a little. The concrete has to set thoroughly, and the roofing was ordered for next week. Besides, we have a little problem at Potsdamer Platz. We're under the gun and need all the hands we can spare. But don't worry, your finish date is in absolutely no danger."

He asked Willenbrock if they could go to his office; he needed another paper signed and didn't want to pull it out in the pouring rain. They went to the trailer, where Willenbrock opened the door and let him in. The engineer was curious to see what it looked like inside but didn't say anything. He sat down when invited, then took some documents out of his briefcase and made a note. He checked his watch, wrote down the time and date, and handed a paper across the desk to Willenbrock, who skimmed it and signed.

"I see we really do need to finish your showroom so you can get out of here. What kind of impression does this kind of setup make on your customers?"

"My customers don't mind at all," Willenbrock insisted. "The new building's for me, not them."

"Of course," said the engineer, quick to agree, "of course it's for you. Customers come and customers go, they don't care one way or another. And people who buy used cars don't put that much stock in appearances, do they?"

Willenbrock didn't respond; he was waiting for the man to leave. He was annoyed that the workers had been pulled off the site, that his job was evidently of secondary importance, but since he couldn't point to any overt breach of their contract he kept silent.

The engineer packed the papers in his briefcase, snapped it shut, and stood up. "Your roof will be here on Wednesday," he said and nodded to Willenbrock.

"What's the problem?" asked Willenbrock.

The man looked at him, taken aback, and Willenbrock explained: "You pulled the workers off my site because of a problem at Potsdamer Platz."

"Oh," said the engineer casually, "that problem. More like a minor disaster. Two idiots ran a truck into a girder and knocked it down. The truck's a total loss, but at least it was insured. Meanwhile, the damage has cost us four days of work, and for that there's no insurance and no mercy. We have to take care of it ourselves, the firm will have to absorb the cost.

"Why don't you get the two idiots to pay for it."

"There's nothing to get. The boss tried. Not from those two jerks."

"That's what happens when you hire cheap labor. You try and cut corners and you end up paying more."

"No, they weren't working for us. It was just two asshole crooks, two brothers trying to make off with one of our trucks. The police hauled them in for a night and then dropped them off at the border."

"Two brothers?" said Willenbrock, suddenly tense. He stared at the engineer, who was a few years younger than himself; the man had taken off his safety helmet inside the trailer, and his blond hair now had an extra wave on both sides of his head.

"Two brothers?" Willenbrock repeated. "From Moscow?"

"No, they were Bulgarians. Or Romanians. You know the sort that crawl over the border."

"I know," Willenbrock said and nodded. He sat back down at his desk.

"You've probably had a few run-ins with these people. A lot full of cars, that should draw the crooks like flies."

"No, I don't have any trouble." Keeping a straight face, he looked the engineer in the eye.

"I'm glad to hear it," the engineer replied. "So we'll see you next week, Herr Willenbrock."

Willenbrock gave a disgruntled nod. He stayed seated,

waiting until the man had driven off. Then he grabbed an umbrella and went out. Taking large strides and avoiding the puddles, he wove his way to the building site and looked it over one more time. Mistrustful, he inspected the recent work and straightened the plastic covering. Then he returned to his office and tried calling Detective Bühler. He wanted to ask about the status of the investigation, find out what had happened to the suspects, what steps the public prosecutor had taken, and whether he was expected to appear in court as a plaintiff or as a witness. He wasn't able to get through to the detective and was told to call back in an hour.

When he finally reached her and gave his name, she remembered him right away. He inquired about the investigation and about the two Russian brothers. There was a long pause, and he asked if she was still on the line and whether she had understood him.

Frau Bühler replied hesitantly, asking if Willenbrock hadn't received a letter from the public prosecutor's office. Willenbrock said he hadn't. The detective took an audible breath and then explained that he should be getting a letter any day now from the public prosecutor in charge of the case, and that she did not want to—was not allowed to—jump ahead of things. Once he'd read the letter he could call her back, if he still had questions.

Her tentative response puzzled Willenbrock, and he asked whether any charges had been brought. As far as he knew, it was a case of attempted manslaughter, so the prosecutor was obliged to proceed with the case, regardless of whether Willenbrock filed charges, which he fully intended to do. Since the detective said nothing, he asked where the two suspects who had been taken into custody were being held—were they still at the local police station, or had they been transferred to a pretrial prison? As he spoke, Willenbrock became increasingly agitated, his voice grew louder and louder, to the point of yelling.

Detective Bühler kept telling Willenbrock to calm down and explained that they had not been able to detain the men any longer. Then she was silent; Willenbrock waited for her to say more. Finally he asked what that meant, that he didn't understand. Once again the detective referred him to the letter due to arrive from the public prosecutor's office and added that the men had to be deported to Poland, by order of the prosecutor in charge, since they had entered Germany illegally.

"Deported?" said Willenbrock, stunned, then added, in a raspy voice: "You mean, two men practically kill me and they're just deported?"

The woman again asked him to calm down and said that she wasn't happy about the decision either but had no choice except to comply. Two days after the brothers had been arrested, she'd had to take them to the eastern border and hand them over to the Polish authorities, on condition that the men return immediately and directly to their home city of Moscow.

Willenbrock was breathing heavily. In a hoarse whisper he asked whether he should assume that the two Russians were already back in the country by now, whether he should be expecting another visit.

"I don't think so," said the detective, then adding: "Let's

hope not, but I can't say for certain. It wasn't for me to decide, Herr Willenbrock. Unfortunately."

Willenbrock hung up. He suddenly felt ill. He held out his palms and watched droplets of sweat form on their surfaces. You're afraid, he said to himself. He was taken aback and overcome by a feeling of shame and resentment. He tried to shake it off, tried to laugh out loud, but all that came out was a rough, toneless croaking.

His wife came home late that evening. Willenbrock was in the kitchen making potato pancakes with diced vegetables. He set the table; they ate in silence. He felt that Susanne was observing him, and he looked at her inquisitively.

"Should we give it up?" she asked suddenly. "Just sell the place?"

She was talking about the country house, and he turned red because he felt caught, because he had been thinking incessantly about the house, the attack, his conversation with the detective.

He only said: "No, let's talk about it in six months. That was the deal."

"What about in the meantime?" she went on. "Somebody has to drive out there to mow the grass and look after the garden. And I don't want to. I'm afraid."

"From a mathematical point of view," he replied, "the chances that—"

He stopped himself, took her hand, and said soothingly: "We'll just have to be more careful, love."

He had decided not to tell her anything about the two Russians being deported, at least not for the moment, so as not to upset her even more, but he knew he wouldn't be able to keep it from her for long. He had checked the mail the minute he got home, but there was nothing from the prosecutor's office; the letter the detective spoke of still hadn't arrived. He didn't know what he would do when it did show up, assuming he managed to get hold of it first.

That night they again woke up at two in the morning. Both felt that the other was wide-awake, but neither said anything.

Three days later he told Jurek he had to go out for an hour, to the post office and to see a wholesale dealer. On the way he stopped to drop off two pairs of scissors to have them sharpened. He parked on the sidewalk outside the shop and stood looking at the wares in the window. A metal crossbow and an air rifle were hanging in the rear of the display; air pistols and signal guns were spread out in front, along with knives and some cans of Mace for warding off attackers and dogs. Willenbrock stared at the window for a long time, amazed that he would even consider buying something like that, that he might actually hold one of these not exactly harmless implements in his hand and point it at another person. The whole idea struck him as absurd. He felt a little embarrassed, too; he had always scoffed at hunters and marksmen: their fondness for beautifully maintained flintlocks and muskets, their need to join clubs where they fired at targets that mimicked animals or even humans had always seemed to him adolescent and undignified. Moreover, there was something unhealthy about it; he saw a morbid desire to kill beneath the game-playing, a murderous drive disguised as macho posturing.

He stepped into the store, where other weapons were on

display in locked glass cases; they were ornately decorated and looked expensive. More than a dozen scary-looking pistols were arranged under the glass of the counter. Willenbrock studied them, unsure if they were actually available for sale. A few seconds later, a tall, stooping man a little older than Willenbrock emerged through a door behind the counter, cued by the bell at the front; slowly and indifferently he made his way toward the customer. He waited until Willenbrock had finished examining the goods and looked up, then asked how he might be of assistance. Willenbrock placed his scissors on the counter.

"They're dull," he said, "could you fix them for me? You do sharpen scissors, don't you?"

The older man took a pair of glasses out of his coat pocket and looked at the scissors.

"What hack got hold of these? They're all nicked to hell," he grumbled crossly.

Willenbrock didn't say anything. He himself had tried in vain to sharpen the scissors in his shop.

"They'll be ready in three days. But I'll have to charge you extra to get these back in shape."

The man tore off a claim check and handed it to Willenbrock.

"Anything else I can help you with?" he asked when Willenbrock didn't leave.

"I don't know," said Willenbrock, looking around the store.

"Take your time," said the shopkeeper without changing his expression, as he waited patiently for the customer to decide.

"I'm looking for some protection against burglars. Know what I mean?"

The man nodded and pointed to the wares under the countertop. "What were you thinking of? A spray, an alarm, a baton, a signal pistol?"

He opened the glass case and took out a shiny black club the length of an arm and held it under Willenbrock's nose.

"Three hundred and fifty thousand volts," he said. "One touch of that and your man's out of commission. Cramps up and drops to the floor, a technical knockout. Here, take it, hold it yourself."

Willenbrock eyed the device suspiciously. "No, I don't think that's what I need. That won't help if they're armed. They won't wait long enough for me to get that close, they'll just pull out their guns."

The dealer nodded in agreement. "Then you ought to buy some acoustic protection, an alarm with a hundred eighty decibels. Makes so much racket it'll bring your roof down."

"That might help if they were easily scared," acknowledged Willenbrock, "but I don't want to rely on that. As a rule these people have strong nerves and few inhibitions."

He looked around the shop, unable to decide.

"You know," he said, "I was recently attacked, at my place in the country."

The vendor nodded indifferently. He showed no sign of surprise and asked no questions, which Willenbrock found appalling. He had expected the man would be shocked by what he'd just told him, moved to show a little more interest, but the dealer merely took it in as though he heard stories like that every day. Maybe he does, thought Willenbrock. Now he was annoyed and upset that he had even mentioned the incident. It was his story, his problem, nobody else was interested; he had to come to grips with it on his own, he and Susanne. Why was he baring his soul to some old guy he didn't know from Adam, who had been perfectly right to react the way he did, as if he were barely listening or had just been made the involuntary recipient of some stranger's confession, which he'd rather ignore and pretend not to hear? I should actually salute the guy, Willenbrock told himself, he's the better man; after all, he refuses to be bothered by the stupidities I keep coming up with.

The man scratched at a small scar on his wrist, then picked up the club he had placed on the counter, returned it to the glass case, and looked at Willenbrock expectantly.

"It's not what I had in mind," said Willenbrock apologetically. He was embarrassed and made a grimace.

"I know what you had in mind. But I can't sell you that. For that you need a weapons license."

"What am I supposed to do with these things? They can't protect me. They're no better than playthings."

"Get a dog," the man suggested impassively.

"No, I can't. My wife, she's allergic to dog hair."

Willenbrock finally bought a little pistol, a small revolver for firing blanks and signal ammo. The shopkeeper showed him the weapon and explained how to load it and release the safety. He reached across the table to hand Willenbrock the gun. Willenbrock felt himself turning red as he hefted it and quickly put it back in the box. He bought a few boxes of blanks as well, and several tubes of signal flares, then paid and hurried out of the store.

In his car he opened the box, removed the weapon and examined it. On one side of the cylinder a warning was stamped in English instructing the user to consult the manual; on the other was the designation "9 mm." A shadow passed across his car window and Willenbrock looked up to see a twelve-year-old boy with a pimply face staring at the revolver with large, wistful eyes. You're getting stranger by the day, he told himself. Do you really think you'd actually point this stupid toy at a human being, even if he breaks in and threatens you? You'd be so worked up you wouldn't even be able to find it, and by the time you got your hands on the thing, it would be too late, and that would only make the attacker more aggressive, so he'd hit you all the harder. Your little toy might even make him reach for his own weapon, and it's doubtful his would be a toy. You'd just be putting yourself in jeopardy, literally sentencing yourself to death. The best thing to do would be to chuck this thing in the nearest trash can, before something really terrible happens.

Willenbrock drove back to his lot. Before he got out, he placed the box with the revolver in the glove compartment, then carefully locked his car. Once in his office, he had to force himself not to look out the window constantly to check on his car. That's one more problem on your hands, he told himself.

At the end of the week the weather cleared up, and on Saturday the sun was shining in a cloudless sky for the first time in days, undimmed by any veil of haze. Willenbrock set the breakfast table outside on the small marble-tiled terrace in the back of the house. He waited until he'd made the coffee before waking Susanne. She went straight from her bed to the table and sat there, wrapped in her bathrobe, delighted to have her husband pamper her.

"We're doing all right, aren't we?" she said.

Willenbrock beamed at her. He knew she was thinking about the attack, and he knew she knew that he was thinking about it, too, but they didn't want to put their thoughts into words. Clearly they'd have to decide sooner or later either to sell the house or drive out there again, and he thought about the signal gun, which he kept squirreled away in his desk. It made him feel ridiculous and embarrassed, owning something like that.

"It's going to be a nice day," was all he said. "A good omen for your show."

Susanne had invited several of her clients to a fashion presentation in the boutique that afternoon, and Willenbrock had promised to look in. The day before he had rented glasses and plates and dropped off several cartons of wine and bottled water at her shop. He planned to help out during the event, taking care of the guests. He had also urged his wife to hire a musician. Susanne had laughed at him and asked whether he was thinking about the brass band he'd twice engaged for his special Sunday sales events—open houses, he called them—but in the end she let him talk her into hiring a solo trombone player from the music academy.

Willenbrock picked up the paper, glanced over the political news, and then turned to the local section. He was looking for the small ad he'd taken out for his wife's show. When he found it, he handed Susanne the paper. She read the announcement, surprised and touched.

"Why did you go and spend money on that?" she asked. "It's just a little show for my clients, not some theatrical performance. What will I do if a few hundred people turn up because they read the paper and want to hear your trombonist?"

"They'll just have to get in line and wait. I'll sell tickets and play the bouncer."

Susanne went to wash up and Willenbrock cleared the table. Half an hour later they drove to her shop in separate cars. The streets were still empty, and they made good time. When they reached the end of Grabbeallee they parted ways with a quick honk of the horn.

Things were quiet at the lot; construction was still on hold. Jurek had jacked up a motor inside the old greenhouse and was busy repairing it. Willenbrock looked in to say hello and, since Jurek was engrossed in his work and didn't respond, went to his office, where he spent nearly two hours designing a solar-powered lighting system for the lot. At ten o'clock he put on some water for coffee and sat down with Jurek to eat the kaiser rolls and cake he'd picked up on the way over. They talked about foreigners working illegally in Berlin and the going rates for apartments. For two years Jurek had been sharing a small apartment with another Pole; a month ago he'd moved into his own one-room apartment. Although his new place was just as small as the old one, the rent was nearly twice as high.

"They're all sharks," said Willenbrock, about the landlords.

Jurek disagreed. "You're mistaking the tree for the nest, boss. With the whole tribe coming over the border, it drives the rents up. Too many people, the prices go crazy. The market's going through the roof."

He spread his arms out wide, his right hand holding the roll he had bitten into.

"The main thing is that we're both doing okay, right?" Willenbrock laughed.

"It's too much. Everything has to have a limit or else it breaks down. And why have a border if it isn't a border?"

"Tell that to your landlord, Jurek. Maybe he'll cut you a deal since you're such a German patriot."

"He doesn't rent to Germans."

"Smart man. At least he doesn't mistake the tree for the nest, as you put it."

"This country's going to burst at the seams, boss. You'll see."

"Have some more cake, Jurek. It'll go stale by Monday."

An hour later Willenbrock came out of the trailer and walked over to Jurek, who had opened the trunk of a car and was explaining something to three customers. While Jurek spoke, one of the men ran his hand almost tenderly over the finish and the chrome trim. As Willenbrock approached, Jurek pointed him out, telling the men that this was the boss. The men looked up and nodded, then turned back to the car. Jurek described the parts he'd changed and pointed out the new tires. Willenbrock listened to him for a moment, then took the mail out of the box by the gate, went back inside the trailer, and looked over the letters. From his window he watched as the men had Jurek show them two more cars and then left.

Afterward Jurek knocked on his door, opened it, and stuck his head inside. Willenbrock looked up.

"Those were Germans," said Jurek.

Willenbrock looked at him, annoyed.

"All I mean is, they were your own countrymen, boss," Jurek explained. "No Russians. I would have let you know."

He closed the door and went down the steps. Willenbrock was now sorry he had told the Pole about the attack. He felt unmasked, and it was true that recently whenever clients showed up in the yard, he went outside to check on them; he found it humiliating that Jurek had evidently noticed. It was a strange feeling that drew him from the trailer, difficult to sort out—a fear, or perhaps a nervous hope, that he might again lay eyes on the young man who'd broken into his house and beat him with an iron rod. Maybe it was also the suspicion that the man and his accomplices really had taken the keys on purpose and would one day show up at the lot—a suspicion that Willenbrock refused to admit but which lingered in his mind nevertheless. He grew flushed whenever he thought about it; the mere notion of seeing the man who had attacked him made his breathing shorter. On the one hand, the very idea sent him into a panic, while on the other hand, he found himself hoping to meet up with his attacker. Time and again he felt his thoughts suddenly turn to the man; in his mind's eye he kept imagining a second meeting in which he was hitting the Russian, stabbing him, wounding him, chaining him up. The fantasies were unpleasant; they always left him in a sweat. Still, there was something liberating about them; he found some release in hurting the man, in paying him back, blow for blow. In his head he played through an infinite variety of confrontations where he hit back violently and with excessive force, sliding from justifiable self-defense into inexcusable excess, beating his attacker even after he lay helpless on the ground, bloody, bound, and unconscious. These battles gave him satisfaction, even as his fantasies of such formidable defense exhausted him physically. When he came to his senses, released from the spell of these phantom encounters prompted by his fear, frustration, and helplessness, he felt overcome with shame. He was shocked at his behavior, stunned by his imaginings, appalled by the hate raging inside him and his consuming thirst for revenge. But the dreams and fantasies kept coming, day and night, without warning, always with the same intensity, sweeping him away. He wondered if Susanne was going through something similar, but he didn't dare ask and was reluctant to tell her about his dreams, his extreme tension.

Half an hour later he watched Jurek walking through the lot with a customer who looked over fifty, a man with very thin hair. When the Pole turned to glance at the trailer, Willenbrock quickly withdrew from the window.

He sent Jurek home before noon. He wrote a note for Pasewald and taped it to the inside of the door, then locked up and drove home to change for Susanne's show.

13

The city was quiet that Saturday afternoon, the streets and sidewalks deserted except for an occasional car. Willenbrock found a parking space close to the boutique, behind a convertible whose owner had the radio turned up full blast while he tinkered with the top.

The door to the shop was open; Willenbrock paused at the threshold to take in the two rows of chairs and handful of guests, but saw no sign of Susanne. As he fiddled with his tie—he wasn't used to wearing one—a young woman came up to see if she could help him. He asked if Frau Willenbrock was in, and she said she would go get her. Willenbrock started to tell her this wasn't necessary, but the woman had already turned around and was headed toward the back, so he followed her in silence past three women whose conversation he had interrupted and who now eyed him with interest.

The small showroom had been rearranged; the sales counter had been shoved against a wall, covered with a white tablecloth, and set with trays of nuts and snacks and glasses for drinks. The racks that were usually hung with blouses, jackets, suits, and dresses had disappeared; folding chairs had been set up in two rows, far enough away from the counter to create a narrow aisle leading to the rear of the shop, which was closed off by a bead curtain.

The girl disappeared behind the colorful beads; Willenbrock stopped in front of the curtain and listened to his wife's voice. She sounded different here than she did at home, more energetic and self-assured, without her usual hesitant tone and the ironic skepticism that made her pronouncements more equivocal than her words suggested and hinted subtly at some other, unspoken, meaning. Now she was speaking in crisp sentences, ending each with a period instead of the less resolute dash or even the rising question mark she frequently used in conversations with him.

Susanne's really in charge here, he thought. She's a different Susanne here, a woman I've never met, one who knows how to take command, decide things, someone who has no trouble making up her mind—who may even have an unpleasant authoritarian streak, which is what you need to run a business, even a small one. Apparently there's a Susanne I don't know, although we've been living together for over ten years, a stranger I'm not sure I want to meet, a woman I don't find so attractive, at least not someone I'd be anxious to jump into bed with. But she does seem to have the store under control.

The three ladies by the snack counter had resumed their conversation and were all speaking at once, or at least that's how it sounded to Willenbrock. He wondered how they were able to talk and listen at the same time—and still manage to keep the conversation going. He was fascinated and amused by this skill, which he considered particularly impressive, this talent for synchronicity, this knack for breaking down speech, for overlapping delivery and reception to the point where the sequence of expressions became blurred, leaving no clear concept of what came first and what followed. As far as Willenbrock could see, it was an exclusively feminine ability: he was reminded of the professional interpreters he occasionally saw on TV translating for expert panels or visiting dignitaries. He never listened to the person speaking, wasn't interested in the VIP, but always focused his full attention on the interpreter, on her ability to translate whatever she had just heard. Even though she needed to hear the whole sentence before she could grasp its full meaning, she would start recasting it in another language before she knew how it would end, deftly handling any unanticipated twists and turns. And while she was bringing one sentence to a coherent conclusion, she was already registering the next—these dignitaries hardly ever paused—holding on to the speaker's words as she waited to finish her own. Willenbrock noticed it was almost always women who did this job, inconspicuously, in the background.

For a moment he thought of asking the three women for a simultaneous translation of whatever it was they were discussing so spiritedly, and with so many interruptions, in three separate languages. He had no doubt they could do it; the only thing stopping him was the thought of having to explain his request. So he simply listened, engrossed, to the chatty tangle of voices, unable to make out more than two or three words.

"It's nice of you to come," said Susanne.

She had shoved the beads aside and was studying him from head to toe. Willenbrock proudly pointed to his tie.

"Why don't you take care of the drinks. You could open the wine and pour some sparkling water. It's all here in back."

Susanne nodded toward the young woman Willenbrock had spoken to before. "This is Kathrin, my part-time assistant. Today she's the star of the show—she'll be modeling the new styles. And this is Herr Rieck, the trombonist.

Willenbrock nodded to both. The trombone player was in his mid-fifties, a large, sturdy man with a bulging stomach and an unkempt beard that came down to his chest. He was wearing blue jeans and a bright lumberjack shirt. Willenbrock reached for the bottles and offered the musician a glass of wine.

"I'll take a beer if you've got one," he said loudly.

Willenbrock looked to his wife, who shrugged her shoulders regretfully.

"Then I'll have the wine. Anything to keep my mouth from drying out."

He took the mouthpiece, held it under his lips, which were completely hidden by the thick gray beard, and blew several times. Willenbrock opened a bottle of wine, poured a full glass, and placed it on a desk beside the trombonist. He asked Kathrin if she wanted something to drink, but she shook her head. Then he carried two bottles of wine and the case of mineral water out to the sales room, where he asked the ladies what he might bring them.

"Just a small glass of wine, please," one of them said.

"Really just the tiniest swallow," her neighbor added. "It's still light out and I can't drink during the day. Are you Frau Willenbrock's husband?"

He nodded silently as he poured the wine.

Shortly after four, Susanne and the trombone player stepped into the room. By then, eight women and one man had taken seats, filling up the second row and leaving just four empty chairs in the first. The women, all middle-aged, were elaborately decked out and made up for the occasion. As Susanne took her place in front, she noticed that three of the women were wearing outfits from her boutique and attempted to grace them with a special smile. The only man among the guests was in his early sixties, very tan and completely bald. He was wearing a light summer suit with a vest and seemed to enjoy being the only male in the audience, apart from Willenbrock. The woman he was with was as suntanned as he. She wore her dyed-blond hair combed back; her flared summer skirt ended above the knee, and her blouse was sheer enough to reveal a black bra. She was much younger than her companion and obviously enjoyed being admired by him and showered with attention. Although he spoke to her constantly, her responses were curt, barely monosyllabic. He hardly ever took his eyes from her face, yet her own gaze was fixed straight ahead; she never turned to look at him, merely jerked her head a tiny bit in his direction.

Susanne greeted her guests by name, addressing the suntanned couple as Frau and Herr Puhlmann. Then she introduced Herr Rieck, the trombone player, to the gathering, invited him to begin, and took a seat in the first row. Willenbrock, who had been standing by the counter, sat down next to her. The musician slowly moved three steps forward. Judging from some disapproving glances, some of the guests were disturbed by the sight of his stomach protruding over his belt and the waistband of his worn-out jeans. The trombonist puffed out his cheeks, let the air escape slowly and audibly, and gave a few ponderous nods, which could be construed either as a greeting or a warm-up for the difficult solo ahead. Suddenly he raised his trombone, brought it to his lips, and blew a loud, wailing tone, fully extending and retracting the slide. Several of the ladies, who, till this moment, were actively chatting away, started in their chairs and stared at him in bewilderment. One rather ample lady in the first row turned to Willenbrock's wife, more puzzled than anything else. Susanne had taken her husband's hand and held on to it tightly while she looked straight ahead.

After the first blast came a violent cascade of notes that repeated to form a theme with a very marked rhythm. Then Rieck set down his instrument and kept time with his feet for several measures before returning the trombone to his lips and producing a prolonged howl that displayed the horn's full range. He had shut his eyes and appeared to be playing the score through in his mind. Suddenly he became quite subdued and began to coax gentle, almost tender tones from the horn, while the rhythm underwent a series of rapid and dramatic changes. After that came a more-or-less melodic passage, a medley containing snatches of familiar tunes—a children's song, the national anthem, a Bach cantata—but this ended abruptly when Rieck jerked the instrument apart, while keeping the mouthpiece fixed to his lips. Cradling the horn in his left arm, he went on buzzing in the mouthpiece. Then he set down the mouthpiece and started making trombone sounds with his lips, as he stamped out the rhythm with his right foot.

Willenbrock had turned in his seat to monitor the guests. The ladies in the first row looked petrified. Now and then someone cast a befuddled glance at Susanne, but she kept her eyes on the musician to spare herself her clients' incredulity and indignation. She gripped her husband's hand more tightly.

The dyed-blond lady in the second row was staring blankly at the sweating musician, her mouth in a tight pucker. She had drawn her arms close to her body and covered her ears with her hands, but it wasn't completely clear whether this was a sign of her disapproval, a way to escape the loud, dissonant tones, or if she was trying to block out her surroundings so as to concentrate more intently on the artist. Meanwhile, her tanned husband was obviously enjoying the performance; he had stretched out his legs and was leaning back in his chair, his buttocks resting on the very edge. When his eyes met with Willenbrock's he responded with a friendly, appreciative nod.

Two other ladies had stopped their ears in protest. One of them stared at Susanne, visibly annoyed.

The musician reinserted the mouthpiece into the horn and began trumpeting like an elephant, arching backward and swinging the trombone high into the air. After a long final cadenza, he laid the instrument down and sang a single concluding note that lasted for several measures, his bass vibrato fading in and out. Then he went quiet and kept his eyes closed while his audience waited to see whether he was done or merely pausing before more foot stamping, or another trombone blast, or renewed rasping and snorting. At last Rieck opened his eyes, nodded heavily several times, pulled a red-checked handkerchief from his pants pocket, and deliberately and thoroughly wiped the sweat off his neck and forehead.

The audience offered reserved applause. The only people truly clapping were the two men. A few of the women moved their hands together but in such a way as to make no sound. The two who had stopped their ears now let their hands drop to their laps; one of them glared at the men. Another of the guests sighed with relief, much to the approval of the rest of the audience. Even Susanne's face relaxed. She stood up and approached Rieck while continuing to applaud.

"That was quite something," she said. "You're really quite something, Herr Rieck."

The trombonist nodded in agreement.

"Definitely not your usual horn solo," she went on. "In fact, some of my guests may have found it a little too unusual. A little too avant-garde, if I might say."

"I realize this isn't the New York Philharmonic," the trombonist conceded. "It's a different audience, for sure."

He bowed curtly to the guests who were observing him with silent disapproval; then he opened the spit valve and very casually drained the accumulated condensation right onto the floor. Carrying the dismantled trombone under his arm, he stepped through the bead curtain and disappeared. As Susanne began to welcome her guests a second time, they heard someone stifle a cry in the back room and all turned to look. Susanne paused, and the musician came back out, his face red, carrying a water glass and a bottle of wine in one hand and signaling to the audience with the other that everything was all right. Still puffing and blowing, Rieck picked up an empty chair from the first row, carried it over to the wall behind the guests, and sat down.

Susanne thanked the visitors for attending and said that now, after the musical introduction—she mentioned the academy where Herr Rieck taught and the orchestra he played with, but avoided any reference to the performance itself—she would like to present a few new styles she had recently acquired and which she was sure would be of interest. Helping her present the clothes was her young assistant, whom she asked the guests to greet with a round of applause. The modest presentation was by no means intended to be a fashion show; she merely wanted to give her long-standing clients a chance to see the new collection outside regular business hours. She was especially happy to have a chance to spend a little time with them socially—and their husbands of course, she added, nodding to the bald-headed man in the second row—since over the years they had become her friends.

Using a remote control, she switched on the stereo and immediately lowered the volume on the upbeat pop music that filled the room. Herr Rieck groaned. Susanne stepped over to the curtain, swept it aside, and asked Kathrin to present the first outfit.

The girl took one or two timid steps into the room and looked around apprehensively. When she saw the trombone player, her face turned red as a beet; evidently when he had gone to put his instrument away he had caught her half-naked. Susanne took Kathrin's arm and pulled her gently into the aisle.

Kathrin was wearing a light-blue summer ensemble obviously meant for a more full-bodied woman; she had to pull her shoulders back to give it some semblance of form. As she paraded slowly in front of the guests, making two trips up and down the aisle, Susanne kept up a running commentary on the outfit, but before she could finish her explanations, the shy Kathrin disappeared behind the bead curtain, much to everyone's surprise.

A short break between presentations was unavoidable, since Kathrin was the sole model and had no one to help her change, so Susanne tried to pass the time by speaking with some of the guests while her husband saw to their drinks.

For three-quarters of an hour, Kathrin modeled clothes that were clearly too big for her. She had pinned them up for a makeshift fit and attempted to correct their loose drape with an overly rigid posture. As she walked back and forth in front of the chairs with flushed cheeks, the guests responded to each presentation by clapping generously—all the more enthusiastic whenever a particular dress seemed especially challenging.

Herr Puhlmann was the most generous with his applause, and although as he talked to his wife he spoke only of the clothes, it was clear he was also rather taken with Kathrin. Each time he tried to persuade his wife that a specific outfit would look good on her, some small remark gave away the fact that his attention was focused far more on the model than on the dress. His wife held her lips in a slight pout, limiting her replies to a repeated, almost imperceptible shake of the head; she kept her eyes fixed straight ahead, without bothering to see whether her husband had registered her rejection.

The other women were freer with their comments, which, after some initial reserve, became louder and lengthier as the presentation continued. Soon they were so vocal that Susanne found herself having to interrupt her own commentary to allow for their chatter. Seeing as she was no longer required to entertain her clients between outfits, she was able to assist Kathrin.

When the show was over, Susanne invited the gathering to stay a while and help themselves to the hors d'oeuvres.

The bald-headed man immediately stood up and bounded over to the table, where he took a plate from the stack and quickly filled it with little treats. Two of the women went up to Susanne to express their appreciation.

"Thank you, thank you," one of them as said she reached out to shake Susanne's hand. "It was charming."

The lady was wearing a cream hat and a number of brightly colored necklaces.

"You know, she's a real gem, our Susanne Willenbrock," she said to the lady standing next to her. Then she reached for one of the plates and helped herself daintily to a single piece of puff pastry.

The trombonist got to his feet and huffed and puffed his way over to Susanne, carrying a full glass of wine. The two ladies standing next to Susanne exchanged knowing glances and drifted off.

"What happened?" asked the musician. "I thought I was going on again after the girl finished with the clothes."

"There's been a change in the program. I think we've all earned a little refreshment. Help yourself, Herr Rieck, please."

"And when do I play?"

"I'll have to figure that out."

"What's the matter? Did I scare your clients? Have your ladies had enough of me?"

"Let's talk about it in a minute, Herr Rieck. Right now I have to attend to my guests."

She turned and went to speak to a client. The trombone player took a healthy swig from his glass, letting the wine roll around in his mouth before swallowing it. He stared at the company, bored, then took some open-faced sandwiches from the table and gulped them down. He looked around for Kathrin and went over to her, still chewing.

"You were mesmerizing, my dear. My congratulations."

The girl blushed with embarrassment and thanked him with a tentative smile.

"Really. You're great. Far too good for this joint. Pearls before swine, if you get my meaning."

Kathrin stared at him with wide eyes and then looked around nervously.

"Excuse me, but my boss is calling."

"Maybe we could get together after the performance? Go out for a coffee?"

"Excuse me, I have to work."

She freed her arm from his grasp and went to Susanne, who was signaling to her, somewhat anxious and worried.

A few of the guests had returned to their seats with full plates and glasses, which they placed on empty chairs or on the floor. Willenbrock strolled through the room with two bottles, replenishing drinks. The bald-headed man, who had sat back down next to his wife, held out his glass without saying a word. As Willenbrock filled it, the man asked whether he was the owner's husband. On learning that he was, the man set his glass down on the nearest chair, stood up, offered Willenbrock his hand, and introduced himself. He said his name was Puhlmann, and that he was here with his wife, who was a regular customer. Today was his first time in the boutique; he liked it. He was impressed by Willenbrock's wife; he liked women who knew how to pull something together, who had energy and imagination and could stand on their own two feet.

Willenbrock nodded.

"My wife likes to shop here. Because your wife has good taste. I have to say I like whatever she buys from her. And I'm not easy to please, either—my wife says I find fault with everything. But you know what my policy is? Demand and deliver nothing but the best. Which is why I like this place. Are you in the fashion business, too?"

"No," answered Willenbrock, and since Puhlmann looked at him expectantly, as if ready to snatch up the answer, he added: "I'm in the car business. A dealer."

That more than satisfied Herr Puhlmann. He tapped Willenbrock patronizingly on the shoulder and nodded, pleased. Then he stuck his right index finger directly under Willenbrock's nose and said: "Somebody's got to bring home the bacon, right? The cow needs a pasture if she's to give milk."

"Did you like it?" Willenbrock turned and asked the man's dyed-blond spouse. She looked at him, surprised, and blinked. Her eyes took Willenbrock in but she said nothing, so he repeated the question, a little impatiently: "Did you see anything you liked?"

"The noise," she said finally, "the noise was atrocious."

"The noise?" Willenbrock bent over a little in surprise.

"I liked the noise," offered Herr Puhlmann. "The man knows his stuff. Takes command of his instrument. It was great."

"It was noise," insisted his wife. She pursed her lips and looked away, annoyed.

"It wasn't Mozart, dear, but it was good. I liked it."

The bald-headed man sat down next to his wife, patting her on the arm to placate her. She kept her head averted and sulked like a teenager. She was fifteen or twenty years younger than her husband and seemed inclined to amplify, or at least accentuate, the difference by behaving like a moody little girl. Her high-pitched, birdlike voice sounded like a child's, her skirt was unusually short for her age, and she evidently relished having her husband dote on her. Willenbrock thought both her behavior and her overall appearance—the clothes, the hairstyle—were inappropriate and discordant. Far from producing the desired impression, the way she presented herself only highlighted the discrepancy between the youthfulness to which she aspired and her true age; the cracks in the veneer emphasized the very passage of years she was trying to mask. Willenbrock, who was, in his way, a connoisseur of women's hopes and desires—though he was less interested in improving his sensitivity than in advancing his own ends—was more amused than impressed by the dyed-blond wife. Willenbrock told the Puhlmanns that he was to blame for the trombonist; he had persuaded his wife to hire the man. Then he excused himself and went looking for more glasses to refill.

Susanne caught his eye to thank him for his help and smiled. She appreciated that he had taken the trouble to dress up, since he seldom wore a suit and never a tie, despite her frequent entreaties that he dress more elegantly. Whenever he put on something remotely stylish, she sought to encourage him by saying how nice he looked. She was talking with two women, trying to tease out their reaction to the new collection, but they both kept returning to the subject of the trombonist, whom they considered, as they whispered to Susanne, absolutely dreadful.

"If that man blows that horn of his one more time I'll have to leave," one of the women was hissing as Willenbrock approached. "It may be full of meaning and all that, and I bet you spent a pretty penny on that racket. I may be from a different generation, though even I know that art doesn't always have to be entertaining—I've been battered over the head by enough performances to realize that—but these days people think art isn't real unless it's boring. They've let these modern artists bamboozle them into buying all kinds of garbage. Call me a philistine, but before I let that elephant completely ruin my hearing I'm getting up and walking out."

The younger woman objected: "I didn't really care for it, either, but he does play with the New York Philharmonic."

"That doesn't mean a thing these days."

Susanne wanted to put in a word for the trombonist, but the woman was too worked up, and before Susanne could say anything, she snarled: "As far as your new outfits go, I'll have to come by during the week. I couldn't make out a thing you said after that ghastly person assaulted my hearing. Not a thing. You didn't do yourself any favors with that entertainment, my dear."

Then she turned to Willenbrock, who was standing one step away, gave him a friendly nod, and said: "I'll have some water, please. And I suppose I'll need a glass as well."

When Willenbrock handed her the glass, Susanne introduced him as her husband. Both women studied him with interest—darting their heads like birds, he thought.

"How nice of you to assist your capable wife," said the younger woman. She was full-figured and holding a lace handkerchief, which she kept using to pat her forehead and neck.

"Should I talk to the trombonist?" Willenbrock asked Susanne. With a gesture of desperation and a hopeful sigh, she said he should.

"That man's no trombonist—he's a terrorist," said the woman who had asked for water.

"Modern art," countered Willenbrock. He meant it both as an explanation and an excuse, a gentle plea for understanding, not so much for the performance as for Susanne's decision to hire the musician for the afternoon—but both women protested indignantly.

"Young man," said the older woman, no longer attempting to whisper or keep her voice down, "you don't have to tell me about art. My husband was a museum director and I've been involved with art my entire life. With true art, though, paintings and literature and music. With genuine music. Which is something entirely different from that pretentious cacophony."

Shrugging his shoulders, Willenbrock repeated that he was

to blame and went on to look after the other guests. Three teenage girls were standing in the open doorway. Willenbrock invited them in, but they laughed; two of them pushed up their noses, which evidently meant something, though he couldn't tell what.

"Good sound," said one of the girls. "The guy blows a mean pipe."

The trombonist was standing near the display window; he had taken Kathrin firmly by the arm and was talking away at her. Willenbrock headed in their direction, but before he could reach them, the woman who'd been so worked up scurried over to Herr Rieck.

"What piece was that you played," she asked pointedly. "Who was the composer?"

"The piece is called 'Sense-non-sense, number 4.' And you're looking at the composer. Made an impression on you, did it?"

"So you're the composer? I thought as much. And if you're asking my opinion, it was horrendous."

"Well, then you understood it perfectly. Horrendous music for a horrendous world, that's the philosophy behind my compositions."

"They'd be better if they were less philosophic and more philharmonic. But, then, that would take talent."

Rieck nodded. "My next piece is even more striking. It's called 'Moments musicaux,' and it's dedicated to Franz Schubert. He wasn't bad either. You like Schubert?"

"Too much to hear what you might do to him." Without waiting for an answer, she spun around and hurried back to Susanne.

Willenbrock raised the bottle; Rieck held up his glass and Willenbrock filled it. "I really enjoyed it," he said to the trombonist. "Thanks."

Herr Rieck merely mumbled: "Me, too," then drained his glass in one gulp and held it out for a refill.

"Not your usual tooting, that's for sure. I suppose it does take a little getting used to, as they say, but you play with real fire and gusto—I like that."

"You're probably the only one here who does."

"No, the man over there liked it as well. And those three girls in the doorway are big fans."

"So that makes six," said the musician, bored.

"I liked it, too" said Kathrin.

The trombonist looked at her, flattered, and blew her a kiss. The girl reddened and turned away.

"This probably wasn't the best audience," Willenbrock picked up the thread again. Susanne had sent him on a mission, and he knew he couldn't risk provoking the portly man into an outburst right at the end of Susanne's show.

"It's definitely not New York," the trombonist agreed. He puffed out his cheeks and gave a disdainful huff.

"I take it you're used to a different crowd," offered Willenbrock.

The trombonist, sweating profusely, gave an emphatic nod.

"But what do you expect?" he said. "Just look at these people. You think they have a clue about art? And these acoustics. There's not enough space; you can't get any resonance. The notes suffocate before they have a chance to unfold."

"I guess it doesn't make much sense to play in a space like this," Willenbrock suggested.

Rieck knitted his brow and suddenly looked at him. "What are you trying to tell me, chief? Do you want to cancel the rest of my performance? Should I pack up?"

"I wasn't thinking that," Willenbrock lied, "but maybe you're right. This isn't the right venue for your music, or the right audience. Maybe we should call it quits for the day."

"What does the boss say? She's the one who hired me."

"I think she'll be amenable. I'll go ask. Naturally you'll receive the full sum."

"Naturally." The musician was chewing indecisively on his lower lip. "But don't think I like the idea. I love playing. I'm good and I enjoy it. You're robbing me of my pleasure."

"More wine, Herr Rieck?"

"Sure, why not. Then I'll just split without a fuss so there's no broken hearts."

With his full glass of wine he lurched after Kathrin, who had draped one of the outfits she had modeled over one arm and was nervously trying to answer a customer's questions. She was so self-conscious that she kept misspeaking and correcting herself, but the lady was completely focused on the dress and didn't seem to notice. Rieck grabbed Kathrin by the shoulder and spun her toward him, but she waved him off, explaining she was busy, as he could see, and asked him to be patient. So the trombonist stood right there, next to her, staring at the client, who shot him an indignant, chastising glance and then walked away without a word. Rieck tried to talk Kathrin into leaving with him, and when she flatly refused, he tried to convince her to meet him later that evening.

Willenbrock had just signaled to his wife that he had averted the threat of a second trombone solo when he was hailed by the well-tanned Herr Puhlmann, who was still sitting, watching the crowd, sharing his impressions and opinions with his wife. She went on nodding curtly without looking at him; or else shaking her head in a way that put an end to any conversation.

"Which car company do you represent?" he asked, gently touching Willenbrock's jacket with the tip of his finger.

"All of them," answered Willenbrock cryptically, then paused a second and added: "I buy and sell all makes—all previously owned."

"Is it a good business?"

"It's a tough one."

"Do you pay well? I have a five-year-old Mercedes I'm thinking of replacing with a Land Rover. You can take a look, it's right outside, the white 600. Make a decent offer and we'll do some business."

Willenbrock declined. "This is my wife's shop, she does the business here. Come to my place on Monday. My mechanic will look your car over, and then we can talk about the price."

He put down the wine bottle, took out his wallet, found a card, and gave it to Puhlmann, who glanced at it, put it in his pocket, then handed one of his own to Willenbrock.

"I'll give you a call, Herr Willenbrock."

"As I said," Willenbrock warned, "it's a tough racket. The seller's hoping to recoup as much of his money as he can, the buyer's looking for a steal, and I have to disappoint both of them. Only one person can get rich off used cars, and the way I see it, that should be me."

Puhlmann laughed out loud. "I like you. You've got the right attitude, Herr Willenbrock. Gitti, I like him."

His wife looked at Willenbrock without saying anything or changing her expression. Willenbrock wanted to go, but Puhlmann held out his glass. "Pour me another, it's so hot here I'm sweating up a storm. Some water, too. And an espresso if you have it."

Willenbrock regretted that he didn't.

"No matter," the bald-headed man said casually, and then asked: "Who do you sell your used cars to? I mean, who actually buys the old crates? Housewives, students, people on welfare?"

"You'd think so. But mostly I sell them to the East. Poland, Russia, Romania. I've been told you can see my cars rolling through Siberia."

"The Russians," said the dyed-blonde. Her voice had no tone. Her husband and Willenbrock waited expectantly, but she again went mute, her mouth puckered into a little beak, and it wasn't clear what she had wanted to say.

"That's a pretty solid client base. And presumably inexhaustible?"

"A bottomless pit," affirmed Willenbrock.

"And you don't have any problems?" asked Puhlmann.

"Nope, everything's fine. I pay cash, they pay cash, no problems."

Puhlmann laughed and said: " 'In God we trust, all others pay cash'—right? And the taxman's none the wiser."

"No. In my business that's impossible. Too dangerous. The tax office keeps a particularly close eye on us. One missing receipt and I get hit with a full audit that costs me a whole week's business. No, I pay what I'm supposed to and sleep the better for it."

"Actually, I was thinking of a different sort of problem," said Puhlmann. "Unwelcome guests. Visitors in the night. You know, the riffraff that spills over the border."

Willenbrock looked at him calmly. "No," he said, "I'm getting along all right."

"You're lucky. If only I could say the same thing. So far we've been spared, but the gangs have been going through the area, looting the houses, one after another. Right in our immediate neighborhood they've hit three villas and beaten one old man half to death."

"Where do you live?"

"Bernadottestrasse, out in Dahlem. My Gitti was so frightened I had the whole house rebuilt just to protect my little treasure. Now I have a safe room right in the middle of my house, an armored security zone impossible to penetrate. If we're attacked, we can barricade ourselves there. It has its own electrical system, independent of the house line, its own water supply, and it's fireproof. You'd need a tank to get inside. Now and then, when I have to spend the night out of town, my treasure sleeps in that room. Don't ask me what it cost. A fortune. A quarter of a million, believe it or not. And all because these days Siberia seems to start right outside your doorstep."

"A dog would have been cheaper."

"A dog? My neighbor had a Great Dane, big as a horse. The Russians cut its throat."

"How do you know they were Russians?"

"Russians, Romanians, Albanians—they could have been Germans, for all I know. Maybe all of them together. They're obviously organized and don't stop at murder. If you've never had any trouble with them going after your cars then you must have been born lucky."

"What would they want with a bunch of used cars?"

"You'd be surprised, Herr Willenbrock. At least you ought to make your home secure. Or get a gun. These days you can buy one anywhere."

Now Willenbrock laughed out loud: "You're not serious, Herr Puhlmann."

"I'm absolutely serious," the bald man said. "I'll do whatever needs to be done to protect Gitti and myself. Self-defense is perfectly legitimate."

"Just don't do something you'll regret," said Willenbrock.

"Asia. The whole world's turning into Asia," said Frau Puhlmann.

The two men looked at her in surprise, but she again withdrew into silence. Willenbrock collected the bottles and moved on.

The trombone player's loud and deep voice came from the back room; he seemed to be arguing with someone. Willenbrock looked around for Susanne and then Kathrin; both were in the salesroom. A second later, Herr Rieck appeared carrying his trombone case, seeming quite pleased. He grinned broadly right and left as he took his leave.

"Hallelujah," declared one woman, acidly and emphatically, when the trombonist reached the door. Rieck paused for a moment, then stepped onto the sidewalk and walked away without turning around. At once the conversation grew louder and livelier, as if a pall had been lifted when Herr Rieck stepped out the door. Susanne noticed the change, the clear relief at the musician's departure, and looked at her husband gratefully.

Two hours later the last guests left, Frau and Herr Puhlmann.

"It was lovely," the dyed-blond lady said to Susanne, kissing her goodbye on the cheek. Then she held her open right hand out to her husband, wordlessly, until he responded to the silent demand and gave her the car keys.

"Maybe we'll do business together," he said to Willenbrock as he stood in the doorway. Only now did Willenbrock notice that the tanned bald man was swaying slightly.

Willenbrock helped his wife and Kathrin fold the chairs and load them into the trunk of Susanne's car. Then he carried the cases of empty bottles to his own car, pushed the counter back in place, and waited until his wife and Kathrin had hung the clothes back on the racks. Susanne asked him to drive the girl home while she closed up and set the alarm, and to meet her back at the house.

Willenbrock held the car door open for Kathrin and helped her in. On the way home he praised her performance. The girl asked if he actually knew the trombonist, since Susanne had told her that he was the one who hired him.

"No, not personally. A friend of mine recommended him. Did you enjoy it?"

"It was fun. I don't understand much about music, but I almost laughed out loud."

"I'm sure he would have liked that, Kathrin, especially coming from you."

The girl turned red and went silent.

"A nice guy, though, right? There's something about him

that reminds me of a hippopotamus. A musical hippopotamus, of course," said Willenbrock, as he turned onto her street and started looking for her address.

"Do you think he's married?" asked the girl, who seemed to appreciate the comparison.

"Hippos never marry," answered Willenbrock. He parked the car, reached across her to open the door, and smiled.

"Would you like his phone number? I have it."

"No. Why?" said the girl pertly.

"You're right, Kathrin. I'm sure he'll show up at the boutique soon enough."

She quickly got out and went inside the building without looking back.

Susanne came home half an hour after Willenbrock. She had a headache and went straight to the bedroom to lie down. After a while Willenbrock went upstairs to ask if she'd like something to eat. She said she didn't. Then she sat up, took hold of his head, and said: "You were very nice today. Thank you. You were a great help. My clients are a difficult bunch, they all want to be babied."

"It was great, love. A success for you."

"But that trombonist! I was so worried. I was afraid there'd be a fight."

"Look at it this way—he was unforgettable. You'll see, your ladies will be talking about him a year from now. Now go to sleep."

He helped her undress and tucked her in affectionately. He switched on the nightlight and turned it away so it wouldn't shine in her eyes.

14

The next week he waited nervously for the builders to resume work on his showroom. When Wednesday morning came and still no one had showed up, he tried to reach the supervising engineer. He dialed every number he had been given, but was only able to get through to a secretary who couldn't tell him anything, and another employee who said he'd never heard of the engineer. According to the terms of the contract, the firm was obliged to begin construction on a specific date and complete it within three months—the finish date was also specified. But when the workers were pulled off the job ten days after starting the shaft work, Willenbrock began to doubt whether they would meet the deadline. He'd spoken with the architect, who confirmed his suspicions, and could only advise him to report every delay to the contractor and deduct a late fee when he paid the individual trades. The one time Willenbrock did get through to the engineer, the man swore up and down that the showroom would be "turnkey ready" by early October. As the interruptions continued, however, the engineer grew increasingly unavailable, and simply ignored Willenbrock's requests to return his calls.

Around noon on Friday a truck arrived with parts for the

roof. The driver pulled up alongside the shell of the new building and uncoupled the trailer. As the driver started to leave, Willenbrock stopped him and asked whether the men were coming that day and where his boss could be reached and why no work had been done on the showroom for almost two weeks. The driver, a young man with thick, shaggy hair, stuck his head out the window, listened to Willenbrock's angry ranting, then took—as Willenbrock waited for an answer—a piece of paper that had been stuck on the window of the cab and held it out to him. It listed Willenbrock's name and the address of his business.

"Is this right?" asked the driver, in a harsh guttural tone.

Willenbrock looked at him, defeated, nodded without saying anything, and went into his office.

When he came to work Monday morning, three workers were putting up the roof. He watched them for a moment before going to see Jurek.

That afternoon Krylov called to say he'd be arriving the next day; he needed three cars. Willenbrock promised to set aside a variety of suitable vehicles. They agreed to meet in the morning. After the phone call, Willenbrock went to Jurek, told him Krylov was coming, and then walked with him around the lot. Jurek pointed out eight cars he thought the Russian could use, and Willenbrock accepted his suggestions. Then he asked Jurek to clean them up for tomorrow morning and move them to the roped-off space behind the trailer.

By closing time he was offered three new cars, all of which he bought, adding one to the eight they had selected.

In the evening he and Susanne drove into town to a small movie theater. They watched a film by a Yugoslav director that Susanne had insisted on seeing. Willenbrock had a hard time understanding it; he found the plot confusing and contradictory, but he liked the shots of animals and salt-of-the-earth farmers, whose joy in life was undiminished in the face of tragedy and who traded coarse jokes even at a funeral. The characters reminded Willenbrock of his grandparents. When the film was over, he and Susanne went to an Indonesian restaurant, where Willenbrock told her about his grandparents, whom she had never met. She enjoyed listening to him; she liked hearing him talk about times past, about his childhood, his hopes and fears. As a rule he didn't speak much about his youth and avoided mentioning his feelings and emotions; she always tried to get him to say more.

At home they both had another drink—she a glass of Spanish red wine and he a beer—and watched the late-night news on TV. She held his hand as they listened, without much interest, to the anchorman. Afterward Susanne went to the bathroom to wash up; Willenbrock followed her in. He took off his bathrobe and joined her in the shower, hugging and caressing her. Then they went upstairs to their bedroom, still naked. Before turning off the light, Willenbrock smoked another cigarette and told her how, when he was little, he'd once gone with his grandfather on a walk through his grandparents' village. At one point they were stopped by a neighbor who started yelling and cursing at Willenbrock's grandfather; Willenbrock hadn't understood what it was about. But suddenly his grandfather let go of his hand, pushed him aside, and hit the neighbor, knocking the man down with one punch. Then he'd waved his grandson back over and they continued their walk as if nothing had happened, taking up the conversation where they had left off, the old man asking the boy about school and his teachers, although Willenbrock would have much preferred to find out why he'd hit the man. Ever since then his admiration for his grandfather knew no bounds, and whenever he read something about a hero, about some fearless, invincible man, either in fairy tales or in his history books at school, the image of his grandfather always came to mind. In reality, though, as the old photos showed, his grandfather was a small man, even frail. Susanne laughed and wriggled beneath his arm; they stayed like that for a while in silence. By the time Willenbrock stretched out his left hand to turn off the light—carefully, so as not to disturb Susanne—her breathing was so deep and regular he thought she was already asleep. But as he lay beside her in the dark, staring up at the ceiling, completely still, thinking about the next day's appointments, she spoke up unexpectedly. "So what about Bugewitz? What should we do with the house?"

Willenbrock took a deep breath. "Right," he said, "we have to drive out there again. Mow the grass, straighten things up. How about next weekend, is it a deal?"

Susanne didn't answer, just turned over on her side. When she finally fell asleep, he felt her body trembling.

15

Krylov showed up shortly after eleven with four young men. Before they could get out of their car, Willenbrock was already headed down the trailer steps. He shook hands first with Krylov and then with his companions, all of whom he recognized from earlier visits. He asked Krylov if he wanted to go straight to the cars, which were picked out and ready to go. Krylov nodded, then paused to look at the construction site, where two workers were standing on the half-finished roof while a third was handing them something from the trailer below.

"Everything okay?" he asked.

"The stone was delivered last week. It's over there—those eight pallets. Excellent quality, and right on time."

"That's the only way to do business," said Krylov, pleased.

"But the construction company's behind. Look at this—they haven't even finished the roof."

"I see," said Krylov. "What's the world coming to when we can't even count on the Germans anymore?"

"And the price is as we said, correct? Three thousand?" asked Willenbrock quietly.

"Of course. Three thousand, plus three hundred for one bona fide German receipt."

He motioned to Willenbrock to lead the way to the reserved vehicles. The other four followed a few steps behind. Krylov quickly selected three cars and said something to his men, three of whom immediately opened the doors and sat in the driver's seats to play with the buttons and switches. Willenbrock suggested a fourth car he thought was worth considering, but Krylov shook his head. He had made up his mind and didn't want to waste another word on the subject. He was accustomed to people accepting his decisions instantly and without question, and quickly became impatient when faced with objections or even well-intentioned advice.

"Don't worry, I'll be back," he said to Willenbrock, less in the way of a promise than to underscore the finality of his decree. Willenbrock asked Krylov to go on ahead to the office, then went to tell Jurek which cars would be leaving, and to put back the parts he'd pulled out for security purposes.

Krylov waited on the lot, watching the workers, until Willenbrock had finished with Jurek, then they both went inside the trailer. Krylov called out something to his four men, who nodded and stayed behind with the cars.

Willenbrock had stacked all the papers on his desk. Leafing through the documents, he selected the ones relating to the cars Krylov had chosen, filled out the forms, recorded the date, and signed them. He pushed the papers across the table to Krylov, together with the keys. The Russian had opened his wallet; he counted out some bills, aloud, and placed them next to the keys. Then he picked the money back up, set aside the price of the stone flooring and the forged receipt, and returned those bills to his wallet. He laid the remaining banknotes on the desk and, with his fingertips, pushed them away an inch or two to signal that the deal was done. Willenbrock put the cash in his desk drawer without looking at it or even counting it. Then he fetched a box of crispbreads from the cabinet and an open bottle of rye whiskey from the refrigerator, set two glasses on the table, filled them both, and handed one to Krylov.

"*Na zdarovye,*" he said.

The Russian took a piece of crispbread, repeated the toast, and drained his glass.

"How's your wife? Everyone healthy at home, my friend?" he asked.

Willenbrock nodded.

"That's good. That's the most important thing," Krylov went on. "As long as you're healthy, everything else falls into place. And the new showroom is coming along, slowly but surely?"

"More slowly than surely. Seems that as far as the builders are concerned, I'm just a two-bit job to fill their downtime. They're doing my showroom on the side. Whenever they need people elsewhere they put me on hold, and when their workers are here they go about things as if they had all the time in the world. They're not exactly knocking themselves out to get the job done."

"I noticed," Krylov confirmed. "They're taking it easy, all right. You wouldn't catch them working that way for me. I wouldn't stand for it. Anybody who dawdled like that on one of my jobs would find himself back on the street along with the other bums disgracing my beautiful city. You have a nice German word for them—*Tagediebe,* daystealers. They can steal all the days they like, but not from me."

Krylov set his glass down to show that he was ready for

another round, and his host refilled it. Willenbrock had only sipped at his; now he drained what was left.

"Not all your daystealers stay in Moscow. Some of them show up here."

"Have you had any more trouble? More stolen cars? I told you that one old man sitting here at night isn't going to scare anyone off. At least not those young punks."

"Worse than that. Two of your compatriots attacked us out in the country. Right in our house. They nearly killed me."

Krylov's face grew dark. His eyes narrowed into slits and his voice turned angry. "Russians, you say? They were Russian?"

"Two brothers from Moscow. The police caught them, but all they could do was deport them. Dropped them off at the border. By now I'll bet they're long back in Germany."

Krylov gave a black look.

"Did anything happen to your wife?"

"No. She got off with a bad scare."

Krylov clenched one hand into a fist and twisted it inside the palm of the other like a ball in a socket. He seemed agitated.

"I'm the one they worked over," Willenbrock went on. "With an iron rod. My wife just had to watch, which wasn't easy either. Now she wants to sell the house, she's afraid, she can barely sleep."

"This isn't good," said Krylov quietly. "No, not good at all, my friend. I don't like this."

He looked at Willenbrock a long time, thinking.

"Two brothers from Moscow, you say. You have their names?"

"Yes. Gatchev. I even have their address, from the police. Andrei and Artur Gatchev. Maybe I should return the visit?"

Willenbrock rummaged through his desk drawer for the address.

"No need for that. What you want to tell them, I can say for you. I'll send someone over to explain that no one attacks my good German friend Willenbrock."

Willenbrock laughed. "You think it would help?"

"I think it would. It always has in the past."

Willenbrock took a bundle of papers from the drawer and began leafing through them.

"I'm not sure that your man could convince these guys not to come back. Even if you spell it out."

"It just has to be spelled out very clearly. If these two brothers had to spend a year without leaving their apartment, then they might just learn to behave themselves."

Willenbrock stopped looking for the address. He held a piece of paper in his hand and stared at Krylov in amazement.

"What would you do to them? Break every bone in their body?"

"You don't have to worry about the details. Consider it a friendly favor—more for myself than for you. If they came from Irkutsk or Petersburg, I wouldn't care so much. But since they're from Moscow, it's a different story. He makes me mad. I love my city, and it upsets me that we have this kind of riffraff. That's not how things should be. No, it's not good. Just give me the address, and then you can forget all about it."

Willenbrock suddenly felt his palms grow damp. Embarrassed, he rummaged timidly through the drawer again, then shut it and said to Krylov: "I can't find the piece of paper with the address. I must have left it at home."

"There's no rush, my friend," said Krylov sympathetically.

"You can give it to me next time we meet. As I said, I take it personally. When gangsters break into your home and attack your wife, that's not good. My mother was attacked once. Four of them broke into our house and raped her, right in front of my father. One year later, she died—because of that, my father said."

"Good God!"

"That was a long time ago," Krylov cut him off, dryly. "A very long time ago. But it's not good."

"Were they ever caught?"

"No."

"So the Russian police aren't much better than the German," said Willenbrock.

"The policeman in our village was very good. Very competent and highly regarded. But he couldn't do anything, there were too many. Too many German thugs."

"Germans?" Willenbrock looked at him, puzzled.

"Yes, Germans. They were billeted in our town. The police couldn't do a thing."

"Germans? What were they doing there?"

"I don't know. I was only two years old."

"I see." Willenbrock swallowed. "You mean they were soldiers. German soldiers. I'm sorry."

Krylov didn't reply. He stood up and stashed the car papers in his jacket pocket, holding on to the keys.

"If someone steals one of your cars, it's annoying. But if they attack you and your wife, that's not good at all. That shouldn't happen. You have to protect yourself better, my friend. I'm concerned for you."

He walked outside; Willenbrock followed. Krylov distributed the keys, which were attached to little medallions bearing the license numbers. Then he said goodbye to Willenbrock and settled into the passenger seat of his own car. Before his driver could start the motor, Krylov rolled down the window and said: "Don't forget that address. I want it the next time I come. Agreed?"

The car drove away, followed by the three vehicles Krylov had purchased.

He'll have those brothers killed, thought Willenbrock. His hands were still sweating. By now he had made up his mind not to give Krylov the address. He went inside the trailer and found the scrap where he'd written it down when the policeman had read the computer printout. For a moment he considered destroying the note, but then he put it back with his other papers and locked the drawer.

Jurek came to ask if it was okay to move the cars Krylov hadn't taken back on the lot. When Willenbrock saw the surly look on his face, he laughed out loud. "Krylov's my best customer, Jurek. Look at it this way: he pays your salary."

"He can't make that kind of money doing honest work. How is he so rich? The Soviet Union falls apart and suddenly he's a millionaire? He has dark sources, boss. That money's not clean. Who knows what's sticking to it?"

"I don't ask my customers where they get their money. I'm not the taxman. We all know nobody ever gets rich by doing an honest day's labor—that's the way the world works. On the other hand, decent people like you and me will be rewarded in the next life. Richly rewarded, I'm sure."

"Don't make fun, boss."

"I'm not making fun, Jurek, but I have to say, you aren't being much of a Christian. Russians are human, too, you know. Even Krylov is one of God's creatures."

"Of course . . . but the Lord created all kinds of creatures. Are you staying on today, boss?"

"I have a meeting at three, but I'll only be gone an hour. Why?"

"A girl was asking for you before. While you were talking to the Russians."

"A girl?"

"Yes. A young woman."

"What did she look like?"

"She looked good, boss, pretty. Like all the women who come asking for you."

"Did she leave a message?"

"She said she'd be back this afternoon. Around two or three, she didn't say for sure."

"Thanks, Jurek."

"So I'll go and move the cars back. Then work on the Mercedes in the shop."

"Sounds good. Do that."

"Was there something else, boss?"

"Yes, Jurek. You don't have to be so polite with me all the time—boss this and boss that. You've been working here too long for that."

"But you're the boss. And my tongue gets twisted. I can't speak your language so good."

"You lie in German like a pro, Jurek. But, have it your way if you prefer."

The Pole tapped his nose in silence and went out. Willenbrock took the records of sale for the cars he'd sold, looked them over, and placed them in a file. Then he removed the money from the drawer, carefully counted it, and put it in his wallet. After lunch—a can of soup warmed on the hot plate, which he shared with Jurek—he went out to the site and observed the three workers suspiciously as they ran up and down the ladders and narrow planks they'd placed on the roof, screwing in the shingles. One of them called down to Willenbrock that he should watch out and not stand there without a hard hat. Willenbrock glared at him but said nothing. For a minute he refused to budge, then he turned around, climbed into his car, and drove to his accountant, whom he'd instructed to apply for a tax deferment because of the costly work on the new showroom. When he came back he asked Jurek whether the girl had come by; the Pole said she hadn't. Willenbrock told him to get her to leave her name and phone number in the event she came and he wasn't there.

16

On Thursday night, a strong gust of wind at the worksite tore a metal plate loose from the upper level of the construction. On its way down, the plate slammed into a lightweight strut, causing it to buckle, and left a hole where it hit the cement floor. When Willenbrock arrived the next morning, the workers were already busy trying to minimize the damage. To protect himself in the event of future problems, Willenbrock demanded that the engineer come on-site to document the incident. The three workmen tried to talk him out of the idea and promised to fix everything on their own time after work. They didn't want the mishap reported because the plate hadn't been properly secured; they were afraid of getting into trouble with the company—but Willenbrock insisted on calling in the engineer anyway. When the workers kept at him, practically begging him to let them put things right on their own and without a fuss, he lost his temper, yelling at them repeatedly to call the engineer. Then he went to his office, stopping in at the shop, where he returned Jurek's greeting with a curt, gruff hello. Once inside the trailer, he sat at his desk, angry at his own behavior, cursing at himself out loud. Half an hour later Jurek opened the main gate and let in the small group of men who'd been waiting outside. Willenbrock sized them up from his office window, careful not to let Jurek see him. He stayed in the trailer until two men had picked out a car and Jurek knocked on his door. Making an effort to be friendly, Willenbrock listened carefully to what the men were saying, and to Jurek's translation, but he couldn't shake his foul humor. He couldn't figure out the reason for it, since he wasn't really all that bothered by the mishap at the site—he was far more upset at his own moodiness and his outburst at the workers, who were probably just afraid of losing their jobs. But he didn't want to go back on his decision to call in their boss, and an apology was out of the question.

The engineer came by a little before ten and, together with Willenbrock, looked over the site. Willenbrock was now calm and controlled as he pointed out the damage, although he continued to scowl, despite the engineer's easy assurances that no real harm had been done. To cheer his client, the engineer told Willenbrock about a competing construction company that had tried to pull off a brazen fraud at Potsdamer Platz, but the story did nothing to dispel Willenbrock's impatient, dour manner. As he listened to the engineer, the three workers watched furtively from the roof.

Willenbrock demanded that the engineer draw up a detailed, binding schedule, since the repeated interruptions and reduced workforce had caused delays that threw off all his plans. The engineer promised to have something for him within the week. He said goodbye to Willenbrock, but before leaving climbed up to speak with the workmen. Willenbrock had the impression they were talking about him, since the men kept glancing down at him during their brief conversation.

On Saturday morning he packed the car for the weekend. Susanne was planning to stay home another hour before going to her shop, so they arranged that he would pick her up there later in the afternoon.

Pasewald had chained his dog outside the trailer and was waiting in the office. He told Willenbrock he'd like to take a brief vacation so he and his wife could visit their children. Willenbrock nodded; it was fine with him. Pasewald said he'd like to go at the end of August and would be away for a week. Since Willenbrock again only nodded his head, Pasewald added that he could send a substitute, a neighbor who'd taken early retirement and was sure to be open to the idea. The neighbor also had a dog, though it wasn't a purebred—one look and you could see right away the dog wasn't worth very much—but he was fierce enough to bite and would do fine as a watchdog. Willenbrock said if it was just a matter of a week, they didn't need a substitute. Word had probably gotten out among the car thieves that his place was pretty tough to crack, and the watchman would be back long before anyone would even know he'd been gone. When Willenbrock saw how uneasy Pasewald was about leaving the cars untended, he suggested that Pasewald's dog could stay on the lot; Jurek would take good care of him until Pasewald came back. Carefully weighing the suggestion, the older man gave a detailed explanation why it wouldn't work: once unchained, the animal wouldn't allow Willenbrock or Jurek or anybody else onto the lot, and would probably even chase the workers off the site unless Pasewald was there to control him. The watchman offered to send his wife on vacation without him—as it was, somebody had to tend the garden and water the flowers, and he did have his other daughter here in Berlin and was so used to spending time with her child he didn't really want to go away. Willenbrock insisted that he go with his wife and forget about the lot. He'd have a security service look after things. He simply asked Pasewald to give him two days' advance notice, then bid the fretful watchman goodbye.

Several people came by that morning; they strolled around the lot and had Jurek unlock this car or that so they could look inside. Most were men, but there were also a few married couples, who would pick out a specific vehicle, ask to see the papers, ply Jurek with questions, hem and haw while casting around for a better deal on another car—then depart, unable to decide.

Three teenagers who looked about sixteen wanted to buy a red coupe. Jurek took them for a spin around the lot but wouldn't let them drive the car before they paid for it. He sent them in to Willenbrock, who said something about regulations and asked the one who wanted to make the purchase for his driver's license and some other ID. When Willenbrock named a price, the three tried to haggle, but he cut them off, saying that this wasn't a flea market; his prices were firm and so closely calculated that he had no room even to offer them a discount. Finally they put five thousand marks on the table and promised to bring the rest on Monday, Tuesday at the latest. Willenbrock agreed; he took the money, wrote out a receipt, put the cash in his drawer, and told them he'd hold the car for them until Monday or Tuesday, when they brought the rest of the money, and would guard it day and night like his most prized possession. The three protested; they needed the car that weekend and claimed that the down payment gave them the right to take it now: the deal was done, the car was theirs, and by law he had to hand it over immediately.

"You'll get your money," said the youngest-looking of the three, who did most of the talking, even though he wasn't the actual buyer. "Don't worry, we'll have it by Monday."

"I'm not worried," answered Willenbrock in a friendly tone. "As soon as you bring the money, you'll get the keys."

They started raising their voices, repeating that they needed the car this weekend; it was today or never. Willenbrock suggested other cars—for five thousand marks he had several they could drive off the lot right then and there, but the teenagers had their sights set on the red coupe and refused to look at anything else.

"The rest of your stuff is junk, man," yelled the youngest one. "We're not buying some old crate."

They asked for their money back and said that other dealers would practically pay them to take junk like that off their hands.

"Then I recommend you go to them. That would save you a lot of money."

On their way out the teenagers tried to slam the plank door, but the solid construction proved too heavy.

By noon he'd sold only one car, and since he knew from experience that hardly anyone ever came after twelve, he sent Jurek home and spent the rest of the workday inspecting the new showroom in peace and quiet, without being observed by the workers. At two o'clock he moved his car off the lot, locked the trailer and the gate, and went to the boutique to pick up Susanne and drive out to the country.

They stopped for lunch at an Italian restaurant in Prenzlau. As they waited for their food, Willenbrock tried to make conversation with his wife, but she seemed distracted and responded in monosyllables.

"Are you worried about something?" he asked.

"Worried? No. I'm afraid," she said quietly.

When their eyes met he saw how exhausted she was. He waited for her to say something more, but she stared at him without saying anything and without moving. She seemed petrified.

"Please don't be afraid," he said, stroking the back of her hand. "It won't happen again, love. I've taken care of things. Half the trunk is filled with alarms and security equipment. I bought whatever I could lay my hands on. I'll start installing everything today, and by the time I'm through, you could drop a bomb on the place and we'd still be safe. The minute anyone starts messing with our house, all hell will break loose and the entire police force will come racing over. Nothing's ever going to happen to us again. Nothing."

Susanne didn't say anything, just looked around the restaurant as if she hadn't been listening and studied the plaster copies of antique statuary strewn about to give the place a Mediterranean atmosphere. After they'd eaten and were back in the car, Willenbrock confessed that he'd even bought a signal pistol. He laughed as he told her, adding that even the thought was grotesque, that he couldn't imagine picking up any kind of gun and pointing it at another human being. He hoped this information would help reassure her, but when he reached for the glove compartment to show her the pistol, she said she didn't want to see it. She didn't want to know anything about it.

They pulled up outside their property, and as Willenbrock got out to open the gate, he scanned the house and grounds. He did so inconspicuously, so as not to worry Susanne, but as he drove the car in, he noticed that she, too, was looking nervously all around. He went into the house ahead of her and quickly checked the rooms on the ground floor before getting their bags from the car and setting them down in the kitchen. Then he checked upstairs. When he came back down, Susanne was standing in the living room, running her finger over the splintered wood in the door and along the slit where the knife had come through the panel.

"All taken care of," he said, in a deliberately casual voice. "I've already talked to Königsmann, the carpenter. He promised to come by in the morning and take measurements. I don't want to have the doors repaired, it's not worth it. In fact, what do you say we replace all the doors, not just the damaged ones? New doors throughout the house, okay, Susanne?"

"He's coming in the morning?"

"Not too early, I told him. He'll be here between ten and eleven."

She unpacked the food basket while he went out to the yard, opened the barn and shed, and searched for signs of anything suspicious. Then he moved the two wooden beams he had propped up against the scaffold on the shed, opened the door, and parked the car inside. He looked over the stacks of lumber, the beams and shingles, the dismantled roof truss that had been lying in the same place for three years, ever since the summer he'd had the barn roof renovated; he had kept the timbers to saw for firewood. The table saw he'd bought for that purpose stood nearby, never used and covered up. Willenbrock sighed as he took in the mess and all the work that awaited him. Someday, he told himself, someday I'll have time for all this. He took three large plastic bags containing numerous items out of the trunk. Earlier that week he'd gone to a store specializing in security equipment and alarm systems. He'd told the salesman what kind of property he had and what size house, and asked for his advice. The man had tried to talk Willenbrock into having his company install a complete round-the-clock surveillance system, but Willenbrock declined. He was less concerned about the high price than the trouble—it all seemed too much; he was afraid that instead of calming Susanne down, the elaborate precautions would only make her even more anxious. He listened carefully to the salesman's pitch and decided to stick with devices he could install himself and that would not be too obtrusive. He bought the ones the man suggested; he got the feeling he was arming himself for war.

"Isn't this a bit much?" he said.

The salesman shook his head. "It only seems like that beforehand. But if something does happen, you'll be glad you did this. Too often people come to us after the fact. Or when their neighbors have been hit; as soon as one house gets cleaned out, the whole neighborhood comes here to get fixed up."

"So business must be booming these days," said Willenbrock.

The salesman looked pleased and nodded. "It's true, every time a place gets broken into, we get new customers. When crime rises, so do our sales."

"You ought to give the crooks a cut of your profits. You're basically living off the fruits of their crime. A silent partner, as it were."

"Well, that's one way of looking at it. But that's life."

He scanned the price codes and packed the boxes in large plastic bags.

"Either way, it's a good investment," he said, holding the door for Willenbrock. "If something happens, you'll be glad you spent the money. And if it doesn't, you won't be unhappy either. Good luck, and many thanks."

Willenbrock worked until dusk, installing security devices on the outside doors and windows and testing them. Susanne looked at him skeptically whenever she passed by but said nothing. Before dinner they walked out to the edge of the forest, which was once again flooded, but came back before dark. Then Willenbrock locked the doors and turned on the new system. Even though they were both exhausted by the time they got to bed, they didn't fall asleep until well after midnight, listening nervously to the noises outside, the nocturnal bird calls, and the soft, light patter of the marten that lived in the rafters of the barn and spent the night roaming the roof and yard. Still, they both woke up again at two o'clock, as they had every night since the attack, and lay next to each other for more than an hour, wide awake. Each knew the other wasn't sleeping, but neither said anything; they just listened to the nighttime noises and tried to get back to sleep.

The next morning, Willenbrock continued working on the

security system. When the carpenter came, he showed him the doors he wanted replaced. Königsmann knew all about the break-in and immediately suggested a way to solve the problem: "Labor camps, like under Adolf. Not everything he did was so bad."

"I know," said Willenbrock ironically, "the autobahn."

"Exactly," said the carpenter. "He had a couple of good ideas, you know. What he got done in twelve years, politicians these days can't come close to doing. They spend that long just talking, but they don't do squat. One thing's for sure: he knew how to deal with the kind of people who did this."

"Along with a few others."

"Even so, Herr Willenbrock, it wasn't all bad."

The carpenter took a pad out of his pocket and wrote down the measurements.

Willenbrock worked through the afternoon, putting in window bars and alarms. He felt Susanne's unease as she watched him, so he tried to make light of what he was doing, joking that by the time he got done, the house would be so secure he wasn't sure *they'd* be able to get in. She asked if this meant he'd already decided to hold on to the property. Willenbrock said he hadn't decided anything. "Let's talk about it half a year from now. And then we'll figure it out together."

The trip home was hard. The country roads were full of slow-moving harvesters that were difficult to pass, the autobahn to Berlin was clogged, and the extensive road construction made the traffic even worse.

That Wednesday one of the workers knocked on Willenbrock's door, came in, and announced they'd be finished with the roof the next day.

When Willenbrock just nodded, the man added: "Tomorrow we're topping off, tomorrow you can celebrate. The worst is over, from this point on it's only small stuff. Like I always say, from here on out it's up to the painters to fix whatever we've screwed up—as long as it's not off by more than two centimeters."

He laughed out loud. Willenbrock didn't react to the joke, but only asked when the engineer would be in to inspect and approve the work.

The next day, a little before lunch, the men took a green plastic wreath they'd brought and mounted it on the roof, then gathered their tools and used push brooms to sweep the new cement floor of the showroom. Half an hour later the engineer arrived to go over the building with Willenbrock and sign the report. Sitting on upturned buckets, the three workers ate their sandwiches as they carefully watched the inspection. Twice the engineer called to the heavyset red-haired man who'd told Willenbrock about the topping-off ceremony and asked him about the insulation.

"It's good work," the engineer finally said to Willenbrock, "your architect will be pleased. And you should be, too."

Before going off with the engineer, Willenbrock had given Jurek some money and asked him to buy a case of beer and some bratwurst from the little kiosk in front of the building-supply store. While they were still checking over the roof, Jurek brought some chairs from the office and the old greenhouse and set them up in the new showroom. After Willenbrock signed the report, the men sat in a circle around the case of beer; Jurek served them bratwurst from a dish. One of the workers pried off a bottle cap with a screwdriver and handed the beer to the engineer, who stood up, raised it high, and congratulated Willenbrock on his new premises. The engineer sat down and everyone looked at Willenbrock, who didn't feel like saying anything, so he just stayed in his chair, lifted his beer in salutation, then put the bottle to his lips. He asked the engineer when the glass panels were coming and went over the deadlines.

The workers had moved closer to Jurek. One of them asked about the red coupe that had been in the yard for two weeks, a car several customers had asked about. Jurek praised the coupe, saying that even though his boss couldn't offer guarantees on used cars, he himself had given this one a really thorough going-over.

"Good car. Not too much mileage, and not too little—a good machine," he said.

The worker asked him about the price, but the Pole referred him to Willenbrock.

"I don't know anything about money," he said.

"Me neither," said the man and laughed.

Half an hour later the workers drove off with the engineer. The construction trailer was picked up later that afternoon. The glass panels were supposed to be installed at the end of the following week, when Willenbrock's handball league was scheduled for a tournament in St. Andreasberg. His team had been training intensely for over a month; they planned to spend the whole coming weekend practicing.

Friday evening Willenbrock dropped Susanne off at the train station. She wanted to visit a girlfriend who was spending the summer on the coast in Ralswiek working as an assistant to the director of an open-air theater. Susanne was afraid there'd be traffic, so she took the train and arranged for her friend to pick her up at the station in Bergen. She'd asked Kathrin to manage the shop on Saturday. Willenbrock placed Susanne's suitcase on the rack above her seat, then went back to the platform and stood outside her compartment. The window was down, a woman and two children had stuck their heads out and were anxiously looking for someone. Willenbrock couldn't see past them to Susanne. When the train started up and the window was raised, he waved, but all he saw was the sun's reflection in the windowpane.

He drove straight from the station to the sports center, quickly changed, and ran to the courts where his team was practicing. They played until the attendant told them it was time to close and afterward went to an Italian restaurant. There they talked about the tournament and women; then Genser, the computer dealer, told them another story about Russia, this one involving a visit to a casino owned by some Austrians. The casino was set up on a boat permanently moored along the Moskva River and connected to the bank by a broad, well-lit pier with a simple railing on either side. Genser had gone there with a Russian girlfriend. They had been sitting at one of the tables when four Russians wearing cheap suits barged in and began arguing with the manager. Genser's croupier took one look at the men, immediately stopped the roulette wheel, and asked the players to take back their bets, since the game had been interrupted. Genser, who was sitting right next to the croupier, took his chips off the cloth and stuck them in his pocket just to be safe. All activity at the other tables stopped as well. When Genser asked the croupier why the games had been halted, the man warily nodded toward the four Russians and whispered in English that the same four gangsters had showed up two days earlier in the company of an elderly gent who had suggested to the manager that they take over the casino's security. The manager had declined, saying that he already had a professional team of trained guards, whereupon the elderly man looked at him uncomprehendingly and walked out, together with his four companions. Now the same four had shown up again and evidently wanted to start a fight. Genser watched the scene, along with everyone else in the casino. The manager tried to make the four men leave. A few seconds later the guards showed up—five very fit, athletic-looking men the proprietor had brought over from Vienna, according to the croupier. The Austrians surrounded the uninvited guests, and for a moment everything was quiet. The manager spoke to the four young men politely but firmly. Suddenly a scuffle broke out; one of the Austrians screamed and pressed his hand against his right ear, which was streaming with blood. When everyone jumped back, a knife was lying on the floor, and next to it, an ear. The four intruders were now standing off to the side, their arms hanging loose, looking helpless and intimidated. They put up no resistance as the Austrian guards shoved them up against the wall and had them raise their arms and spread their legs. The Russians said nothing, submitting to the screaming manager and the gesticulating guards, and allowed themselves to be jostled. A few minutes later, two squad cars arrived with shrieking sirens and flashing blue lights; six policemen jumped out and stormed across the pier onto the boat. The manager and the proprietor, who'd arrived shortly after the guards, explained to the police what had happened. The police put handcuffs on the four Russians and seemed to be cursing them out. An ambulance came; three men in white brought a stretcher on board. They took the wounded Austrian, who was sitting in one of the armchairs, howling with pain, carried him off the boat, and drove him to a hospital. One of the croupiers had picked up the severed ear and put it on ice in a champagne cooler, which he covered with a napkin. He handed the silver bucket to a paramedic. The police captain spoke for a while with the casino owner and made some notes. Then he interrogated all the Russian-speaking witnesses. Finally he summoned his men with a commanding gesture, and the policemen led the handcuffed young Russians out of the casino. Several guests immediately cashed in their chips, paid the waiter, and asked for their coats. Only a few people remained at the gaming tables, and none played. They'd seen what had happened and now watched as one of the barmaids wiped up the blood and polished the floor with a rag. Genser and his girlfriend followed their croupier to the window; they looked out over the pier toward the riverbank and the two cars with the flashing lights. The policemen were heading slowly across the white gangplank over the water toward the city. When they reached their cars, they stopped; they seemed to be talking among themselves. Then they took the handcuffs off the men in custody, stood around with them a while and smoked. At one point the four young Russians vanished; the police casually climbed into their cars and drove away.

When Genser asked the croupier what it all meant, he replied matter-of-factly that the elderly gent would visit the boss in the morning; a few hours later the bodyguards would fly back to Vienna—except for the man in the hospital—and starting at noon the next day, the casino would have a new security team, a Russian one. That's terrible, said Genser, but the croupier disagreed, saying that, on the contrary, they'd finally have some peace, no more incidents, no more attacks, no more trouble with drunken guests—no worries whatsoever. After the elderly man's first visit, the croupier had told his boss that Russian guards were very good and highly effective. The manager hadn't wanted to listen, and as a result the poor Austrian had lost an ear. The croupier looked Genser in the eye and said: "When in Rome . . ." Then he went back to his table and spun the roulette wheel to signal that the table was open for business. Genser and his friend stayed another few minutes, but they didn't continue playing; after the bloody ear, they'd lost their appetite for amusement.

One of the teammates made some witticism about the ear. Willenbrock immediately got up and said he had to go.

"So soon?" asked Genser.

"I can't listen to any more of your stories. I've had it up to here with them," Willenbrock snarled and left.

The conversation stopped at once; his friends stared at him, appalled.

Back home, Willenbrock moved the empty garbage can into its place behind the chipboard wall. Before turning off the outdoor lights, he went inside, examined the windows and both doors, and wondered whether he should install a security system in this house as well.

Both Saturday and Sunday he spent four hours training with his team. He noticed that the extra-long playing time was hard on him; for the last half hour he was completely out of breath, and he wasn't reacting quickly enough. But he noticed that his teammates, too, were panting, constantly wiping their foreheads, and frequently stopping to rest with their hands propped on their thighs. Dieter, their captain, a lecturer at the university, kept trying to fire the men up, but their playing continued to get slower and slacker. Later, when they were having a beer at the pub and the captain complained about their performance, Willenbrock said: "We're old men, Dieter."

His exhausted teammates nodded in agreement and grinned, but when Dieter suggested pulling out of the tournament, they protested and promised to give it all they had.

After Sunday's practice, Willenbrock drank nothing but water; he left the pub ten minutes early to pick Susanne up at the station. As he parked the car and received his time-stamped ticket, he noticed three men watching him. Their clothes were torn and dirty; they were sitting on a cement ledge and had a huge German shepherd at their feet. For a moment Willenbrock considered parking elsewhere, but then he slipped the ticket behind the sun visor, locked the car, and walked to the station. As he passed by the three men, one of them stood up, along with the dog, and blocked his way. The man had a bunch of newspapers draped over one arm and asked if Willenbrock wanted to purchase one, for the homeless. Willenbrock took out his wallet and gave the man a mark, but declined the paper, saying he'd just bought one the day before. The man thanked him very politely. An additional parking charge, Willenbrock told himself—his only reason for giving the man money was to make sure none of the three bums, who didn't exactly inspire trust, would start messing with his car.

Susanne was in a good mood when she got off the train. She asked how he'd spent his weekend and then, bubbling over with excitement, told him all about her visit and the open-air theater in Ralswiek. The whole way home she talked about her trips around the Isle of Rügen, the chalk cliffs and the lighthouse, a three-hour sail on the Baltic in her friend's boat, and the disappointing theater production. Evidently the audience only applauded for the scenery, the equestrian show, and a trained sea eagle; the play itself was a muddled and stupid affair, made worse by the fact that all the actors were miked, so it was never clear who on the huge stage was speaking.

"The only person who really enjoyed every bit of it was the owner," she said. "He just keeps raking it in, and the prices are outrageous."

Willenbrock pointed out that a theater like that had a pretty short season, and if the weather didn't cooperate, the owner could easily find himself in the red. But Susanne countered that the show went on rain or shine, since the audience wasn't about to let a little weather interfere with their plans. Besides, since all the refreshment stands belonged to the same owner, he never lost a penny even when it did rain; on the contrary, storms were a godsend for him, since with every cloudburst he sold hundreds of cheap ponchos at jacked-up prices. Willenbrock was impressed.

"Now that's the way to do things, that's the way to live," he told Susanne.

"I don't see what *you* have to complain about," she

answered in an insinuating way. "Looks to me like you're living pretty well yourself."

Willenbrock whistled and drummed contentedly on the steering wheel.

At home she asked whether he was still going to the handball tournament. He said he was and added that the sport was the only real fun he had these days, he needed it to unwind, and hoped he'd be able to keep on playing, for a few years at least. Sooner or later he'll have to stop, he'll be too old and slow, and then he'll probably take up stamp collecting.

"I'd lose my mind if I didn't have something outside the car business."

As he lay next to her in bed, she told him about her friend who was working at the theater, and he reflected on the fact that he'd spent the whole weekend by himself and hadn't seen or even called a single one of his girlfriends. He wondered when the last time was that he'd passed up such an opportunity but couldn't remember.

"I must be getting old," he said suddenly.

Susanne, who was still talking about her friend, looked at him, puzzled.

"What's got into you?" she asked.

Willenbrock did not respond.

17

On Tuesday morning Feuerbach showed up at the lot, hoping to sell his old car. Jurek spoke with him and led him to the office to see Willenbrock, who hadn't realized it was his former colleague until he saw the two men heading his way. He presumed Feuerbach was unaware which dealer he had come to. Willenbrock quickly sat at his desk and spun his chair to face the wall before the men came in. He waited for Jurek to address him before turning around, then stood up and said in a friendly voice:

"Hello, Willi. What brings you here?"

Feuerbach blanched. He stood there a moment with his mouth slightly open before he was able to mumble a greeting. Willenbrock focused on Jurek while he reported on the car: "An Opel Kadett, twelve years old, five owners. The clutch rattles and the tires are pretty shot. Lots of rust, boss, needs a lot of work."

Willenbrock nodded, and the Pole left.

"Have a seat, Willi. How did you manage to find me?"

"I honestly had no idea this was your place. I've been thinking about selling my car and was driving by when I saw the buy-and-sell sign. I didn't know you—"

"What a coincidence that of all the used-car lots you should wind up at mine, Willi."

Willenbrock propped his elbows on the desk, folded his hands together, rested his chin on them, and looked at Feuerbach expectantly.

"How's the family? How's work?"

"So far so good, we're getting by."

"And the party, Willi? Fighting the good fight? Onward and upward?"

"It's a lot of work, lots of paper pushing. And all on our own time."

"Still on the chatty side, Willi?"

Feuerbach pressed his lips together, then asked frostily: "Do you want to buy the car?"

"You heard what my mechanic said. It's not worth much."

He glanced out the window at the car.

"Don't you even want to have a look?"

"I can see it from here. And I trust Jurek completely."

He paused, looked outside again, and said: "One thousand five hundred. Is it a deal?"

Feuerbach made a skeptical face.

"You won't get more for it anywhere else, unless you take out an ad. Who knows, maybe you'll get lucky and find some guy who's deaf and blind and happens to be in the market for an ancient Kadett."

"I don't think I can accept what you're offering, Bernd, it's not enough."

Willenbrock shrugged his shoulders and said sympathetically: "Things a bit tough on the financial front?"

Feuerbach hesitated, then said defensively: “I’m getting along all right.”

“You always did.”

“No need to get insulting.”

“Insulting? I’m sorry, it’s just that I have a hard time forgetting, Willi. I can’t forget that because you couldn’t keep your trap shut, I didn’t get to go to London, or anywhere else after that. My name never came up again, that was it, I was out of the running. I’d been blacklisted and had no idea why. And now it turns out it was all because of you, you and your goddamned snitching.”

“I never meant to hurt you, Bernd. I had no idea my assessments would be used for that. I treated the whole thing as a lot of stupid paperwork, it never even occurred to me anyone actually read my reports.”

“What did you think they’d do? What were you hoping for with all your denunciations? Some kind of medal?”

“I didn’t denounce anyone. My job was to write a yearly assessment of the personnel. Everybody knew that.”

“And the fact that I met my sister and her husband in Prague, because it was impossible to meet them anywhere else, that was all part of a professional review?”

“You told everybody that you’d met them. The whole factory knew it. If I hadn’t mentioned it, they would have hauled me over the coals.”

“You see, that’s the difference: the whole factory knew it, but you’re the only one who passed it on. That’s precisely the difference between Herr Doktor Feuerbach and a human being. You make me sick.”

"What do you want me to do? Apologize? Fine, I'm sorry. Happy now?"

"You asshole. Get out of here. I'm not doing business with you. I wouldn't want that old crate even if you gave it to me. I've had it up to here with people like you. Denouncing me, robbing me, trying to beat me to death. I'll show you, pal. I won't take it. Get out of here."

Feuerbach's sarcastic response had gotten Willenbrock so worked up he jumped out of his chair, charged from behind his desk, and planted himself directly in front of Feuerbach, shaking with rage. Feuerbach stood up, looked Willenbrock in the eye, and said, quietly and nonchalantly: "I only did what I had to do. Writing assessments was part of my work, you all knew that. Sure, people look at everything differently now. Everybody's smarter with a little hindsight."

"You goddamned snitch!" Willenbrock roared.

And then he punched Feuerbach in the face. He hit him right in the nose, which immediately started bleeding. Before Feuerbach could get out his handkerchief and hold it up to his face, his shirt and one lapel were smeared with blood. Holding the cloth in front of his mouth, his eyes burned with anger as he took several deep breaths and then walked out the door without closing it. "You idiot," he said, calmly, before going down the stairs.

Willenbrock was shocked at himself. His rage disappeared as quickly as it had come over him.

"Get the hell out!" he yelled across the lot at Feuerbach as he was climbing into his car, but he was shouting more from shame than rage, and because he didn't want to apologize to

Feuerbach. He was shouting because he was so shocked at what he had done.

"That asshole," he said aloud to himself as he closed the door, "has the nerve to show up here, on my lot. Of all places he comes straight to mine."

Willenbrock bit his lip. He was so flushed with embarrassment he was sweating. Jurek opened the door and stuck his head in.

"Everything okay, boss?" he asked.

"Yes," grumbled Willenbrock, without looking up from the papers he was pretending to work on.

He couldn't stop thinking about Feuerbach all day. He didn't understand what had come over him, why he had hit the man. By the time he went to his handball practice that evening, he had concluded it was all Berner's fault, since he was the one who'd told him about Willi Feuerbach. He cursed Berner, and he cursed the phone call that had, he now believed, put him in such a frenzy he'd lost control of himself. He was sorry about Feuerbach, not because he'd punched him in the face, but because the guy was essentially a poor dumb sap who'd been shortchanged; he probably only wrote his reports because they gave him a feeling of power and importance otherwise missing in his life and work. Willenbrock resented Berner's uninvited intrusion. He hadn't asked to be told about Feuerbach, he would have happily gone on not knowing who'd dragged his name in the mud, especially now, ten years after his old firm had gone under. Sure, he would have been interested at the time, back then he would have let Feuerbach have it, but now the whole thing was ancient history, he'd forgotten all about those trips, and it was only because of Berner that the whole stinking mess had been brought up again. I should have punched Berner out instead of this pitiful little wimp of a Feuerbach. By the time he parked at the sports center, Willenbrock was resolved to call Berner and tell him exactly what he thought of him and that from here on out he wanted nothing more to do with him.

Dieter broke the news that the team's best pivot player had pulled a ligament and would be out for the next three weeks. He introduced a tall man named Michael, whom he'd asked to stand in, a colleague of his from the mathematics department whose hair was cut so short he almost looked bald. They played nearly three hours with only an occasional break, and since the new man was fast and a dangerously good shot, they were all over him after practice at the pub, praising him and congratulating one another on their lucky replacement.

Thursday morning three men delivered the huge glass plates and the doors for the showroom in a special truck with a hydraulic arm. As they inspected the site, the men stopped in front of a particular opening, which they measured repeatedly. Willenbrock went over and asked if anything was wrong. They said there wasn't. Then he asked how long it would take them to install the glass panels and doors, and one of the men said that they had to be in Rostock on Monday, so they would definitely finish up here over the weekend, regardless of how many hours they had to put in. Willenbrock walked to the truck, rapped on the glass, inspected the labels, and then went back to his office. Around noon he said goodbye to Jurek, drove to the Kaiserdamm, and spent a long time searching for a halfway decent place to eat. Then, taking his bags from the car, he made his way to the appointed meeting place. Four of his teammates were already waiting in the rented minibus, where Dieter greeted him with the news that Genser had had to cancel: something unexpected had come up and he had to go to Munich for four days and would miss the tournament. So they'd all have to play as hard as they could and avoid getting injured at all costs—they couldn't afford to lose a single player.

The rest of the group filtered in over the next ten minutes; Dieter started the minibus and got on the autobahn. The men spent the first part of the trip cursing Genser for leaving them in the lurch, and analyzing their chances in the tournament, but once they were out of the city the talk turned to business, women, and the Formula One Race.

In St. Andreasberg they had booked rooms in the Waldfrieden Hotel, which had made special arrangements with the tournament. After setting their luggage in their rooms, they took a stroll around town before having a bite to eat. Then they went to the high school gymnasium where their first game was scheduled. The team they were up against was from Uelzen, and they beat them easily. They also managed to beat their second opponents the following afternoon. On Saturday morning one of the opposing players slammed Michael so hard the player was disqualified, but the mathematician was limping and had to change places with their goalie, since they had no one to replace him. They lost the game in a rout and were eliminated from the tournament. A doctor examined Michael, bandaged his leg, and advised him to get it X-rayed right away, since he suspected it might be broken. The young man casually took in what the doctor was saying, lay down in his hotel room for half an hour, and then joined his disappointed teammates in the hotel restaurant, where they sat drinking beer.

That evening they watched the game from the bleachers. They all agreed that if they'd had a reserve player they would have made it to the finals and possibly even won the top prize, or at least second place, which also included a cash award.

After the game they went to the hotel restaurant. The men on the two surviving teams had gone to their rooms to rest up before facing each other the next morning, so the only players in the restaurant were those who'd already been eliminated. They reviewed the matches; Dieter suggested that the guys chip in and pick up Michael's travel expenses—at least for the moment—and then present the bill to Genser. Gerd, Willenbrock's tax advisor, thought that since the computer dealer had left them in the lurch, he should pay the whole team's expenses, on which point the rest of the team was in agreement, since they blamed him for their early elimination. Willenbrock considered skipping the final play-off and taking a taxi out to Goslar the next morning to visit his brother. They hadn't seen each other in years and had fallen completely out of touch. Willenbrock only thought of him when he thought about his childhood—that was the only thing that connected them. But he dropped the idea and decided to stay with his team.

Right after the play-off they drove back to Berlin. Somebody had to carry Michael's bag, since his leg was extremely swollen and it was clearly very painful for him to move. They said goodbye at the Kaiserdamm. Willenbrock said he hoped Michael hadn't broken anything and that his leg would mend soon, and asked him to consider joining their team. The other players also tried to talk him into signing up.

"It has other advantages, too," said Gerd. "Since almost all of us run our own businesses, we're able to help our teammates out in various ways here and there. Just ask Dieter."

The mathematician laughed and said he'd consider the invitation. Dieter dropped him off at his apartment in the minibus.

Willenbrock got in his car and drove to the lot. He looked over the construction; all the glass and doors had been installed and were reflecting the afternoon sun. He liked the way the showroom was shaping up and felt pleased with himself. He tried going inside, but the new doors were locked. Hoping the workmen had given the keys to Jurek and that Jurek might have left them in the office, he went inside the trailer, but didn't find anything. He took another walk around the building, then called Susanne and told her he'd be home in an hour. She was surprised to hear from him so soon; she hadn't expected him until evening. As soon as he hung up he thought about calling her right back; something about their conversation bothered him, but he couldn't put his finger on it, and he just shook his head, confused. He turned on the computer and spent some time browsing the Internet.

Susanne had just put dinner on the table when he came in. He told her about the tournament, about Michael's injury and their team's early elimination. She looked at him, strangely absent, listening in silence. After dinner he brewed some tea in the kitchen. When he took the tea service into the living room, Susanne was holding an open letter for him to look at. It was the official communication from the prosecutor's office informing the Willenbrocks that the inquiry against Andrei and Artur Gatchev had been dropped and that the accused had been deported to Poland on July 28, as there was insufficient incriminating evidence to hold them any longer. The Gatchev brothers had been ordered to return immediately and directly to Moscow, their city of residence. A public prosecutor by the name of Tesch further informed the Willenbrocks that the evidence uncovered at the scene of the crime had not been adequate to ensure positive identification of the perpetrators, such that no indictment could be obtained for the persons in custody. The prosecutor had decided to forgo submitting an official request for the matter to be taken up by a Russian court, since there was little chance of success, particularly as the address on file for the brothers was incomplete. The letter was accompanied by a short form outlining the appeals process and listing the address of the attorney general.

Willenbrock read the letter twice, then put it down on the table and looked at Susanne, who had turned pale and was waiting for him to say something. He had trouble keeping calm; the tone of the letter, the prosecutor's explanation, the glibly official language informing them that their case was being dropped, that the accused had been deported without the slightest effort to bring them to justice, even though they'd tried to bludgeon him to death—it all upset him tremendously, but he didn't want to worry Susanne and managed to force a sneer of disgust.

"They're both back out on the streets," said Susanne. "They were released the next day."

"Deported," he corrected.

"They were sent to Poland the very next day. And could have been back at our place two days later. And we didn't even know they were free again."

"It's true, they could have. But they wouldn't come near our place again, not after I chased them away so heroically," he said, trying to calm her down. "Besides, our house is now completely secure."

"You knew all about this, didn't you? You've known it for a long time, right?"

"Yes," he confessed, "I spoke with the detective a few weeks ago. That's when I bought the pistol, but that was dumb, just a hysterical reaction. I think the security system I've installed and the alarms are better protection. Guys like that don't like taking risks. When they see how difficult our house is to crack they'll go elsewhere."

"To a neighbor's."

"Maybe. Or to another village. There's nothing we can do about it. I talked to the patrolmen—they all have families and are afraid to go on their beat at night. One of them told me about the difference between the rookies and the older, more experienced cops. Evidently the old-timers take longer to get to the scene of the crime, they make a point of first driving around an extra block or two—to avoid running into the criminals! They'd rather show up just to register the damage. That's easy enough to understand, don't you think?"

"They could have attacked us last weekend, those same two brothers, Bernd."

Willenbrock laughed out loud. "They'll think twice about doing that. And so will everyone else. We're safe as a bank out there, Susanne."

They took the teacups to the kitchen and loaded the dishes and silverware in the dishwasher.

Early that evening they drove out to Krampnitz to visit Susanne's cousin and his family. They hadn't warned him they were coming, they just took their chances, and wound up staying late into the night. They sat outside, eating grilled meat and vegetables, looking out over the lake and talking about the family. The cousin apologized for not making it to Susanne's mother's funeral; the news had reached him when he was in Milan, at a sporting-goods sales exposition. He hadn't been able to get away; in fact he only heard about it on the day of the service, so he wouldn't have been able to make it anyway. Then the men talked about their work, Willenbrock told about his new showroom, and the women disappeared. When they came back, two hours later, they just said they'd been putting the children to bed. As she drove back home, Susanne asked whether he had told her cousin.

"Told him what? What do you mean?"

"I mean the attack. Did you tell him?"

"No, why? Did you?"

Susanne shook her head.

"It's probably better that way."

"I just asked Ingrid whether they weren't afraid to live in such a big house, all by themselves, with that huge garden. But she didn't understand what I was getting at. She didn't see that there was anything to be afraid of."

"Stop driving yourself crazy," was all he said. "It's happened. It's over and done with. It's behind us now. Those two won't be coming back, and neither will anybody else. The chances of that happening are about the same as winning the lottery twice."

"But what is it you always say? The devil always shits on the biggest pile, in good things and in bad."

"Then let the devil come—and I'll light a firecracker under his ass."

Willenbrock closed his eyes and leaned back in the passenger seat. The strenuous tournament and the alcohol they'd drunk at Susanne's cousin's were causing him to doze off. Susanne turned down the radio. The highway was still crowded, and the traffic was slow.

At home Willenbrock went straight to bed and fell asleep right away, but at two o'clock he woke up. He couldn't get the prosecutor's letter out of his head. He wanted to go read it again, but he sensed Susanne was lying awake next to him, and if he got up neither one would be able to fall back asleep. He tried focusing on something else, on Susanne's cousin and his lakefront house, his team's defeat in the tournament, but he kept coming back to the letter. He didn't get back to sleep until four, and when the alarm went off, he felt unrested and worn out.

18

Krylov called three days later to say he would come by the following afternoon. When Willenbrock said he was happy to see him again so soon and asked how many cars he wanted this time, Krylov replied that he was traveling in the other direction, that he wasn't coming on business, but as a friend.

"No cars at all?" Willenbrock asked again.

"No," Krylov said and hung up.

He showed up at four. His driver stayed in the car while Krylov walked to the office carrying a small, beat-up cardboard box. Willenbrock, who'd been waiting for him and seen him pull up, held open the door. He had set out a bottle and glasses, but Krylov just sat down and gestured with his hand to decline when Willenbrock started to pour.

"I don't have the time, my friend," he said. "I'm on my way to Madrid and have to be at the airport in half an hour."

"So, what brings you here to see me, Herr Direktor?"

"Friendship," said Krylov and laughed. Then he turned serious and said: "Do you have the address for Gatchev?"

For a moment Willenbrock didn't understand.

"Gatchev?" he asked. He had taken it for granted that Krylov would nevertheless be placing another order, so after the Russian had called, he and Jurek had gone through the lot and picked out a few cars he thought Krylov might want. Now he was caught off guard by Krylov's question. Krylov merely looked at him in silence until Willenbrock realized what the Russian was after. He was surprised Krylov remembered the name of his attackers.

"No, I must have lost the address. I thought I had it somewhere in my papers, but I couldn't find it anywhere. I probably heard it at the police station and just imagined that I had it written down. But the fact is I don't, and I can't remember what they told me. I'm sorry, I forgot all about it."

Krylov nodded sympathetically.

"I thought that might happen," he said. "I knew you wouldn't be able to find the address. You're a good person, my friend. But it's not always smart to be so good. There are too many bad people in the world, and they need help. It's up to us to help them, and to help ourselves. Maybe the brothers don't have a father, maybe they've grown up on the wild side. Maybe the family couldn't get a foothold in the new order, or they went downhill and became asocial. In cases like that you have to step in and lend a hand, teach the young men a lesson. I would be deeply saddened if anything happened to my friend Willenbrock."

He placed the bruised-up box on the desk and looked at Willenbrock.

"What's that?"

"A present."

"A present? For who?"

"For you, for my friend."

Willenbrock reached tentatively for the package, but

Krylov shook his head and said: "Before you touch it you have to give me three hundred marks."

Willenbrock looked at him, surprised, then leaned back in his chair and gave an awkward grin.

"I don't understand," he said, as Krylov watched him in silence. "Maybe you should explain it to me, Direktor."

"Three hundred marks and the present is yours."

Willenbrock forced a laugh. He rested his hands on the desktop, unable to decide. He looked out the window at Krylov's car, where the driver was sitting in the open door, smoking a cigarette. He didn't understand what Krylov wanted from him; he had the feeling the Russian was playing some kind of prank. Maybe it was some Russian custom he was unfamiliar with. He had no idea how he was supposed to react.

"Don't you trust me, my German friend?"

Willenbrock looked him in the eyes, then reached for his jacket, which was draped over the back of the armchair, removed his wallet, counted his cash, lay three hundred-mark bills on the table, and put away the rest.

"There," he said, pointing to the money. "Of course I trust you, even if I don't have a clue to what's going on."

Krylov nodded, took the money, and casually stuck it in his pocket. Then he pulled back the top of the box; inside was something wrapped in newspaper. Grabbing the box with both hands, Krylov lifted it up and deftly flipped it over. Something heavy thudded onto the desk, and the Russian took the empty box and set it on his knees.

"There," was all he said.

Willenbrock carefully unwrapped the strange gift. Under

the layer of newspaper he found an olive-green oiled rag; when he picked it up with his fingertips, a small heavy carton slid out onto the table. He carefully placed the rag and its contents back on the newspaper and picked up the carton, which was marked with numbers and barcodes and had some words printed in English: AMMUNITION, CAUTION, CARTRIDGE. He looked up at Krylov, who had folded his arms and was observing him. Seeing Willenbrock hesitate, he glanced at his watch and gestured for him to continue.

"I think I know what it is you want to give me," said Willenbrock, reaching for the bundle. Slowly he unwrapped a shiny dark revolver. Picking it up carefully by the barrel, he turned it over to look at it from all sides, studied the grip, the cylinder, the hammer and trigger.

"Smith and Wesson," he read out loud.

He looked at Krylov, baffled.

"Model 586," said the Russian, "clean as a whistle, never been fired, a virgin. No more need to worry. What's wrong, my friend? Does the price give you a headache? I was assured it's worth a whole lot more—the three hundred marks are just to cover my expenses. And I don't like expenses, even for presents. Anyway, I'd have to ask you for some money, you can't just give someone a knife or a gun, that's bad luck. But it's all right if you turn it into a small purchase."

He stood up, put his hands in his pockets, and peered at Willenbrock as the latter cleared his throat.

"Well," he said, drawing out the word, "what can I say?"

"Just say 'Thanks, friend,'" answered Krylov. "Now I have to get going, the plane won't wait. And we'll just forget about all this, right? We'll forget I was ever here today. My driver can always testify that I wasn't. We didn't even see each other. But don't worry, the weapon's clean, not a single fingerprint."

He took the newspaper, put the box under his arm, and went to the door. Willenbrock stood up to walk him to his car, but Krylov pointed at the weapon. "No, you stay here. You shouldn't leave something like that lying around."

He nodded meaningfully and stepped out of the trailer.

Willenbrock watched him through the window. The driver flicked his cigarette away and opened the door for his boss. The car roared off the lot, came to a quick stop at the street and then squealed into the traffic. Willenbrock turned to the weapon on his desk and eyed it with concern. He wrapped it back in the rag and placed it in a desk drawer together with the box of ammunition. A little later he opened the drawer and peeled back the rag, without touching the gun. He wondered what he should do with it.

"For God's sake, Krylov!" he said out loud. The revolver lay on the small stack of sex magazines he occasionally handed out to his customers. The barrel was dark blue, almost black, with the trademark Smith & Wesson stamp. He reached in and held it, without taking it out of the drawer. The weapon was cool and pleasant to the touch. He thought about how he'd registered years ago as a conscientious objector, how he'd served in the Construction Corps to avoid having to carry a weapon. And now here he was, the owner of a Smith & Wesson, a serious firearm, highly dangerous, lethal, illicit. He felt confused, burdened. Buying the signal pistol had made him feel ridiculous; now he was holding a gun that fired live ammunition, a real revolver he had to hide where no one could see it, let alone touch it, a weapon that indisputably provided effective protection, but also posed a constant danger. Willenbrock didn't know what to do, where to keep the thing. The idea of carrying it with him all the time was grotesque, but he would be negligent if he left it at home or in the office, where someone else might find it. He wasn't so much afraid of the legal consequences as he was scared of what could happen if someone, especially a child, stumbled upon the gun and started playing with it. He should never have touched the gun, he should have immediately given it back to Krylov. He should have asked him to return the money and told him he had no use for the deadly piece. The Russian would have laughed at him and offered a few general pronouncements about the Germans, and some specific ones about his German friend, but Willenbrock would have been relieved. He resolved to keep the revolver safely stored until Krylov's next visit, and then return it, no matter what. He wasn't the man for a gun like that, he didn't have the nerves for it, and took no pleasure in having one around. He didn't want to be forced to possess something he didn't want. Willenbrock slammed the drawer so hard that he heard the revolver bang against the wood, and he jumped—hoping it wasn't loaded. He had no experience, wasn't sure how to check. After work he put the revolver in his briefcase; he didn't want to leave it in his office unattended.

He got home before Susanne, and sat down in his study to get a better look at the revolver. Cautiously he picked it up, flipped open the cylinder to peek in, then snapped it back in place. He aimed the gun at pictures on the wall, at a photo of himself climbing into a glider plane—carefully, trying to keep his hand steady, never touching the trigger. Then he removed some cartridges from the box, loaded them in the chambers, and took them back out, rechecking several times to make sure the cylinder was completely empty. He thought about the prosecutor's letter, found it and read it one more time. Then he took the revolver, pointed it at the letterhead, and pulled the trigger. He heard a metallic click. Aiming carefully, he pulled the trigger a second time, and then a third, making noises with his mouth as if he were actually firing. Playing like that gave him a sense of relief. Finally he put the gun and ammo back in the briefcase—all the while shaking his head in wonder.

There were three messages on the answering machine in the living room. Willenbrock pressed the button to listen. The first sounded like a fax; then he heard Susanne's cousin asking them to call back. The third caller was a man saying hello to Susanne and something about a pine forest he would never forget, thanks to her. Willenbrock didn't recognize the man and had no idea what he was talking about. As he replayed the message he was amused to note how oddly intimate the man sounded, almost affectionate, tender.

When Susanne came home they had an aperitif; after she'd phoned her cousin back, Willenbrock asked what he had wanted. Then he asked who the other caller was, and she said it was the husband of one of her clients, she'd helped him pick a present for his wife. Willenbrock saw right away she wasn't telling the truth; Susanne was incapable of deceit. Whenever she needed to tell a lie, it was so transparent that Willenbrock had actually offered to instruct her.

This time she turned red and ran her hand nervously

through her hair. She went to the kitchen so as not to have to look at him and asked whether he'd already fixed dinner or if there was anything he particularly wanted. Willenbrock followed her and said that all he'd done in the way of cooking was open the bottle of wine. He tried to look her in the face, which was still flushed, and she maneuvered to avoid his gaze, pretending to search a long time for something in the silver drawer. During dinner they watched a film about the mating habits of wild cats. Now and then Willenbrock glanced at his wife, who hardly took her eyes off the TV.

Madame is having an affair, he told himself, she's cheating on you. Maybe it really is a client's husband, but he wasn't thanking her for a present, at least not one for his wife—no, my darling Susanne must have given him an entirely different present, a very special kind of gift, didn't he say something about a pine forest, what kind of present does a woman give a man in a forest, in an unforgettable pine forest, a special place for a special present. So she's expanding the business, opening a new branch, which no doubt I'll also end up subsidizing, the guy could scarcely control himself on the phone, you could literally hear his mouth watering, oozing with charm, just too sweet, I only hope I don't come off like that every time I call up some woman, all sticky and sugary and dripping with flattery, it might be just right for young schoolgirls, but not Susanne, she can put two and two together, she wouldn't fall for that kind of crap, she has taste, and besides she knows better, my God, Susanne, a sappy voice like that should set off all sorts of bells, that's not your style, girl, it can't be, I'm worth my weight in gold compared to that, okay, I'm not exactly one to forgo pleasures myself, but come on, Susanne. Well, now I'm curious to see what you'll tell me, you're bound to see that I've caught on—right, love?—you'd have to be off your rocker not to notice that, or do you think I'm senile, come on, you know I've heard the message, so what are you thinking in that pretty little head of yours, what's going on in there, are all your wires overheating while you watch these lions fuck away nonstop, are you thinking about this guy in the pine forest, about the forest he'll never forget thanks to you, or are you getting your story straight, working out what to say in case I ask if there's another man, some happy poacher on the lookout for the game warden? I know, I know, what right do I have, none at all, I can't say anything, it would be pretty funny for me to start playing the wounded husband, I'd have to bite my lip to keep from laughing, well, I hope it was an experience for you, angel, a little bone you can gnaw on in your old age, something to brighten up the twilight, as you like to put it. This little pine forest, is that where you went when you visited your friend in Ralswiek, a special open-air performance just for two? I hope he wasn't a disappointment, hope he wasn't as much of a wimp as he sounded on the phone, just think, a hundred years ago I would have had to challenge him to a duel, well, at least I have a weapon, love, little do you know, I could shoot him dead, gun him down in a fit of passion, with a good lawyer I could get off with two years, tops, or I else could shoot you, my angel, with my brand-new Smith & Wesson, polished and blued, with its beautiful smooth cylinder action and a grip that molds to your hand. That wouldn't cost me much more, either, not with the right lawyer, I'd just have to explain where I got the gun, the court would want to know, they'd want more then "I just found it somewhere," too, and if they caught the Russian, it would be goodbye to my car business, they'd smell a rat, and even if I did just get two years, I'd lose my license for sure, and if the court didn't put me out of business then Krylov would send his boys if I ever mentioned his name, no, that's not a good idea. So you don't have anything to worry about, love, and I'll be getting rid of the revolver soon anyway, it would be best if Krylov came this week and took the thing back, oily rag and all, I'm sure he can find other people who'd be happy to take it off my hands, the metal's burning my fingers. Of course I could shoot myself, that would be easy enough, no consequences, at least not for me, no need to explain anything, it would be suicide out of jealousy, the tabloids would love it, the weapon would remain a riddle, the woman would be well taken care of, maybe the guy with the sappy voice would take my place, hmm . . . not a very comforting thought, best thing is to keep quiet, not say a word—after all, if I'd come home an hour later, I wouldn't have found out a thing, wouldn't know a bit about it, I would have heard a fax and her cousin, and the rest would have been erased. I could sit here calmly watching these horny cats and have no more to worry about than what to do with this revolver that's suddenly popped up in my life. That's it—I just came too early, I'm just too damn domestic, I ought to go out drinking more, maybe do something with the team, a few of those boys hit the town a good three times a week, or else take Jurek, he's getting grumpier and grumpier, that's it, I should take him barhopping sometime, cheer him up a little, after all I am his boss and I should be looking after my only employee, a Christmas bonus isn't enough, maybe he needs a little affection, something Susanne obviously thinks she's missing, too, well, she's gone and gotten herself some, I wonder how old the guy is, probably ten years younger, hard to tell from his voice, but she wouldn't have gone for some old geezer. Maybe she just needs a little consolation and reassurance, and conversation of course, my dear Susanne needs a lot of conversation, long and deep ones about life and eternity, maybe they just talk with each other, hour-long walks through the unforgettable pine forest and nothing else, it's possible, he's probably one of these cultured types, operas and exhibits and everything Susanne raves about and I'm completely ignorant of, though I have other qualities, my love, I rake in the money, that's nothing to sneer at, right? It's easier to live with money, and it's lots easier to live with lots of money, and I think you realize your boutique would have gone under at least twice if dear old Bernd hadn't been helping out all the time, and no sooner is he out of the house than you get the itch, not nice, my girl, not nice, but I'm not saying anything, no questions, you don't have to worry, there won't be any inquisition, that went out with the duels, I don't want to know what happened, and please don't start telling me, no admissions or confessions or anything, no tears, you'll have to deal with it on your own. I wasn't there, I wasn't in the pine forest and I don't want to be dragged there after dinner, you two did your little number, so don't expect me to make you feel better about it, no jealous scenes from me, you'll have to deal with whatshisname on your own. As far as I'm concerned he's some client's husband and you helped him find something for his ample wife and that's why he's so boundlessly grateful, and if he slipped you a little on the side, I don't want to hear about it, and if you drew a dud—and he must be some kind of loser, judging by his voice and the way you're sitting there looking sad as sin—that's your problem. You shouldn't drink so much, women can't handle it, they're missing an enzyme or something, just like the Japanese, they get drunk right away, too, but I'm going to treat myself to a brandy even if you disapprove because it doesn't go well on top of this fine Bordeaux, but then what does go well together in this world, even the two of us only fit together now and then.

Susanne kept her gaze fixed on the TV, where the two lions copulating in the yellow savanna grass were more easily imagined than seen, as the host explained that during this time each male would mate with a female every half hour. Willenbrock got up, saying that he was impressed, the host must be some kind of stud if he could treat a feat like that so casually. Then he asked Susanne if she wanted to go on watching the film, and when she just nodded her head and didn't say anything, he walked over to the answering machine. He wanted to replay the third message, but Susanne had already erased them all. She glanced up at him when he pressed the button. When he looked her way she had already turned back to the TV. Willenbrock went to the kitchen.

After they were in bed, he turned toward her and said she must be very tired.

"Yes," was all she answered.

19

Willenbrock was already out on the lot when the electricians came on Wednesday. He took the master electrician through the showroom and went over the work order, consulting the list he'd drawn up, while two journeymen carried in ladders and rolls of cable and began connecting the underfloor heating. The master showed Willenbrock an assortment of plugs and switches he had on display in the back of his van and made note of Willenbrock's preferences.

At noon Jurek came over to the trailer, rapped on the door, and tried to open it, but found it was locked.

"Just a second," called Willenbrock.

He had taken the revolver out of his briefcase, as he had during the previous days, and spent several minutes playing with it, loading and unloading the chambers. To avoid being surprised, he'd locked the door. Now he quickly stashed the revolver and the cartridges in a desk drawer and let Jurek in.

"Is there a problem, boss?" asked Jurek, surprised, as he entered. He glanced around the room and looked at Willenbrock, who never locked up unless he was going out, and then always left the keys with Jurek in case he had to use the phone or locate the keys to a particular car.

"Everything's fine," said Willenbrock. He felt like a little boy who'd been caught red-handed. He pretended to pay attention as Jurek went over what needed to be ordered and reminded Willenbrock to contact the supplier to have the wheel-balancing machine inspected before the warranty ran out. Taking the list from Jurek, Willenbrock nodded his head and made a few notes, but all he was really thinking about was the fact that his employee had come within a hairsbreadth of catching him playing with the revolver. He cursed Krylov and his miserable present. As Jurek turned to leave, Willenbrock mentioned that he hadn't meant to lock the door. The Pole nodded indifferently.

An hour later, Willenbrock went to find Jurek in the shop. He inquired about the oil supply, and together they went over the tool inventory. He asked about Jurek's family, what his son was doing and how his wife was getting along.

"Fine, just fine," said Jurek bitterly.

Willenbrock looked at him in surprise. He put the plastic box he was holding back on the shelf.

"What's wrong?"

Jurek picked up an oily rag and wiped his hands so thoroughly they became a uniform gray, then said without raising his head: "My son has his own business. He earns three times as much as me. When I ask what kind, he just says it's import and export. And then he laughs. He's moved out of the house. Doesn't need my money anymore. And my wife is doing great. She wants a divorce."

"For God's sake, Jurek, what happened?"

"Nothing happened, boss. No problem. I'm here, she's there, that's how it is. She's all by herself. I'm not home in the evening. Not like you, boss. I'm here, she's there, we don't see each other. She wants a divorce."

"Is there another man?"

"I don't know. She says there isn't. Swore on the Bible. But how can I know? I'm not home."

"That happens, Jurek. Some couples live under the same roof forever and it still doesn't help. Marriage is a difficult business."

"Marriage is a sacrament, boss. Till death do us part."

"What are you planning to do? Refuse to give her a divorce? Can you do that? What are your laws like back home?"

"If the woman wants it, then there's no hope. It'd be a disaster for me to say no. And there's no hope if I stay here."

"Do you want to go back, Jurek? Back to Poznan?"

"No, boss. What would I do? I don't have any work there, and that's no good for the marriage, either. My neighbors aren't my neighbors anymore. I no longer fit in, because I work for a German, because I'm living in Germany. They think I'm a rich snob. I'm no longer one of them. I've become a German as far as they're concerned."

Willenbrock didn't like hearing Jurek grumble and didn't know what to say. He thought of telling him about Susanne, about her lover with the high-pitched sappy voice, but that wouldn't be any consolation.

"Find somebody else," he said. "You're a good-looking guy, you earn good money, women go for that, in Poland or in Germany."

"No, boss, I'm married. I'm not through with my marriage or my wife."

"Well," said Willenbrock, drawing the word out, "anytime

you want to go home, just tell me. I can manage by myself for a few days."

"Go home? What for?"

The Pole was cleaning a spark plug with a wire brush; he held it to his mouth, blew hard, and rubbed it with a rag. Willenbrock picked up a broken screw and tossed it in the trash can. He looked at Jurek another few seconds, then went back to his office to write a letter to the prosecutor. He'd made some notes over the past several days and now sat down at the computer to formulate his appeal. Half an hour later, he read and reread the letter he'd composed on the screen, but wasn't satisfied with the result; the language didn't say what he wanted it to, and the letter sounded angry, almost hysterical. He decided to put it aside for a day and called his lawyer to request an appointment. All he needed was a few minutes, he said, but the matter was urgent.

"No," he answered over the phone, "it's not about a payment notice. I'm drafting a letter to a public prosecutor."

The lawyer said he'd be free in an hour and asked Willenbrock to come by then. Afterward, Willenbrock tried to reach the entomology student he'd taken to Bugewitz, but he kept getting the answering machine, and since the voice was a man's, he hung up without leaving a message. Then he called Rita Lohr at the hair salon. She seemed piqued when she heard who it was and reproached him for not having called in so long, but agreed to meet him after work in the hotel at the Gendarmenmarkt. Willenbrock told Jurek he was going out for two hours to see his lawyer and packed the revolver in his briefcase so as not to leave it unattended.

The lawyer listened to Willenbrock's story with an expression of concern. He read the letter, shaking his head and sneering with indignation.

"This is a clear violation of the law," he said. "We have no choice but to file an appeal. It was attempted murder, or rather manslaughter. They can't just sneak away from their responsibilities like that. Not even out there in the middle of nowhere."

But when Willenbrock asked what chance he had of winning such an appeal, and whether they could then really force the prosecutor's office to resume the investigation and possibly ask the Russian authorities for assistance, the lawyer only shrugged his shoulders.

"At the very least we should try," he said. "The case is too important. A crime of that magnitude has to be prosecuted ex officio—the prosecutor is supposed to pursue it on his own, but all they do is sit around on their lazy bureaucratic duffs. Those dogs won't hunt unless you make them. I think we can get the court to do that. But I'm sure you realize, Herr Willenbrock, that German courts are no different from the high seas—either way, we put ourselves in God's hands."

He looked at Willenbrock with concern and asked if he wanted some coffee. The phone rang, the lawyer gestured to excuse himself and picked up the receiver.

"No, I don't want to be disturbed," he said, "but go ahead and put this one through."

He asked Willenbrock to pardon the interruption and proceeded to speak with a client who evidently owed back taxes in the amount of twelve million marks. The lawyer explained that their firm's accountant hadn't discovered any errors in the official audit.

"But I still think there's something we can do," he explained. "I have an idea, but I'd prefer not to explain it over the phone. When could I come over? When would you have time to see me? Fine, I'll be there right at ten. And I'll bring a colleague, if you don't mind, our tax whiz Herr Scheibler—I think you know him."

"Other people, other problems," he said cheerfully when he hung up. He scrawled something on a piece of paper, then turned back to Willenbrock.

"So, have you decided? Shall we teach these hicks a lesson in German law? I'd like that. Prosecutors all think they're little gods, that their decisions are holy writ, and they consider us lawyers a bunch of troublemakers. I'd love the chance to haul one of these guys up by the ears, some jackass who thinks he's headed for the Supreme Court. Shall we do it, Willenbrock?"

He straightened his tie and drummed on the table, his eyes sparkling with pleasure below his bushy eyebrows.

"Maybe I should just file a protest first," said Willenbrock, hesitatingly.

The lawyer nodded. "Do that. And if that doesn't bring anything, then we can put the screws on."

He stood up and went over to Willenbrock, shook his hand, and walked him to the lobby.

"This could be the trial of the century, Willenbrock."

He gave an encouraging nod, then asked his secretary to send for Herr Scheibler.

Willenbrock drove back to work, uncertain what to do next. When Jurek said goodbye at the end of the day, Willenbrock asked him if he'd like to come over sometime, just for a private visit.

Jurek looked at him and thought a moment.

"No," he said, "I always have a lot to do in the evening. Taking care of things for my friends, my house, my wife, always busy."

"For your wife?" asked Willenbrock, surprised.

"Well, maybe," said Jurek, then broke off the conversation, gave a quick nod, and went to his car.

Willenbrock took his razor out of the desk drawer and stood in front of the little mirror. When he finished shaving he daubed on some cologne. Then he packed the papers and keys in his briefcase and locked the trailer. Pasewald was due to arrive in an hour and would stay on through the night until eight, when Jurek showed up for work.

In the middle of the hotel lobby, an elderly lady wearing a huge hat was standing next to a mountain of luggage—two trunks and half a dozen suitcases—and snapping away, incensed, at both her escorts and two women from the reception desk. She was speaking Spanish, which Willenbrock did not understand. He went into the lounge; the tables were all taken, there was no sign of Rita. When he asked for the key to his room, the two men at the counter asked for a moment's patience, since they, too, had to take care of the Spanish lady. Evidently something was wrong with her room. They kept asking her to step up to the counter to explain what had gone wrong, but the woman insisted on issuing her demands, loudly and imperiously, from the middle of the lobby. The guests in the lounge had stopped talking and were following the scene, as it was impossible to ignore. The two young women from reception kept pleading with the lady in Spanish, trying to calm her down; both had turned bright red.

One of the two men at the counter was on the phone; the other was banging away at his computer keyboard. By the time Willenbrock finally retrieved his room key, he had learned that the woman was a Spanish countess who claimed to have reserved two suites; the hotel employees were trying to find out whether the reservation had been booked with another hotel.

Willenbrock picked up a newspaper and sat down in an armchair. An older man, presumably the hotel manager or director, came out from some back room, spoke to his staff and afterward to the countess, then stepped behind the counter, took two keys, and hurried back to the lady. With extreme deference, he asked her to accompany him to the elevator. The countess followed, still complaining loudly. Her two escorts and the four hotel employees ferried the luggage over but did not get in; they waited for the countess and the manager to go upstairs before they called the elevator back down.

Willenbrock leafed through the newspaper, keeping an eye on the entrance. He was still brooding over the letter from the prosecutor, wondering whether he really should follow his lawyer's advice. A waiter came and he ordered a whiskey.

Rita showed up half an hour late. Instead of apologizing, she told him that he smelled of alcohol; then they went up to the room.

Two hours later they were drinking an espresso at the hotel bar. Willenbrock promised to call her again soon and apologized once again for having been out of touch, but he had a lot on his plate at the moment. The young woman looked at him mockingly and said he should be careful not to overexert himself; after all, he wasn't the youngest anymore. When he leaned in to kiss her goodbye on the cheek, she coldly turned her face away and strutted out of the lobby, head high, without once looking back at Willenbrock, who went to the desk to pay for the room.

He didn't get home until ten. When Susanne asked why he was so late and why he hadn't called, all he said was that he'd spoken with his lawyer and would try to talk to the prosecutor.

The next day at work he called the public prosecutor's office in Neubrandenburg and asked to be put through to Herr Tesch, explaining that it was in regard to an important case of attempted manslaughter. He was told the prosecutor was out of the office and that he should call the criminal investigation department. When Willenbrock objected to being brushed off, the receptionist merely repeated what she'd said and hung up. An hour later he called back, this time identifying himself as the Willenbrock Car Company. He was immediately put through to Herr Tesch's secretary, who asked whether the call was official or private; Willenbrock replied that he wasn't sure, he had no idea how his clients used his cars. The secretary told him that the prosecutor would be in court all day, but that he could be reached tomorrow late in the morning. She asked for Willenbrock's number so the prosecutor could call him back, but Willenbrock said that wasn't necessary, he'd call again tomorrow, and asked whether eleven-thirty would be a good time.

Over lunch Jurek informed Willenbrock that he'd decided to go to Poznan for a few days after all and wondered if he could have a week off. Willenbrock asked him when he wanted to leave, and when Jurek said as soon as possible, Willenbrock asked that he wait until Friday, since he had an appointment that day he couldn't postpone and that would probably last all afternoon. After that Jurek could take off as soon as he wanted, and if one week wasn't enough, he should feel free to call and they could make arrangements. Jurek just nodded and muttered some curt replies as Willenbrock went over the schedule for the week he'd be away. When Willenbrock asked him if he really loved his wife so much, the Pole looked at him uncomprehendingly.

"We're married," he said defiantly.

Willenbrock reached Neubrandenburg at eleven. He had a hard time finding the right address and a place to park. A little before eleven-thirty he was standing in front of Herr Tesch's secretary, who asked the purpose of his visit. He introduced himself as owner of the Willenbrock Car Company and said only that he needed to speak with Herr Tesch. She asked Willenbrock to wait a minute while she went into the next room. A few seconds later she came back, held the door for him, and invited him inside.

The prosecutor looked up when Willenbrock stepped in the room. He was in his mid-forties, his hair cut fashionably short and the tips dyed blond. His shirt and tie were carefully coordinated with his suit; a handkerchief was nonchalantly folded in his breast pocket. He bent back over his papers and asked in a quiet, bored voice: "So, with whom do I have the pleasure?"

"The name is Willenbrock. You wrote to me."

"Of the Willenbrock Car Company, my secretary said. I'm afraid I don't understand why you've come to see me. I don't need a car at the moment."

"You wrote to me," Willenbrock repeated, as he sat in the chair facing the desk.

He opened his briefcase, carefully, so the revolver didn't fall out, found the letter, and handed it to the prosecutor. Tesch merely glanced at it and handed it back.

"I see. My secretary must have made a mistake. If this is what you want to speak to me about, you'll have to have her set up an appointment. But I really don't know what there is to say. That case was cleared a while ago. If you want to appeal my decision, kindly take it up with the attorney general's office. But in writing, please, we all have a lot to do."

He returned to his papers. Willenbrock just stayed in his chair, unfazed, so that a few moments later Herr Tesch again looked up, stared at Willenbrock in silence, and pointed to the door.

"Please leave," he said.

"They tried to kill me," said Willenbrock.

The prosecutor nodded curtly.

"The detectives did find evidence. Crystal-clear evidence, they said. And here you claim it wasn't sufficient. All you did was have the guys deported and shelve the case. It was attempted manslaughter."

The prosecutor kept busy with his papers and said quietly: "Please leave."

"No," said Willenbrock defiantly, sitting up in the chair. "I demand that the criminals be punished. That's what you're paid for, with my tax money. That's why you're here!"

He had raised his voice. The door to the next room opened and the secretary appeared. She stood in the doorway, looking at Tesch. He came out from behind his desk and took a step toward Willenbrock.

"Listen, Herr . . ."

"Willenbrock," said the secretary.

"Right, Herr Willenbrock, I'm sure you've gone through a terrible ordeal. But now you have to put your trust in the Justice Department and leave me to my work. If you wish to appeal the decision, my secretary will inform you about the appropriate procedures. But don't make things worse than they are by refusing to leave. If I have to have you removed from my office, that could have serious consequences. I'd rather not have to charge you with attempted coercion."

"A crime of this magnitude has to be prosecuted ex officio. You can't just shrug it off like that."

"Are you trying to instruct me in German law, Herr Willenbrock? I assure you, the investigation can always be reopened if new compelling evidence is presented. But at this juncture, there's no point in addressing the Russian magisterial court. Besides, it probably wouldn't bring much. Requests like that eat up a lot of time and money. And now, if you'll be so kind."

Seeing it was hopeless, Willenbrock gave in and headed for the door.

"You'll hear from me," he said threateningly to the prosecutor, who noted it but remained unrattled. When Willenbrock stormed out of the room, the secretary called out to him but he didn't catch what she was saying. On his way downstairs, as he was muttering curses out loud, he ran into a courier coming up the steps with a bundle of files who eyed him warily. Willenbrock gave him a reassuring smile. Before leaving the building he put the letter back in the briefcase, his hand grazing the revolver in the process. Maybe this Herr Tesch, this fop playing at being a prosecutor, would have been a little nicer, a little more forthcoming, if he'd known what was in the briefcase. Willenbrock got back in his car and drove to Berlin.

By four o'clock he was on the lot and told Jurek he could leave to go home.

"Take along something nice for your wife," he said, as they parted.

"She already has everything. More than all the other wives."

When Jurek got in his car, Willenbrock noticed it was so packed that even the passenger seat was crammed with boxes. He went into the office and turned on the computer to continue drafting his letter to the attorney general, in which he protested the prosecutor's decision and described his visit to Tesch. In conclusion, he asked to be issued a weapons permit, since the Justice Department was evidently either unwilling or unable to punish violent crime; consequently he had no choice but to take his family's security into his own hands. Satisfied with what he'd written, he reread the letter, thought for a moment and typed "Respectfully yours" at the bottom. As soon as he'd printed and signed the paper, he felt relieved.

He didn't say much to Susanne about his trip to Neubrandenburg, only that he'd filed an appeal on the advice of his lawyer, although he doubted the brothers would be brought to trial, since so much time had passed.

That weekend they stayed in town. Willenbrock managed the lot by himself and didn't come home until late. During the few days Jurek was away, he failed to sell a single car. He couldn't figure out if this was because of the season or because his customers, who were predominantly East European, trusted Jurek more than they did him. In any case, he was relieved when Jurek returned.

They ate breakfast together on the lot. Willenbrock had set up a table and some chairs outside the trailer and made some coffee. He waited for Jurek to say something about his wife and the situation at home, but the Pole just held his face in the sun and chewed the bread he'd brought from home. Finally, when Willenbrock asked him, Jurek said that he and his wife had come to an agreement, a truce, as he put it; she promised to think it all through again, in peace and quiet, and meanwhile he'd keep his job with Willenbrock.

"Did you talk to your son, too?"

"I saw him in a café. He saw me but acted as if I was air. He was sitting with his friends. The scum of Poznan."

"They're young," said Willenbrock.

"They're gangsters," said Jurek.

"We used to play cops and robbers, too. Children's games, he'll grow out of it."

"These kids aren't playing at robbers—they *are* robbers. They have pistols, real pistols. They run around the city with them at night. They attack other kids and take their money. Did you use to do that, boss?"

"No, but I wasn't exactly an angel. Were you?"

"Of course not. Who says we were angels? Back then some of us kept pictures of Pilsudski, others were fans of the Beatles, and we all still kiss the shadow of the Pope. But my son's idol is Al Capone. He dreams of becoming the Godfather of Poznan."

Willenbrock thought of telling Jurek about his revolver, but that probably wouldn't cheer him up. He could have said that he ran around with a pistol, too, that he took it wherever he went, that he'd even carried it into a public attorney's office—because he didn't want to leave it in his car—the kind of stunt only a dangerous criminal or a movie hero could pull off. But all he said was: "We were real children back then. These days they're different, a lot more mature than we used to be, more hardened."

Jurek snorted with contempt and carefully peeled an apple.

20

The electricians were still working inside the showroom. They had been joined by two pipe fitters, whom Willenbrock could hear cursing as they got in each other's way. The doors and windows were now usable, although the fittings were still taped off, and Willenbrock walked through the site every evening, inspecting the progress and enjoying his new building. He imagined how he would arrange his future office, which was set off from the workshop and salesroom floor. The bathroom with the shower was still a jumble of cables and pipes, while in the shop, the storage shelves were already assembled, waiting only to be mounted once the walls were painted.

In early October Susanne announced she wanted to close the boutique: she'd been losing money since the beginning of the year—even the end-of-summer sale had failed to turn things around. Willenbrock spent a long time persuading her to stay open at least through the Christmas season. He also tried unsuccessfully to talk her into keeping Kathrin, pointing out that without any help she'd be tied to the shop, that every time she needed to run an errand she'd have to close down, and that she'd have to spend every Saturday and Monday in her boutique, which would mean fewer trips together to their house in the country. He realized right away that this last argument might produce the opposite of his intended effect, by giving Susanne another reason for limiting their trips to Bugewitz. Susanne refused to change her mind. She explained to Kathrin that she could keep her on until the end of the year but no longer and encouraged her to look for other work.

Willenbrock had taken to playing the messages on the answering machine as soon as he came home, punching the button even if no new calls had been recorded. His wife noticed this new habit—and he was glad she did—but neither said a word about it. Now and then his behavior struck him as childish, especially since the caller he was checking for—Susanne's "client"—was unlikely to phone again, following that first bizarre message. But he didn't change his habit, partly because he was suspicious, and partly because he wanted Susanne to know he was on to her. His daily practice of playing the messages the minute he got home began to resemble an obsession, as did the way he kept sizing up the customers while they examined the cars, listening to Jurek. His compulsion, his mania for checking things, both amused and disturbed him. He was afraid they were the quirks of a grumpy old man, a sign of approaching senility—especially when he realized they were beyond his control, that he'd become completely addicted. If he heard unknown voices on the lot and didn't rush to the window to check, or if he suddenly realized that he had forgotten to play the answering machine, he would become so anxious that he couldn't concentrate on his work or the evening's activity until he had done so. You've become a genuine obsessive-compulsive, he told himself, so now you just have to deal with it—but the idea of growing old and eccentric bothered him.

A mason showed up at the end of September and in four days had built a red brick porch at the entrance to the showroom. Willenbrock's architect had suggested that the brickwork would give the metal structure a welcoming character, a nice complement to the shiny, silvery metal. The painters came two days after the mason and painted the showroom's hung ceiling and plasterboard walls.

At the beginning of October, Willenbrock pushed Susanne to go with him to Bugewitz. Because they hadn't been going very often over the past months, and since he didn't know when he could talk her into making the trip again, he decided to drain the water from the outside lines and prepare the barn for winter. She was already starting to prepare for the Christmas sales season and soon would have plenty of reasons not to leave Berlin until the end of the year.

That Sunday morning he put on his workclothes and went in the kitchen to make some tea. Susanne was sitting at the table, holding the revolver. In a flash he was standing next to her and wrenched the weapon out of her hand.

"That's not a plaything," he said, alarmed.

"I was looking for a pen. I'm sorry, I thought you had one in your briefcase."

"Please don't touch that, Susanne."

"It looks like the real thing. Like a real pistol."

"Uh-huh," was all he said.

"It gives me the shivers."

"That's the point. It's supposed to look real. It feels the same, it sounds the same, except it's not—and it can't hurt anybody."

"It's awful," she said. "What's it doing in your briefcase? Do you always carry it around?"

"I don't know where else to keep it. I have to make sure it doesn't fall into the hands of a child or some dumb teenager, you know."

The revolver wasn't loaded, but seeing it in her hands had given Willenbrock the scare of his life. Once again he cursed Krylov and hoped he'd come back soon so he could return the ominous present. He wrapped the Smith & Wesson in its rag and put it in the briefcase.

Back in Berlin he searched his desk for the little key to the briefcase and locked it. From then on he locked it every evening before leaving the lot. Every day on his way home, he now checked the briefcase, feeling with his fingers to make sure it was locked.

By mid-October the painters had finished. The building was nearly complete, and Willenbrock and Jurek set up the furniture that had been delivered two weeks before. Together they mounted shelves along the walls inside the shop.

On October 22 the showroom was officially handed over. Willenbrock's architect and the supervising engineer came and walked through the new building, pulling the switches and levers, turning the faucets on and off, testing the windows and doors one final time, and knocking on the walls. Then the engineer congratulated Willenbrock with a formal little speech he seemed to be reciting from memory. Willenbrock opened a bottle of champagne.

"What do you plan to do with your old trailer?" the engineer asked. "If you want to get rid of it, my company would be interested."

"Nope," said Willenbrock, "not for sale. That trailer's what I started out with—it's going to be the first exhibit in my company museum."

Jurek had asked if he could live in the trailer; he wanted to give up his small apartment; for the five nights he spent in Berlin every week, the trailer would do fine, especially now that he could wash up in the new building. Besides, his current apartment wasn't any bigger. Willenbrock had agreed. That way he wouldn't have to worry so much about his watchman, since Pasewald would have help nearby in case of an emergency.

The engineer again lauded the construction, calling attention to the quality of his firm's work. In the end everything had come out more or less on time, despite the considerable difficulties. Martens, the architect, had to leave early since he had an appointment with the Berlin Senate; Willenbrock walked him to his car. As they said goodbye, Martens reminded him to withhold his final payment as a guarantee against any builder's errors that might pop up in the next few weeks, or to have the bank hold it in escrow.

That evening Willenbrock waited for Pasewald, in order to give him the keys to the main entrance and to his office. When Willenbrock asked after his family, Pasewald started talking about his grandchild and didn't stop until Willenbrock, who wanted to leave, interrupted him. Susanne hadn't come to the opening ceremony; she had arranged to attend a fashion presentation that an Italian firm was putting on in a

Berlin hotel. She'd been selling their clothes for three years and didn't want to miss the event, but she promised Willenbrock she'd visit the new building soon. Willenbrock knew she wasn't really interested in his showroom and didn't insist.

At home that evening he found a letter from the attorney general. Willenbrock was annoyed to see it in the mailbox, since he had expressly asked that the reply be sent to his office address. He didn't want to upset Susanne. He went in the kitchen, put some water on for tea, and uneasily opened the envelope. A certain Herr Meier informed him that despite his careful review of the case, he saw no reason to continue with the investigation, since there was not sufficient grounds to justify preferring charges. The earlier information obtained by Willenbrock, namely, that international assistance would not be sought for reasons of time and cost, was misleading; the real rationale for declining to pursue this was the lack of hard, factual evidence. Willenbrock's appeal, therefore, was considered to be unsubstantiated and would have to be declined. This decision could be contested in court, though the intent to do so would have to be filed within one month, and the petition needed to be signed by a lawyer and not the petitioner, although the latter would nevertheless have to bear the costs of filing. Willenbrock was further informed that the attorney general's office did not issue weapons permits, and that, moreover, these were never issued for reasons of personal protection but exclusively for sporting purposes and were only valid under the auspices of licensed sports associations and within the parameters determined by them to be sufficiently safe. As a precaution, he was reminded that even someone entitled to use a legally obtained weapon was bound by specific regulations, and that the use of a weapon in defense against a real danger would necessarily lead to an inquiry by the criminal investigation department and the public prosecutor's office, since even in self-defense the use of excessive force, if so determined, was an offense punishable by imprisonment.

The letter ended with the formula "Respectfully yours, on behalf of the Attorney General"—which Willenbrock pondered for some time. He wasn't at all upset that his appeal had been denied; he had expected as much. He crumpled the paper and tossed it into a corner of the kitchen. Then he smoked a cigarette. A moment later he retrieved the letter and smoothed it out so he could add it to his papers. He had no desire to mention the contents to Susanne, or to his lawyer, for that matter, nor did he have the slightest intention of filing an appeal. If his attorney liked the idea of taking on a public prosecutor so much, let him do it at his own expense. Willenbrock no longer saw any sense in trying to force the prosecutor to do something he obviously was unwilling to do, even if it was his clear duty, at least according to Willenbrock. The attack in the night was history; he just wanted to forget it. He'd installed various security systems in the country house—gadgets he called them—that should do the trick. He thought about Krylov's revolver and wondered if maybe he shouldn't keep it after all.

At the beginning of December, Willenbrock made one last trip for the season out to the house in Bugewitz. Susanne had so much to do she was working even on weekends, so he went by himself. He'd thought of calling up one of the young women he knew from his car lot and inviting her to spend the weekend. He'd even gone so far as to open his address file, but then he was overcome by a strange reluctance. So instead he packed two books about World War I flying aces and stayed up reading late into the morning. He'd taken the revolver out of his briefcase and laid it next to his bed. After owning the weapon all this time he felt tempted to try it out, to fire it at some target, but he was afraid he might attract attention and get into trouble. Since he didn't feel like cooking just for himself, he drove over to a restaurant in Anklam for his midday meal.

Four days before Christmas, he shut down the lot. Jurek was planning to spend the first few days with his mother in Warsaw, then wait until after Christmas to go to Poznan. Willenbrock handed him an envelope with his Christmas bonus, and a dress for Jurek's wife that Susanne had chosen from her boutique and wrapped up. Jurek tried to decline the gift; he didn't feel like giving his wife any presents this year, whether from himself or from anyone else, but Willenbrock insisted.

"Buy her something nice," he told him, "Women are like children, they adore presents—you know, pretty little packages make them feel loved."

"I've given her everything," Jurek muttered. "There's nothing I haven't given her. I even bought her a lawnmower."

"You gave her a lawnmower? Women want something they can wear—clothes, jewelry . . . What's your wife supposed to do with a lawnmower?"

"It's a big help for her."

"I'm sure it is. But why don't you buy her a gold necklace or some pearl earrings? Women are different, Jurek, completely different."

"That's for sure. My wife's different, all right. And my son, too."

His voice was flat and embittered. He stuck the present carelessly under his arm and said: "Thanks, boss."

On their first day of vacation, he and Susanne drove out to Goslar to visit his brother, Peter. When Willenbrock called to suggest the idea, his brother's reaction had been fairly reserved: he said merely that they were welcome to come and could stay at his place. The two brothers had never gotten along very well, and after their parents died—both in the same year—they had dropped out of touch completely, which neither perceived as a great loss. Now and then Susanne urged her husband to keep up the contact, or rather to renew it, and it was she who sent the birthday cards, but the families never did get together. So when Willenbrock suggested in mid-December that they spend Christmas with his brother, since Susanne's mother was gone and he had no desire to see her brother, Fred, she was surprised but immediately agreed.

It was late afternoon by the time they arrived. The brothers greeted each other formally, much to the irritation of their wives, who embraced each other warmly. After vespers they went for a walk through town and looked at the brightly lit window displays—some of the Christmas decorations had already been taken down as soon as the shops closed for the holidays. They spent the evening in the family's spacious home, which overlooked the Petersberg mountain, a local landmark.

When he was twenty-four, Peter Willenbrock had taken a glider belonging to their sports association and flown it over the border into West Germany. He had been competing in a championship at the Neustadt-Glewe training center; he'd let his tow plane take him up like everyone else, but as soon as he was out of sight of the airfield, Peter had left the prescribed southeastern course and, taking advantage of some favorable thermals, had steered directly for the border. He flew at a safe altitude—very high, since the gliders were too small to show up on radar and the only danger was being spotted by a border guard.

After he had flown what he thought was twenty kilometers, he landed in a meadow. He hadn't noticed the electric pasture fence until it was too late, and despite some aggressive last-minute maneuvering, one wing was completely destroyed. When he brought the machine to a stop he was so shaken that he just sat there for several minutes and only got out because he had to vomit. Some farmers found him. Nervously, he asked where he had landed. When he heard that he was just eight hundred meters away from the border zone—in other words, that he had completely miscalculated and must have gone into a curve sometime after crossing the border and just barely missed landing back on the eastern side—he felt sick all over again.

His friends from the training center in Neustadt-Glewe didn't learn about his escape until two days later, and then only because it was reported on West German radio. When Peter Willenbrock didn't show up, they had been worried, and when air-traffic control was unable to provide any information, they had gone up in a few little prop planes to search the countryside for the missing glider.

Peter had gone on to study law and economics in Hannover, after which he tried to set himself up as an independent financial consultant. Four years later he took a job with the Goslar municipal administration and was soon granted tenure as a civil servant.

Peter's flight had put a strain on his relationship with Bernd, who accused his brother of abandoning their parents, not to mention harming himself, and selfishly and inconsiderately destroying Bernd's own ambitions. After his brother's illegal flight, Bernd Willenbrock was accused of being an accessory and barred from the flying club. Until then he had devoted all his free time to flying gliders. He was considered his club's great hope and had a good chance of becoming provincial champion—his pals had nicknamed him "Foka 6," after the famous glider model. As a further punishment, he was expelled from the technical college and had to spend two years working in a factory before he was allowed to resume his studies.

He shrugged off the expulsion—he'd never been very interested in his studies—but being barred from the flying club and put under an indefinite ban from flying was a painful blow. In revoking his license, the board cited his brother Peter's reckless and irresponsible departure from the prescribed route, which constituted an act of criminal endangerment to international air traffic, and his purloining of a glider, which displayed a gross disregard of the law. Bernd Willenbrock protested vigorously: he was not his brother and could not be punished for his brother's offense; that would be guilt by association—clan liability—and was therefore inadmissible. But the regional head of the Ministry for Sports and Technology advised him that it was pointless to appeal, since the decision had come from high up. He himself had done what he could—after all, he didn't want to lose his "Foka 6"—but it was hopeless: his brother's escapade meant Willenbrock could forget about ever flying again.

One year later, Bernd Willenbrock requested that he be allowed to resume flying sports planes, and he repeated his request two more times over the next two years, but always in vain. After that he gave up. He still bought every book he could about old planes and the latest models, and went on reading biographies of pilots, but he never went back to the training field, nor did he attend air shows or watch the air force demonstrations.

For a while after Peter fled to West Germany, the brothers exchanged angry, accusatory letters, then they broke off all contact, until both had married and their wives prodded them to get back in touch, which they did very tentatively. This visit was the first time they'd seen each other since their parents' funeral, seven years before.

It was also the first time Bernd and Susanne had ever seen Peter's two children—the daughter, who studied in Munich, and the son, who still lived at home and who'd been trying for years to get into a program to study sound engineering, while he held various odd jobs and played the occasional gig with his band. Peter and his wife showed pictures and a video of a two-month trip to China, and the brothers talked about their parents and their childhood. Both did their best to avoid delicate subjects and not get into a fight; their wives got along easily and well.

Peter talked about his plane, a Cessna, and offered to take his brother out to see it, but Willenbrock declined. He had no interest in flying anymore, he said. Susanne looked at him, surprised, but didn't say anything.

"You don't fly anymore?"

"No."

"So Foka 6 has hung up his wings. Well, that's a surprise. I mean, there's nothing to stop you now. You could even buy your own glider, I'm sure you could afford it."

"No interest."

"So what do you do? I mean, in your free time."

"I sell cars. That's my hobby."

"Money isn't everything," said Peter. "You need some kind of hobby. Otherwise you'll waste away. Anyway, I'm glad I have my machine. Every time I go up it saves me any number of trips to the doctor. I just can't see why you haven't started flying again, Bernd, now that it would be so easy. Back then you were the best. Foka 6 was always number one."

"That was back then, a long time ago."

"I'm sorry, but I don't get it."

"Well," said Willenbrock, "that's how it is."

Peter wanted to show him photos and videos of his Cessna and some flights he'd taken, but his brother was so adamant that he dropped the idea, annoyed.

The next day Willenbrock and Susanne went back to Berlin, since his team had four games scheduled before the end of the year.

21

On December 29, Willenbrock didn't get home until late. After the game he and his teammates had gone to their pub for a few hours. Willenbrock had had some beer, so he drove home as carefully and calmly as he could to avoid being pulled over. Here and there people were already setting off firecrackers. One red-glowing rocket grazed his car, but he didn't stop, and he waited until he was parked in the garage before checking the paint for signs of damage. Then he quietly entered the house, which was completely dark, undressed in the bathroom, and lay down, naked, next to Susanne. He quickly fell asleep.

Shortly after eleven he woke up. He had heard a noise that sounded like wood splintering. At once he was fully alert, his ears cocked. He heard two firecrackers go off, one right after the other, and then a different noise, a metallic banging, as if someone were shaking a sheet of tin. In the dark, Willenbrock carefully got up and left the bedroom. Not wanting to turn on any lights, he groped his way to the bathroom, reached for his robe, and put it on. Then he tiptoed to his study, picked up his briefcase, and went to his desk. Nervously he rummaged in the drawer for the key; when he finally found it, he opened the briefcase, took out the revolver and the box of ammunition, and quietly entered the hall, where he slipped into his shoes and grabbed a scarf. Then he unlocked the door to the house and stepped outside. After he'd gone two steps he went back and relocked the door. Then he walked on slowly, very slowly, careful not to make any noise. When he reached the corner of the house, he cautiously peered around and saw that the garage was wide open. It occurred to him that the motion detector hadn't turned on the outdoor lights; he figured someone had cut the cable.

In the garage he could see a tiny beam of light. Someone was trying to break into his car: Willenbrock could make out a silhouette bending over the driver's door. Keeping close to the corner, he looked around to see if there was anyone else, but all he saw was the figure in the garage, and all he heard was the person trying to get the door open.

Willenbrock stepped back, put the revolver in one pocket of his robe, and opened the box of ammunition in the other pocket, letting the cartridges slide out. Then he took the revolver in his left hand, carefully swung out the cylinder, and quietly loaded all the chambers. One cartridge fell clinking onto the ground. Willenbrock froze for a few seconds, then peered slowly around the corner to make sure the figure was still in the garage. He couldn't find the cartridge. He snapped the cylinder back in place and, switching the revolver to his right hand, walked around the corner toward the garage, still trying not to make any noise. He glanced up at the bedroom window; it was dark, Susanne was probably still asleep. Willenbrock wanted to make it to the garage without being noticed so he could turn on the light, but before he reached the driveway, the figure straightened up. For a moment

Willenbrock was caught in a weak flashlight beam, then it went out. Now the garage was pitch dark and Willenbrock couldn't make out a thing. He took two steps back, his eyes fixed on the place where he had last seen the figure.

"Come on out," he said.

His voice sounded husky and hoarse. A rocket went off somewhere in the neighborhood; a bundle of red stars came shooting out and slowly drifted to the ground. At the same moment a man came charging out of the garage, wielding a club or iron bar in his raised right hand.

Willenbrock held the revolver in front of him, ready to shoot; he felt his hand go suddenly wet and tightened his grip. When the man was a few meters away, he fired. It was just a reflex; he was pointing the gun at the man, and when the man came charging at him so fast, his finger sought the trigger practically of its own accord, out of fear. It was nothing more than a defensive reaction. He could just as easily have thrown his arms up to protect his head, and indeed the instant he fired, both arms did go up to protect his face and ward off any blows.

The figure jerked back a moment as if it had been punched in the chest, but then advanced again on Willenbrock, though more slowly than before and with heavy steps. Willenbrock was still grasping the revolver tightly, his index finger cramped around the pulled trigger. He stepped back and called out—a warning, or a cry for help, he wasn't sure what he said. He was panicky with fear when he saw the man still coming at him. So Krylov's conned me, he thought, this really is just a loud toy designed to scare people. He cursed himself for never having tried out Krylov's revolver, for never having fired a test shot in the seclusion of his country house or in the woods.

The man stopped just two or three steps away from him and stared at him with big eyes. He's a child, thought Willenbrock. The man was eighteen or nineteen years old, his head was shaved, he was wearing a cheap dark suit over a sweater. He had wrapped a wide headband around both ears. The man dropped the rod onto the cement driveway, it rang against the pavement, loud and metallic. Then he fell to his knees, a little blood came dribbling out of his mouth, he tipped forward onto the ground, propped himself up with his arms, and stayed that way without moving and without saying anything. Four or five more drops of blood spilled out of his mouth or his chest.

I've hit him, thought Willenbrock, both shocked and relieved.

"What do you think you're doing here!" he yelled at the man, who was kneeling in front of him, gasping loudly.

As Willenbrock lowered the revolver, his finger released the trigger, which snapped back into position with an audible click. The man raised his head; he looked at Willenbrock, his mouth half open. He had turned pale, and his eyes were staring incredulously into space.

A light went on in the bedroom; the curtains were shoved aside, a bright beam fell on the lawn beside the driveway. Willenbrock was afraid Susanne might open the window and look out, but she didn't; he could see her behind the closed panes.

Pointing the gun at the young man, he anxiously looked around right and left: he was afraid an accomplice might show up, or someone who'd been alarmed by the shot. But everything was completely quiet, no steps, no sounds—no one else was there.

Slowly, very slowly, the young man stood up. Once he was on his feet, Willenbrock saw that his jacket was drenched with blood, a wet black stain below his shoulder. Clutching his right side with both hands, he stumbled down the driveway; Willenbrock followed at a distance. When the man reached the street, he rested on one of the cars parked along the curb, supporting himself with both elbows. A few seconds later he hauled himself up and slowly trudged away. Willenbrock placed his hand with the revolver under his robe. He stayed by the garden fence until the man disappeared from sight.

He walked back toward the house, glanced at the lit bedroom, then went to the garage, closed the double door, and stopped it with a stone, since the metal bolt appeared to have been broken off. He didn't want to set foot inside the garage.

Now, for the first time, he felt cold. Back at the house he was startled when he turned the handle of the door and it wouldn't open. Despite the temperature he could feel he was sweating. He jiggled the handle hard until he remembered that he had locked the door himself. He pulled his keys out of his pocket and tried to fit the right one in the lock, but it was difficult because he was shaking and couldn't find the keyhole. He switched the revolver to his left hand and tried with his right. When he finally managed to open the door, he took another look around and listened. A rocket went hissing somewhere into the sky, a dim light emerged over the trees.

He stuck the revolver in his pocket, went inside, and locked the door, breathing heavily.

"Everything's fine, Susanne," he called from the bottom of the stairs.

He stepped into his study and hid the revolver, the empty ammunition box, and the remaining cartridges in the display case behind a stack of airplane albums. Still in his street shoes, he climbed upstairs.

Susanne was sitting up in bed, afraid. When he came in, she looked relieved. He sat down next to her and put his arm around her shoulders; she was ice cold, shivering.

"Everything's all right," he said soothingly. "Go back to sleep."

"What was that? A gun? I heard a shot."

Willenbrock told her it was only firecrackers for New Year's. He thought he'd heard something else outside and had gone to check. The garage was open; he'd probably forgotten to close it when he came home, that can happen when you've had a few beers. While he was locking the garage, three dumb kids came down the street; they lit a firecracker and tossed it right at him; the thing had gone off next to the house, making a hell of a racket, of course.

"My God, Bernd, I thought you'd fired your pistol. I was afraid something had happened to you."

"Come on, let's get some sleep. Nothing happened, everything's okay."

Willenbrock lay awake a long time. He kept seeing the childish face of the intruder, as he kneeled on the ground, staring wide-eyed at Willenbrock. He didn't get to sleep until three o'clock; three hours later he was wide awake again. He got up quietly, washed, and got dressed. Then he went outside. A light snow had fallen, the sidewalk and the driveway were covered with a thin skin of white; it was still dark, and Willenbrock could sense more than see the snow, it crunched beneath his shoes. At the corner of the house he bent down and groped around for the fallen cartridge. He had to search a long time until he found it in the half-dark and snow. He walked up to the fence and onto the street; there was no one in sight; the neighborhood was completely quiet.

Back inside, he took the revolver and emptied the chambers. He picked up the cartridges and packed them back in the cardboard box, then put everything in his briefcase, which he locked. When Susanne came down, at seven-thirty, Willenbrock was sitting in the living room, reading about the Yak 9, a single-engine fighter plane from the Second World War. While his wife washed up, Willenbrock made coffee. Over breakfast they talked about the previous night. Susanne asked once more whether he really hadn't fired the gun and whether there'd been anyone outside, or even in their house. Willenbrock reassured her.

"It was just a firecracker," he said, "that's all, and we'll be hearing more of those in the next few nights. Plus, I forgot to close the garage. We're still on edge, Susanne."

"I hope you're telling me the truth. Don't lie to me, Bernd."

He just nodded. When it was bright enough he went back outside to look for traces of the previous night. The snow had covered everything. Where the intruder had fallen he found a metal bar, an angle iron he had used to put up some shelves in the basement and had left in the garage. He picked it up and blew off the snowflakes: he could see blood, dried or frozen blood. Careful not to get anything on him, he picked up the iron by opposite ends with two fingertips and carried it over to the garage. There he kicked away the stone and inspected the doors. The faux wood had been damaged, the screws were twisted and partly torn out, one bolt could be moved without the slightest effort. The other door was intact. Everything in the garage looked unscathed, both cars were locked, he saw no dents or scratches—only the weather stripping had been pulled from the driver's window, but he was easily able to press that back in place. He checked the locks on both cars; they worked perfectly.

He unscrewed the damaged door lock, wrapped it in some newspaper he had stored in the garage, and started to take it into the house. When he saw the bloody angle iron he'd left outside, he put down the lock, took another old newspaper, unfolded it and wrapped it around the iron. Then he laid it on the shelf; he would dispose of it somewhere the next time he drove into town.

He told Susanne that he'd wanted to replace the garage latch for a long time; it wasn't stable enough and had gotten twisted through use. She said she hadn't noticed and eyed him suspiciously, but said nothing and drove off to her shop.

After she left, he swept the snow off the driveway. He fetched two buckets of hot water from inside and poured them over the dark stains, then swept the area once again. Then he headed out for the building-supply store to buy a new lock and a new electrical cable—the intruder had, indeed, cut the old one. Looking carefully around, he backed out of the driveway, then cruised up and down the streets in his neighborhood, but nothing caught his eye, so he headed into town.

That afternoon he drove to his handball practice. He left as soon as they finished playing at eight o'clock and went straight home. As he parked in the garage, he felt his heart catch in his throat. He kept looking nervously around, quickly locked the driveway gate and the door to the garage, and hurried into the house, bolting the door behind him and securing it with a chain.

He slept fitfully and badly. While Susanne was in the bathroom he unlocked the briefcase with the revolver and set it next to his bed.

The next morning they left very early for Bischofswiesen, in the Bavarian Alps, where they had arranged to meet some friends—a former classmate of Susanne's, his wife, and their daughter, who was nearly grown up. Willenbrock had reserved a hotel for five days. They didn't take much luggage and went without skis, since they planned to rent them there. Originally Willenbrock had planned to drive through the Czech Republic and Austria, but then he decided to take the revolver, both because he was reluctant to leave it behind in the empty house and because he didn't want to travel without it. Afraid a customs official might search his luggage and find the weapon if they crossed the border, he told Susanne he had decided to drive by way of Nuremberg, since the radio had warned of heavy traffic delays on the route they had originally planned.

On their way out of town he stopped at a gas station where he tanked up and bought four newspapers. He leafed through them as he stood in line waiting to pay, but found nothing about the previous night's incident, no mention of a shooting—only ads for sales and other New Year's announcements. He tossed them in the trunk. Susanne asked why he needed so many newspapers; he told her that he'd taken out some ads and wanted to keep up-to-date on the going prices in the used-car market.

When they got to the hotel in Bischofswiesen, their friends were already waiting; they'd arrived two hours earlier. Susanne's friend was surprised that Willenbrock had come the long way and said that the route through the Czech Republic and Austria had been completely clear. He had already reserved their skis for the next morning.

The Willenbrocks settled into their room. While they were unpacking, Susanne asked him why he'd brought his briefcase, and he explained he had a few tax forms to fill out and was hoping to find a couple of hours to take care of it. She was indignant; she didn't want to spoil their short vacation with work.

Half an hour later they met their friends and took a stroll through the small town, which was full of tourists admiring the houses and window displays. Susanne's old schoolmate had called ahead from Berlin to reserve a table at a restaurant he'd been to several times the previous year. They ended up staying there until two in the morning, eating and dancing. The man flirted with Susanne as they reminisced about old times.

Willenbrock wasn't very talkative. He danced with both women, and even the teenage daughter, who looked outraged when he pressed her against him on the dance floor. After midnight the schoolmate's wife told Willenbrock he should loosen up; she tried to get him to kiss her, which he grudgingly went along with. He was amazed to see how unbridled Susanne was with her old friend, to the point of kissing him, and how closely the two danced together. He wondered whether this was her secret lover, the man who'd left the message on the answering machine some months before.

When they got back to the hotel, Susanne collapsed onto the bed, half-dressed, and fell asleep at once. Willenbrock sat in a chair and read through all his newspapers. He found nothing about any gunshot wounds.

The next morning they picked up their skis, and Susanne's schoolmate drove them out to the slopes. Susanne and the other couple took a lift to one the man had chosen, while Willenbrock went with the daughter to a beginners' slope. They took some food along and arranged to meet back at the car at four o'clock.

Later, at the hotel, Willenbrock excused himself, saying he had to go to his room for an hour to do a little homework for the taxman. Susanne's friend was sympathetic; he, too, was self-employed—an independent dealer in garden tools and pumps—just the other night he'd been complaining about taxes and cursing the finance minister. The women decided to stay in the bar until dinner.

Willenbrock went up to his room and turned on the TV to watch the news from Berlin. There were pictures of several people who'd been injured and a number of interviews with doctors about the dangers of fireworks, but nothing about his intruder.

Over dinner the girl asked Willenbrock if he was an alcoholic, explaining that every time he'd reached the bottom of the slope, he'd had a shot of brandy. Then she lectured him on the disastrous effects of alcohol, how every drop kills such-and-such a number of brain cells, and how you can tell people who drink by their skin. Her parents found this hilarious, and Willenbrock responded that he only drank when he was bored, then asked the waiter to bring him a scotch.

The next morning before breakfast he went to a nearby newsstand, where he bawled out the saleslady for having only one Berlin newspaper. He paid for it and went back to the hotel. Instead of going to his room, he went into the phone booth next to the reception desk, picked up the receiver, and thought for a moment who he might ask in Berlin to buy the papers he wanted. He called information and requested the number of a magazine shop a block away from his car lot where he frequently bought things. He dialed the number and explained awkwardly who he was and asked if they could save all the Berlin papers through Monday, as he was looking for some ads and would be gone for a few days. The vendor remembered him as soon as Willenbrock mentioned that he occasionally bought porn magazines by the stack. The man promised to save the papers.

Willenbrock went to the breakfast room, ordered a coffee, and searched the paper for the dreaded news. Here, too, there were many reports about accidents and injuries, but nothing about the man who'd broken into his garage. If he had gone to a doctor or a hospital with a gunshot wound, Willenbrock reasoned, the police would surely have been informed, and the press would have reported it. Either the wound was so slight that he didn't need a doctor or else he was afraid he might get hauled in—it was likely that he already had quite a record. It's also possible he was a foreigner, an illegal immigrant making his way across the country stealing things, and wanted to avoid drawing attention to himself at all costs. Or maybe he had friends who were taking care of him, in which case Willenbrock could expect another unpleasant visit. He'd have to be more alert in the future; most of all, he couldn't mention anything to Susanne or give anything away.

As he set the paper on a chair, he considered another possibility: that the man was dead, that he had killed him. The intruder had lost blood and had dragged himself through the streets despite the open wound. Maybe he got as far as the edge of the forest and died there. It had snowed that night. If the man had found shelter in some secluded place and had collapsed there and been snowed under, it could be a while before he was discovered by a dog or someone out walking. It might be a matter of days or weeks—or, under certain circumstances, even months—before they found him.

Susanne's friend appeared and asked jokingly if he'd already had his morning scotch. Willenbrock forced a smile. Over the next few days he made a point of going to his room every evening, ostensibly to work on his taxes, and in reality to watch the Berlin news, but nothing was reported about his intruder.

On Sunday Willenbrock drove back through Nuremberg, over the protests of Susanne and the others; he wanted at all costs to avoid having his luggage searched. As soon as they reached the city he stopped at a gas station and bought all the local newspapers they had in stock. By the time they got home it was evening.

Monday morning on his way to work he stopped at the newsstand to pick up the papers he had reserved as well as the current issues. He had the salesman pack them all in a bag, since he didn't want to have to tell Jurek the story about the ads.

The Pole was already busy in his new workshop, working on a carburetor. Willenbrock asked him about his holidays and how things were with his wife.

"Her mother died over Christmas," said Jurek. "She passed away on Christmas Eve. Elżbieta loved her very much."

"I'm sorry to hear it."

A shy smile flitted across Jurek's face. "Elżbieta cried a lot. On Christmas all she did was cry. But what can I say? Her mother's death brought us closer again, no problem. We're going to have another go at it."

He looked down at his hands, slightly embarrassed.

"Life's full of surprises," was all Willenbrock said.

They smoked their cigarettes in silence.

Inside his new office he quickly leafed through the newspapers, then carefully searched them one by one, but didn't find the news he was hunting for. He called the store where he had bought the security system for his country house and asked about wall safes. The salesman told him they had four models on display, though there were others he could order. Willenbrock said he'd stop in that afternoon.

The next week he had two small wall safes installed, one in his new office and one in his study at home. He explained to Susanne that a sales rep had cornered him and talked so long he'd finally given in. He laughed at himself and what he'd ordered, but then described all the advantages of having a safe at home. Susanne remained suspicious and again asked what happened that night before New Year's Eve; there was an urgency to her voice as she asked why he was afraid to tell her the truth. He laughed at her and said he could barely remember what had happened, some dumb kids playing a prank.

He covered the safe in his study with the large framed photograph that showed him as a young man in flight gear, climbing into a glider. A date had been inscribed in the lower right corner with a broad-tipped pen: 12 JUNE 1974. Next to the date were the words: FOKA 6. The ink was very faded.

Willenbrock had an additional lock put on the door to their house, a massive steel deadbolt that reminded him of the entrance to a bank vault.

At the end of January he stopped searching the papers for news about the wounded man. It was probably nothing major, he told himself; after all, he hadn't really aimed, the gun had just gone off because he was on edge and scared. The fact that the man had bled a little didn't mean a thing. Anyway, he'd probably given the burglar enough of a scare to think twice about coming back, so to that extent the revolver had proven useful.

22

In mid-February Krylov showed up on the car lot. They talked about the world and the Russian president, whom Krylov claimed was really a golem created by accomplished Russian doctors. He said that in this area Russian medicine was outstanding, and very sophisticated. Brezhnev had been a golem like that, too—he'd gone on ruling the country four years after his natural death. After all, what's a golem for the nation that conquered space before anybody else? Willenbrock laughed, but Krylov was serious: "Believe me, my friend, even if it sounds unbelievable. Russian scientists are geniuses, true artists. With everyday things, they're useless. If you catch a cold in my country, you can die from it. But with things that aren't so everyday, with supernatural things, our scientists and artists are unbeatable. Think about *Sputnik*, the Bolshoi, Tchaikovsky, Pushkin and Chekhov, Plisetskaya and Nureyev. No other country in the world can do it. One day they'll dig up the remains of the tsars and discover that they were all machines, wonders of technology, masterpieces of Russian genius."

"I'm guessing," said Willenbrock, laughing, "that you don't exactly love your president."

"Of course I love him," Krylov insisted. "We all love him.

We worship him, he's priceless. Another triumph of Russian science."

He congratulated Willenbrock on the new building. Willenbrock wanted to give him a tour of the showroom, but Krylov declined. He paid for the two cars he'd chosen. Neither he nor Willenbrock mentioned the revolver. It was too late to give it back, now that it was no longer a virgin, as Krylov had put it. Besides, he didn't want to. There was, after all, at least one person apart from the two of them who knew he had it—the young man who'd been wounded, and if he or one of his cohorts ever paid him another visit, Willenbrock would need a weapon.

As Krylov drove away, he nodded to Willenbrock patronizingly from his car. Suddenly Willenbrock hated the man. Without so much as a by-your-leave, Krylov had given him a weapon that had turned his life completely upside down. He had shot a man and for weeks had been expecting either that the same man would show up to take his revenge or else that the police would pay him a visit. And if they decided to look for the revolver, they would search his house, his country house, and his car lot until they found it. There was no place where it would be absolutely safe and hidden. And he was reluctant to get rid of it, to toss it into the Spree.

On the last Friday in February, Willenbrock and his wife were already in bed when Susanne suddenly sat up, afraid. She put away the book she was reading and jumped out of bed. Willenbrock looked at her in surprise.

"I left today's cash in the car," she said. "I didn't take it to the bank since I was running so late. I just remembered it's in the car. I'll run and get it. I don't want to leave it there overnight."

Willenbrock asked her not to go out, it was already midnight, too late to leave the house. Besides, he'd already locked up, it was too much trouble to unlock everything again.

"What's wrong with you?" asked Susanne. "Why can't I go out? Are you afraid of something? Are you afraid we could get attacked here, too?"

Willenbrock said no, he wasn't. "But there's no need to be reckless. Just stay here, nothing's going to happen to the money."

"You're hiding something from me."

"I wouldn't know what."

"There's something you're not telling me, Bernd. For weeks you've been coming home every evening right after work. You're always here waiting for me. All of sudden you stop going out at night. Even after your beloved handball, you come straight home. You never used to come home before one o'clock after a practice."

"I can't keep up anymore," he admitted. "I must be getting old."

He took her hand and pulled her back into bed.

In March, when the snow melted, he got progressively more uneasy. He started buying tabloids once again and leafing through them anxiously whenever he was alone in the office. If he found an item about an unidentified body, his apprehensiveness rose and he had trouble keeping it hidden from Jurek and Susanne.

In spring, they again started going out to Bugewitz. His

wife was surprised that he always took along his briefcase, but she stopped asking him about it. By now they'd gotten used to staying in after dark, both in Berlin and in the country. When this was impossible, because one of them had an appointment or was held up at work and couldn't get home until late, they would each hurry to turn off the car and get inside. If it was Susanne who came late, Willenbrock would rush out as soon as he heard her pulling up. He would open the door for her, drive her car in, lock the garage, and run back inside, then lock and bolt and chain the door.

They seldom mentioned the break-in, but now and then he noticed a look or gesture that proved that she hadn't forgotten about it, either.

He never read or heard anything about the man he had surprised and wounded two days before New Year's. He told himself the wound was probably insignificant, nothing to worry about, maybe he'd just grazed the man. In time his memory of the nighttime incident faded, and he began thinking that all he'd done was give the man a good scare and chase him away. The blood he thought he'd seen was probably just a figment of his imagination, brought on by his own fear, by the panic that had come over him when he saw the intruder suddenly charge, and by the noise when the gun accidentally went off.

At the beginning of April, Willenbrock quit his handball team. After a game they'd gone to the Italian restaurant, where he told them that for personal reasons he'd have to leave the team, effective immediately. He sounded so determined that no one tried to talk him out of his decision.

"But you'll be there if we need someone to fill in, right, Bernd?"

"I'm not moving to the other end of the world."

Susanne was surprised by his decision and remarked that she never would understand him. He just nodded.

She kept her boutique open through the spring, even though it still wasn't turning a profit; she'd be happy if she broke even by the end of the year. Willenbrock's car business practically ran itself; he relied completely on Jurek, who had given up his Berlin apartment and moved into the old trailer, which they'd set up in back of the new showroom. At night, Jurek and Pasewald played cards or watched sports on TV until Jurek went to bed and the watchman walked over to the new building.

23

On the last weekend in April, at Susanne's request, they drove out to Güstrow to see Ernst Barlach's studio and the Chapel of St. Gertrude. Willenbrock accompanied Susanne through the exhibit, then left her to her own devices while he went outside to smoke a cigarette. He was sitting on a bench when all of a sudden he saw the young man he'd caught in his garage and fired at. The man was holding hands with a young blond woman and heading straight toward Willenbrock; both were wearing backpacks and engaged in a lively conversation.

Willenbrock went up to them and said in an agitated voice: "What do you want from me?"

The man looked at him in surprise, then said, in English: "Sorry, would you mind repeating that?"

"Why are you following me?" asked Willenbrock, still in German.

"I'm sorry . . . is something the matter?"

Embarrassed, Willenbrock realized his mistake, and said, this time in English: "Excuse me"—and quickly backed off.

The couple kept looking at him, bewildered.

As Willenbrock walked away, still appalled at his misjudgment, he heard the man say something about him—he thought he caught the word "crazy." When he'd calmed down, he went back and tried to catch another glimpse of the man, from a distance. He couldn't say for sure how closely the English-speaker really did resemble the intruder; he could no longer remember the other man very well. The face of the man he had fired at was beginning to blur with the face of the Russian who had attacked him. Confused, he waited for Susanne so they could go out to eat.

Two days later, when Willenbrock was taking the revolver out of the safe to put it in his briefcase, Jurek saw it. He looked at his boss in surprise, but said nothing. Willenbrock started to explain, but then just locked his briefcase without a word, closed the safe, and said: "So see you tomorrow, Jurek."

On the way home he thought about the Pole's dismayed look and wondered what Jurek must have thought, whether he could possibly imagine that his boss had actually fired this weapon at a human being. Willenbrock remembered a lieutenant he had read about in one of his biographies who'd been called before a court martial at the end of 1917. After a successful dogfight, as he was flying back to base, he had taken his Albatross D5 biplane under one of the bridges on the Rhine. He was charged with endangering the war effort and abetting the enemy, without intent of treason, by deliberate and reckless dereliction of duty. During the proceedings, the lieutenant had said something that struck Willenbrock as both so incomprehensible and so enlightening that he'd never forgotten it. When asked why he'd performed such a dangerous and daring feat, the lieutenant had said only: "If you look long enough into the abyss, the abyss looks back."

Despite the admonitions of the court and the urging of his own counsel, he refused to say anything more.

Another driver passed Willenbrock, shaking his fist; apparently Willenbrock had cut in front of him without realizing it.

He turned onto his street and saw his house; the windowpanes were glowing reddish in the setting sun. The sight of his house and the garden in front that Susanne tended made him happy. He stopped at the driveway to open the gate. He saw his neighbor, Herr Wittgen, digging away in front of his home, and next to him several woody shrubs or trees with thick plaits of roots he was evidently in the process of planting. When Willenbrock said hello, Herr Wittgen looked up and waved across the fence. Willenbrock checked his watch, parked the car in the garage, and went inside.

In the kitchen, he fixed cabbage soup for dinner. He cut up some bacon, onions, and sauerkraut, chopped three cloves of garlic, and cleaned the peppers. He poured a can of beef bouillon into the pot, placed it on the stove, added a few spices, and set the soup to simmer. He brought a bottle of white wine up from the basement, felt the temperature, and put it in the refrigerator. Then he listened to the messages on the answering machine and went into his office. He looked at the wallpaper and made up his mind to call a painter and have at least some of the rooms redone before summer. His eyes rested on the black-and-white photo of the young glider pilot. Susanne had once told him that the only reason she had married him was because when he proposed to her he'd shown the exact same combination of jaunty pride and childishness as he did in this picture. But that was a long time ago; now the large, yellowed photo seemed out of place in his study with all its modern furnishings. Gerd had repeatedly urged him to go to a gallery and buy some paintings. It didn't have to be a Rembrandt, but he could take the expense as a deduction; and, besides, art was a good investment, it would pay off in the future. What's more, he had said, a few pictures would spruce up both his office and his study at home—Willenbrock could see how Gerd's own office was practically plastered with modern art.

Willenbrock looked at the photo and thought: it really does look out of place. A nice landscape would be better, or a portrait of Susanne that he could commission from the painter whose car he'd bought last year, whom his wife had not only recognized but even held in high regard. He took down the photo, then opened the safe and removed the revolver. He pulled the trigger, producing a sharp metallic click. He ran his fingers over the shiny dark metal; now he was relieved to have it. It was fun to own a real gun.

He heard a car pull up and went to the window. His wife was turning into the driveway. She stopped at the gate and got out to say hello to Herr Wittgen, who was still busy planting. Susanne reached over the fence to shake hands; they had an animated conversation. Willenbrock watched her as he played with his gun. He was surprised how friendly she was with the neighbor. He wanted to open the window to hear the man's voice. Maybe it was him, he thought, maybe he was the sappy caller on the machine. But before he could unlatch the window, Susanne saw him and waved. Willenbrock waved back, keeping his left hand down to cover the gun that was lying on the windowsill so neither she nor the neighbor could see it. Then he stashed the Smith & Wesson in the safe, locked it up, and hung the picture back on the wall without looking at the laughing face of the young man beside the glider. Before returning to the kitchen, he again glanced out the window at the garden. Susanne was no longer in sight; Herr Wittgen had gone back to his plants. The fruit trees were in bloom, the pinkish tint of their new leaves intensified by the evening twilight.

about the author

Christoph Hein, a novelist, poet, playwright, and essayist, is one of the most respected literary and political voices in Europe today. A former president of German PEN, he is the author of the internationally acclaimed and award-winning novels *The Distant Lover* and *The Tango Player,* which have been translated into seventeen languages. He lives in Berlin.